TERRIBLE CHOICES

Published in the UK in 2022 by BryherHouse Publishing
www.bryherhousepublishing.com
Copyright © Calum Kerr 2022

Hardback ISBN: 978-1-8382583-6-8
Paperback ISBN: 978-1-8382583-8-2
eBook ISBN: 978-1-8382583-9-9

Cover design and typeset by SpiffingCovers

TERRIBLE CHOICES

CALUM KERR

Foreword

"Nearly 250 suspects were arrested by the Met Police and dozens of 'county lines' networks out of London were smashed as part of a fresh crackdown. The raids ran from 7 March to 13 March. 2022. They joined forces across the UK carrying out synchronised dawn raids seizing cash, drugs and firearms from properties used to run drug operations.

The National Police Chiefs' Council said the week of action saw over 1,400 arrested and 671 vulnerable people safeguarded across England and Wales.

County lines is a distribution model that involves urban gangs expanding their markets for crack cocaine and heroin into smaller towns by setting up phone lines through which they sell Class A drugs.

The Met's Deputy Assistant Commissioner Graham McNulty described county lines as an 'abhorrent crime.'

'We know the supply of drugs is inextricably linked to violence and causes misery to those impacted by it' he said.

Those in charge of the phone lines, known as line-holders, often recruit children and vulnerable adults into trafficking the drugs all over the country in order to avoid detection themselves. These drug runners are often threatened with violence and are unable to escape.

In the latest raids, more than 100 vulnerable children and adults exploited by county lines operators are now being helped by police and social services. Officers also made 25 referrals to the National Referral Mechanism, which assesses individuals as potential victims of human trafficking/modern slavery.

Police also seized £284,000 in cash, 2.4kg in Class A drugs and 14kg in Class B drugs. They also found 56 knives and one firearm in the raids, as well as making 249 arrests in the capital."

CHAPTER 1

It was a large office in a very modern building in Cornhill, in the middle of the 'square mile' district of the City of London. It was traditional; old prints on the wall, some shelves with leather-bound books and a bureau with crystal decanters of sherry and port. There was no computer or telephone on the antique desk. Sitting behind it was a small man, about five feet five inches tall, grey hair and of slim build. His voice was soft, his accent posh, his suit Savile Row and his tie MCC. He was a qualified solicitor, a Mason, a member of the Carlton Club and an MBE for services to a charity supporting disabled children.

The man's name was Edward Bond. And most of the media described him as 'A pillar of the establishment'. When Chief Superintendent Jackie Starling, a very senior officer in the UK National Crime Agency, described him, her words were less flattering: "He's a fucking evil bastard criminal". And her description was one hundred percent accurate. He was a mean man, a *very* mean man. Ruthless and sadistic, he enjoyed being able to hurt people but he always used someone else to do the dirty work. He had never been arrested, let alone charged, for any offence, in spite of being responsible for about fifty percent of the heroin, cocaine and ketamine sold in the UK and the murder of nineteen men, three women and a six-year-old child.

On the other side of the desk was Leroy Reid, a big man, a dangerous man, with dark skin and dark eyes that seemed empty of any emotion. He was Bond's executive assistant and his roles included driver, bodyguard and senior enforcer. He was wearing a casual Armani suit with a white button-down shirt and he looked like a management consultant. He had survived for twenty years with only a short stretch in Wandsworth prison and a couple of knife wounds so far, and was completely relaxed. The assignment they had been discussing was fairly routine; they both knew it was time to make the decision.

Bond sighed. "I agree. We need to draw a line in the sand. It's not about the money. It's a question of principle. We cannot allow this fellow to go unpunished. Word will get around that we have become weak, soft, vulnerable or whatever. The question is how best to deal with him. Take me through the options again, Leroy."

"Of course, Mr Bond. His name is Teddy Anderson. Option one is just to shoot him in the head. Very little risk. Option two, kill his wife as well."

"Understood. But will those options resonate? People might think some criminals were responsible; it might not look like retribution for stealing our money."

Reid nodded. "Agreed, Mr Bond. That takes us to option three: More complicated as you know but it will certainly resonate. Rape the wife, rape Teddy, cut off some fingers and video the whole thing. But, it's not without risk. We will need to involve other people, but in a way that's a good thing as word will get around. So will the video. Alibis are sorted, technology is sorted – all we need is your decision."

Chapter 1

Bond didn't hesitate: "In my view, simplicity usually trumps complexity. Let's go for option two, Leroy. Just kill him and kill his wife. Who will you use?"

"I'm glad you asked. You may remember that girl, Sally, who joined the team a few months ago, ex-army and pretty tough. Probably a good time to find out how tough?"

"Agreed."

CHAPTER 2

Leroy was pleased to see that Sally had already arrived for the meeting they had arranged and had chosen a table away from other customers at the café in the huge Westfield shopping centre. She looked like an attractive young housewife taking a break from her shopping and the two carrier bags on the floor added authenticity. She seemed completely relaxed. He wondered how relaxed she would be when he explained the mission. He got a coffee and joined her. There was no small talk.

"Remember when Viv introduced us and you described your background and army experiences?"

"Yeah."

"Well, after he left, I described the sort of experiences you could expect if you joined our team. How is it going so far?"

Sally shrugged. "To be honest, a bit boring. Almost as boring as the army."

"Well, I understand you had a bit of excitement last week."

"Oh, Eric?"

"Yes, Eric. The big, black teenage motherfucker, as stupid as they come!"

"In the army we had to describe such people as 'Vulnerable and having difficulty processing information.'"

"Vulnerable! Eric? He is as vulnerable as a Rottweiler!

Anyway, tell me what happened."

Sally remembered the incident very clearly. "Viv told me that the London market is oversupplied with product and the competition is increasing all the time, hence all the violence and the need for county lines to extend our market. He said that we have two boys in the Feltham Young Offenders Institution, three older boys on remand in Wandsworth, two others dead and two in hospital – one of whom is a thirteen-year-old girl. He told me that in the last twelve months seven of our kids have been killed and thirty stabbed. So, we have had to widen our net. He said that he had taken over a number of houses and there were two guys cooking crack in Plymouth where the homeowner is getting as much as he wants. Apparently, we now need more distributors and he told me to send Eric and his two pals down there. I caught up with the boys and girls in the Tower Hamlets house and gave them the background. When I spoke to Eric it didn't go well. It was like: 'Plymouth! Where the fuck is Plymouth? If it ain't in London I'm not going. I live in London and I'm staying put.' I could hear a bit of mumbling from the kids behind me so I spoke slowly and loudly to Eric using my Diane Abbott voice."

Leroy laughed out loud. "I know just what you mean. Assume the audience are stupid. In this case, highly appropriate!"

Sally smiled. "I explained it all again and told him what had been arranged and that Viv would not be changing his mind. It seemed to me that this had to be fixed now or we might be in serious trouble." She looked nervously at Leroy. "I hope that was the right thing."

He nodded.

"Anyway, he gave me that stare he has and I can remember exactly what he said: 'No fucking way, babe; no fucking way!' The room was silent. I could hear Eric's breathing, almost panting; his eyes were wild and red, glaring at me. Trust me, it was about to kick off."

Leroy nodded. Sally continued.

"When I was promoted to Corporal in the army I was trained in dealing with this sort of situation. I guessed, no, I knew that Eric was not going to back down and lose face in front of the other kids. So, I said: 'Eric, if you don't do what Viv wants you to do, you will be in serious trouble. Why don't we step outside and talk this over?' He replied: 'Fuck you, bitch!'"

"That was the right thing to do, Sally. Did it work?" asked Leroy.

"No. He pulled a knife out and started waving it at me. I stepped back and he smiled. He's about a foot taller than me, almost twice my weight and was waving a knife. As I stepped back, he came forward. Very confident! I shuffled my feet and got ready. When the distance between us was perfect I breathed in. And I shouted out as I kicked him in the balls as hard as I could. He screamed but didn't collapse. I closed in and punched him in the throat. But he was still standing so I punched him in the solar plexus and put him on the floor. He tried to get up but couldn't make the count. I stood over him and said: 'OK, Eric, let's have that chat later. In the meantime, why don't you get some fresh air?' The rest of the morning went smoothly."

Leroy smiled. "Sounds to me that you handled that very well, Sally. Good to hear and very timely as the boss and I have decided that it's time for you to get some additional experience in the field, if you know what I mean. So, we have been tasked with a very important mission and it involves firearms. Back then I think you told me that you had received thorough firearms training in the army. Is that correct?"

"Correct!"

"OK. I'm going to describe the mission, but first of all I want you to listen very carefully to what I am about to say." Leroy sipped his coffee and looked at her straight in the eye. She met his gaze.

"I understand."

"Right. Now is the time to tell me if you are prepared to kill someone and not even know why. If you are not prepared then just get up and go. No hard feelings."

Sally continued to look relaxed. "I'm prepared to kill someone. But I would draw the line at killing the kids. Most of them were fucked up before they were even born."

He smiled, although the smile didn't reach his eyes.

"No children will be harmed. How about you get us two more coffees and I'll explain more."

Sally was less laid-back than she looked and as she waited in the queue she felt her hands were shaking a bit as her mind was whirling. She remembered her father talking to her about 'a crossroads in your life', a situation where your choices take your life in different directions: 'Keep going forward, turn left or right or turn around and go back', and now she was standing there. Uncertain. One road could take her to wealth and excitement, but if there was a God her final destination could be an eternity of damnation. The other road looked boring. She made up her mind.

"One double espresso, one black Americano, please." Then she returned to the table, sat down, put her elbows on top, rested her chin on her thumbs and looked at Leroy's dark eyes. "Tell me more."

Leroy spoke so quietly Sally had to lean forward.

"First thing, Sally, I need to check your phone, your bag and those carrier bags. I also need to use this little gizmo to check for any listening devices. This is our standard operational protocol and if and when you are sitting where I'm sitting, you will adopt them. They are not optional."

He was very thorough and then passed everything back to Sally.

"Good. OK, here is what you need to know. We have discovered that one of our senior team members has been stealing from us. We have proof; there is no doubt and quite a few people know about it. So, we have to put a stop to it and make sure no one else is tempted to try it. We have decided to kill him and his wife."

"His wife! Why his wife?"

"Have a think about it then *you* tell *me*."

Sally closed her eyes for a few seconds.

"Yeah, I get it. She will possibly tell the police who she thinks did it." She paused. "She will definitely tell the police."

"Correct. In fact, she would definitely know who killed him and tell the police because she will witness the shooting. The safest place to kill the guy will be in his house and no doubt she will be there tomorrow evening."

Sally went a little pale. "Tomorrow? Why so soon?"

"Why not? But actually, there is a valid reason. We have reason to believe that sometime soon he will be going back to Jamaica and we sure as hell won't be able to waste him over there."

Neither of them spoke for a while. "Can I assume you have never shot anyone?" asked Leroy.

"Only cardboard cut-outs."

"Well, they don't try and jump out of the way, scream with fright or maybe try and get hold of the gun. So, what will you do?"

"In the army we were told to fire a shot to the body as soon as possible and finish with a shot to the head, but if we are looking at two people that's four bangs. Isn't that dangerous?"

"It would be. But you will be using a Beretta M9A3 handgun and it will have a SoulArms SF-M9 silencer. It's quite a light gun and holds sixteen rounds. You won't get a chance to fire it before we go into the house, but don't worry, you will have plenty of time to get used to handling it. One of my colleagues will be sorting out a car for us and will pick you up outside the Ladbroke Arms pub in Notting Hill at three o'clock tomorrow. Bear in mind that everything you will be wearing other than underwear will be burnt that evening, so bring a bag with spare clothes and shoes. Make them suitable for a restaurant because we are having dinner together."

"Dinner?"

"Yep. Part of our alibi."

"OK. One question: What's in this for me?"

"You keep your job and you get ten grand if all goes well."

"What if it *doesn't* go well? What if I fuck up?"

"Let's not go there, Sally."

"No, seriously. I need to know!"

Leroy frowned. "OK. Let's put it this way, Sally. If the job doesn't go well, things won't go well for you."

Sally found it hard to get to sleep that night. Leroy's last words kept going round and round in her head: 'You keep your job and you get ten grand if all goes well, if the job doesn't go well, things won't go well for you'. She decided that she wouldn't hesitate to kill these people no matter what happened.

CHAPTER 3

At exactly three o'clock the next day a car pulled up opposite the pub. Sally walked across the road to meet it. Leroy was in the front passenger seat, she didn't recognise the driver. She got in, they pulled away and Leroy passed her a carrier bag. It was fairly heavy and she knew immediately what it contained.

"Take a look," he urged. "It's fully loaded and of course the safety is on. Keep it in your lap; we don't want someone seeing it through the window. Try and become familiar with it."

She weighed it in her hand, feeling but not moving the safety. It was lighter and the barrel was longer than all the handguns she had fired in the army, but it brought back memories: The smell of cordite in the interior range, the banter afterwards and her pride when winning a competition, but this was going to be different – killing two people! Her stomach churned and she was having difficulty breathing steadily. She tried to calm down; worrying that Leroy could hear, then finally she got her panic under control.

Ten minutes later, Leroy spoke again.

"Let me introduce you to Bill." Bill spoke; it was clear that English wasn't his primary language and Bill was unlikely to be his real name as his skin colour suggested he was from the Middle East.

"This is my car but it has false number plates today. I shall drop you off where Mr Reid has instructed and you will return to that place in due course. In the meantime, I will be driving around. If there is any change of plan Mr Reid will call me."

Leroy looked backwards to meet Sally's eyes.

"That gun is your responsibility until I ask for it back. If I shout 'Gun!' at any time you give it to me immediately – no questions, no delay – just give it to me. Hold the barrel and pass the handle to me. Understood?"

"Understood. What else do I need to know?"

"Bill will drop us about ten minutes from the house; we will be wearing caps and here is yours." He passed it to her. "And here are some latex gloves, you don't want any firearm discharge on your hands. It's getting quite dark now so there's very little chance that any CCTV will enable anyone to identify us when we walk to the house, but put on this face-mask. I don't know if the guy will be at home but I have met his wife who will let us in and we can chat until he arrives. Kill him as soon as possible when he does, then kill her."

"What happens next?"

"We check we still have our face-masks on, then walk out of the back of the house and make our way to Bill's parked car. Our routes here and back have been planned to avoid CCTV as much as possible so it will be a bit up and down, but better safe than sorry. As I mentioned yesterday, when we get in the car you will need to take off your clothes and put on the stuff you have brought. I'll be doing the same. When we get dropped off we shall be looking like a couple on their first date and I guess there is an element of truth in that!"

CHAPTER 4

Teddy Anderson was exhausted and as his driver had finally stopped talking he closed his eyes. Thinking back on his day. Talks with the six primary dealers who were responsible for his county lines totalling over a hundred kids and calls with guys cooking the crack cocaine in Cambridge, Norwich and Birmingham. Every day there were problems – kids getting arrested, kids stealing cash, kids stealing the drugs, using the drugs, overdosing on the drugs or just disappearing with the drugs, not to mention kids crying and kids dying. And the primary dealers were even worse. Still, in a couple of months he would be out of this. He had been averaging about five thousand pounds a week from Viv and skimming another thousand a week for the past couple of years. Their house was on the market and they had already exchanged contracts on a wonderful place in Ocho Rios. They were going back to Jamaica and it was all under control.

When Teddy let himself into the house and called out Valerie's name a different voice responded, a voice he recognised – Leroy Reid. His heart sank and when he walked into the living room there he was. He saw a girl emerge from behind him and she was holding a gun. Then something exploded in his chest and his head hit the floor throwing his vision into blackness. He didn't hear or feel the second bullet. Valerie's mouth dropped open; she was sitting on the sofa, frozen with fear. Sally took a deep breath, walked behind the sofa and put a bullet in the back of her head. There was blood all over the place. Teddy and Valerie's heads had exploded; she thought she was going to be sick.

"Gun!" said Leroy quietly. She put on the safety and passed him the gun, handle first as instructed. "Thanks. You did well, Sally. Let's get out of here. We are going to leave through the back door and the gate at the bottom of the garden."

Five minutes later as they walked along a quiet road, Sally's head began to feel odd, then she felt vomit rising and all of a sudden she was sick – coughing, spluttering, nose running and eyes weeping. She was also feeling the breathless and panicky effects just as she had in the car earlier. Leroy took a few steps away and waited patiently. He didn't say a word.

Twenty minutes later they were in Bill's car struggling to change their clothes in the confined space and by seven o'clock they were in the restaurant. The owner was a good friend, the reservation on the system was for six o'clock and, in the unlikely event that the police enquired, he would be happy to confirm that they arrived on time. Sally started to feel a bit better and after two vodka martinis the memories began to fade a little.

Leroy was pleased. Everything had gone to plan, although Sally should have put the first shot into Valerie's chest before the headshot.

"No need to explain, Sally, but the plan was body, then headshot for both of them. I appreciate you didn't feel the first shot for Valerie was necessary, but let's agree something:

You always stick to the plan unless the plan isn't working. Quick question: Could you see her hands?"

"What do you mean? What about her hands?"

"What did she have in her hands?"

"Nothing."

"Are you sure?"

"No!"

"Precisely. One of her hands might have been holding a gun and she could have shot me as you walked over to the settee."

"Why would she have had a gun?"

Leroy smiled. "Too late to ask her now! But it's not impossible, is it? Anyway, you've got a bit more colour in your face now; let's have some wine and order some food. They do a good steak here."

The steak and a bottle of Côtes du Rhône arrived with the bill. Sally was puzzled.

"Why the bill so soon?" she asked as Leroy glanced at it and put a card on it.

"Remember; we arrived here at six o'clock and I am using a card to pay the bill because, in the very unlikely case that the police are interested in our alibi, they can obtain the payment details from the issuer and that will contain the time the bill was paid. Hope for the best. Plan for the worst!"

CHAPTER 5

William West, very fit for a seventy-year-old, was running along the Thames Path at six-thirty on a Friday evening. After a warm day he was grateful to feel a cool breeze off the water and he felt great. As always, he was wearing his Garmin and the heart rate monitor showed that he was in the threshold zone; more than aerobic, less than maximum. Perfect. It also told him that the last mile had taken nine minutes and twenty seconds. He felt even better when he drew level with the runner in front. He took a surreptitious glance, the man looked to be in his thirties. William wasn't a modest man and increased his pace to overtake him.

Ten minutes later William was running through Hammersmith Terrace, past the Italian deli and into Chiswick Mall. His home, like most of the others in the Mall, had a small garden on the riverside to his left, with the house on his right, which also had quite a large garden behind it. He opened the gate to his river garden to do his stretching and checked the Garmin again. The six miles had taken about fifty minutes; not a record by any means but not bad at all.

William's house was lovely but ridiculously large for a single man, and his housekeeper, Tina, who came in five days a week, was always telling him to get something smaller.

"You've got a huge bedroom, a dressing room that is

bigger than most people's living rooms, and a massive bathroom. And you have two more bathrooms and three more bedrooms, plus all that empty space in the attic. I know Ina uses one of the bedrooms and one of the bathrooms when she stays over, but why do you need more?"

William was completely comfortable with his house; it was exactly as he wanted it and he hadn't changed it much since Ryoko had died. Dining room, library and kitchen on the ground floor, a huge living room on the first floor with lovely views of the river, and the garden at the back. He also had an office above the garage at the end of the back garden in a clapboard building that looked like one he had seen in Cape Cod. No need to go there this evening. Friday night was date night and La Trompette in Devonshire Road, Chiswick, was booked for eight-thirty. So plenty of time for a shave and a shower and a couple of sharpeners before his cab arrived at eight-fifteen. As usual, his drink was two-thirds Sipsmith vodka from the freezer, one third diet tonic, three ice cubes and no fruit.

CHAPTER 6

When Ina walked into La Trompette the lady at reception immediately took her little wheelie case and another lady escorted her to William's table. He stood up and they kissed before they sat down. Ina picked up the glass of Rosé de Blancs Champagne, which William had ordered for her. It was her usual drink and was still nicely chilled – he knew she would be on time.

She smiled. "Thank you, darling; just what I needed, but actually, I am feeling a little spoiled. As I told you on Wednesday, I have got the promotion and I am now the UK CEO of a FTSE 100 bank! Give me another kiss!" He did and put his hand on her thigh under the table.

"William, I didn't take the tube tonight."

William pretended to be shocked.

"Don't tell me you splashed out on a taxi all the way from Canary Wharf?"

"No. I now have a driver. And he is available twenty-four-seven! But I will not be taking the piss. The last thing I need is some journalist suggesting that I'm wasting shareholders' money. But, apparently, trips in the direction of home are par for the course."

The dinner was delightful and they got back to Chiswick Mall at eleven o'clock. They had a couple of drinks and a couple of lines of coke before going upstairs to make love.

Chapter 6

Ina was up at the crack of dawn to play golf at Royal Mid-Surrey and her pal, Ginny, picked her up at eight. William got up after they had gone, had breakfast and drove to Richmond Park for a run. Then he had a quick shower and a short drive to Chiswick Quay Marina. His pal, Robert Boyd, was waiting for him, the harbourmaster was at the lock gates and ten minutes later Robert's boat was approaching Kew Bridge. William had put a couple of bottles in the fridge and all was well. It was the first time he had been back on the boat since a pretty wild trip a couple of years previously when Freddie and Sky were aboard and he couldn't forget all that had happened since. But he felt at peace as he opened the first bottle.

Chapter 7

Missed call: Monday. Voicemail – Freddie Findlay, brief, as always: 'William, could we meet sometime this week for dinner or maybe lunch? I need your advice'.

Freddie went on to suggest dinner at Gymkhana in Albemarle Street, Mayfair, and they agreed on Wednesday. William had already enjoyed a large vodka with a small splash of slimline tonic before Freddie breezed in and ordered a gin and tonic for himself.

"And another of these, please," added William, "but no need for another tonic."

"So, Freddie, how are things at the firm? I'm still doing those 'Welcome to DPK' talks to the new intake of grads, but no one ever updates me on what's going on."

"Same here, mate and I'm a partner! What I *can* tell you is that we have increased our market share at the expense of the two other 'Big Three' accountants. We are on about forty percent of the global market of large businesses now and so it won't be long before there is another Government initiative to make life even more difficult for us. And talking about life being more difficult, everyone is shit-scared about the woke police."

"Woke police?"

"Yeah, talent management, people architecture, diversity department, ESG principles, CBT, UBT; the list goes on."

William sat back. "What the fuck are CBT and UBT? Thank God in my presentations I just talk about how things actually work and why we embrace diversity. It's simple: It's the right thing to do and it makes the firm money."

"CBT is cognitive behavioural therapy. UBT is unconscious bias training. There are loads of other acronyms so don't get me going. Let's order; I love the food in this place. They do a thing with kid goat, which is great."

Later on, William asked Freddie, "What advice? You said you needed some advice. So far, my advice has been restricted to the wine list!"

Freddie looked a bit embarrassed. "The thing is is that it's a very personal matter and I had forgotten how intimate this restaurant is. Could you bear to come back to my flat for a chat?"

In the cab, William said, "Freddie, I look forward to exploiting your now infamous wine room and don't keep pretending it was already in the place when you bought the penthouse you call a flat. Just like your hot tub – it's a Freddie Findlay life statement and I expect to see the whole place in some colour supplement in due course! But isn't the whole place a bit sterile? I mean, do you know your neighbours or are they all kind of remote?"

Freddie thought for a moment. "Yeah, you could be right, but I have now met some interesting people in the gym and swimming pool."

William guffawed at that. "And would one of the interesting people be single and attractive?"

"Well, since you ask; yes. First thing in the morning I go to the ground floor pool, which has six lanes. And most of the time there are five of us occupying them at six-thirty. I have to admit that there *is* a charming and rather attractive actress whom I lusted after during my teens and who played a part in my dreams. She still looks the part and I still lust after her. She has an amazing body, very fit, very slim – almost too thin – but looks great in a high cut Lycra swimsuit. Her first name is Vanessa; I can't remember her last name and I don't dare ask her. There is also a retired doctor called Adrian who is a bit of a nutcase. All I know is that he has seven motorbikes and more than thirty guitars."

"More than thir*teen* guitars?"

"No, William, more than *thirty* guitars! Then there is another lady, difficult to guess her age, but pretty lively, who wears a full body swimsuit. She walks with a stick but swims like a fish. It looks like she has had a lot of work done on her face and her boobs don't seem quite right."

"What do you mean her boobs don't look right?"

"They look a bit too perfect. Anyway, her name is Sheila. I think she might also have been an actress, I think I've seen her somewhere before. There is also a retired engineer, Steve, who is charming. He's spent most of his life in Hong Kong and Singapore. We all tend to talk a bit before and after the swim and meet up for coffee most weeks. I kind of like it. Perhaps I'm getting old."

CHAPTER 8

It was a warm evening, so when William and Freddie were dropped off at Fulham Reach they decided to sit on his terrace that overlooked the River Thames, the Harrods Depository site, now exclusive apartments, and Hammersmith Bridge. Two friends, two wine glasses and one bottle of 1983 Château d'Yquem.

William took a sip. "Fantastic, Freddie. Wonderful. The best sticky I have tasted for years. So, come on, spit it out – what's the problem?"

"It's those terrible brothers in Scotland, the twins. There is some collateral damage."

"Collateral damage; what on earth do you mean? You killed both of them."

Freddie sighed. "It's a long story, William, but I'll try and make it short. Back in the day when I was in the SBS, I went on a mission that required a UK passport and they issued us with genuine documents. I remember it well. The paper-pusher must have been a chess player; my name was Bishop, the boss' name was King. I forget who was called Castle. No idea what the half-dozen other ranks were called. Anyway, the mission took place in the Middle East and was accomplished without too much drama: Father with heart attack; Eton,Oxford and Sandhurst educated son installed. All good. I kept the passport until someone asked for it and no one asked! So, I kept it and polished it and have had a clean alias called Miles Bishop for many years."

"What? Why?"

"Well, you never know when such a thing might be useful. I won't bore you with the details as to how I have maintained it or used it, but that brings me to the problem and the need for your advice."

"Sounds serious, Freddie, but I need a pee."

When William came back to the terrace, Freddie had topped up the glasses.

"I know what you are going to say, but let me tell you, the lavatories came with the place," said Freddie.

"Yeah, I have never seen anything like them in the UK. Water spray and drier buttons just like hotels in Japan. Anyway, Mr Bishop, tell me more."

Freddie winced. "The thing is, I used the Bishop alias when I was dealing with those twins and, through some unfortunate coincidences, the National Crime Agency have made the connection. Actually, not the NCA but Chief Superintendent Jackie Starl–"

"Jackie Starling!" interrupted William. "Were you not having an affair with her last year?"

"Yeah, but this is business."

William couldn't see Freddie's face but if he could he was sure he would be looking sheepish.

"So, Freddie, is this 'Hell hath no fury like a woman scorned' or is it really business?"

"I really don't know, but I am getting the impression that she is going to ask Mr Bishop to do something off the books or expose me. I'm pretty sure that they would be unable to make a solid case for me to be involved with the twins. But the question is, what do I do? Play along with her, come clean, get a lawyer or whatever? If this goes to court I will be finished with DPK. And if I was convicted, Christ, I would be in prison for God knows how long!"

William picked up his glass, stood up and walked around for a couple of minutes, thinking things through, then he sat back down, poured what was left of the wine into his glass and frowned.

"Freddie, the first thing you need to do is ensure Mr Bishop evaporates if you haven't already done that. Second, you need a first-class alibi for the date that the second brother was killed. Am I right that the first one, Gordon, simply disappeared?"

"Yes."

"I'll have a look at my calendar later to see if I can help with the alibi. Text me the dates. As far as Jackie Starling is concerned, here is my advice. Play along but don't admit you have used the Bishop alias, record all calls with her, record all meetings with her and have as much sex with her as possible. If you can record that too it might well be helpful. Just go on Amazon and you will find loads of devices that facilitate secret recording. I used one sometime ago at DPK and it defused a problem I had with partnership protection."

"Hang on… record sex?"

"Yep. I doubt she will want a court to hear that, let alone her husband!"

CHAPTER 9

Friday at one-thirty and William was looking forward to his lunch with 'Two Lunches' Lionel as he stepped into the lift at Coq d'Argent. As the door was closing, a Gucci shoe shoved itself into the gap, the doors stuttered and then opened. A young man with a beard and a bright blue suit walked in followed by an attractive girl. She mouthed 'Sorry'. The young man simply ignored William and looked at the closing doors.

William smiled as the lift rose and then stopped. The young man waited for the door to open but William, smiling to himself, walked out as soon as the door opened at the rear of the lift, and onto the terrace and right there was legendary Lionel. Round table for four but only two places set, large brolly to protect them from the sun, an ice bucket on a little table within his reach and a wide grin on his face.

"William, dear boy. How wonderful to see you! It's been ages and I have to say you are looking pretty chipper. I also gather that you are going steady with the CEO of a major audit client, so I think the firm will be prepared to stump up for lunch. Let me pour you a glass of this Minuty, I think you will find it agreeable."

William sipped the dry rosé and smiled again.

"Thank you, Lionel. How are you?"

Chapter 9

"I had my first lunch here and the client doesn't drink at lunchtime. So, let's get stuck in!"

Food ordered, plus a decent red to go with the main courses and Lionel opened up.

"The reason I invited you for lunch was of course that I always enjoy our get- togethers, but there is something I need to tell you, William. The powers that be are a little concerned about your pal, Freddie Findlay."

"What? Freddie? What's that got to do with me? He's a partner, you're a partner; the 'powers that be' are all partners. I don't even work for DPK anymore apart from the occasional 'Welcome to DPK' talk to graduate trainees. What could I know that you guys don't?"

"Well, let me tell you what has been worrying the bosses. First, when Freddie was stabbed outside Fulham Football Club it was put down as a case of mistaken identity but apparently the police were not one hundred percent convinced and some clients are a bit disturbed by the whole thing as well. Second, Freddie is pretty high-profile after that incident a couple of years ago when he rescued you and shot that guy and I think people are adding two and two and seeing five. Third, the firm hasn't forgotten his use of cocaine, and fourth, there is his new apartment in Fulham Reach. As you know, I was at the housewarming and, to be frank, it looked over the top to me. Apparently, it cost around four point five million. Where on earth did he find that sort of money? Between you and me, the firm has checked and no mortgage lender has asked us for proof of earnings."

William sat back and beamed.

"Good to know that the firm hasn't changed since I left. Partners still paranoid! I'm tempted to ask you to tell them to fuck off but if you order another bottle of this excellent Pinot Noir and promise me you will put it on expenses, I will tell you where Freddie found the money."

"Done!"

"It's very simple. Freddie's parents lived in a very substantial house in Hartington Road, Chiswick, and it passed to Freddie when they died. He sold it a while ago for eight point five million. Are we done?"

"There is one more thing. The firm is a bit worried about his relationship with a girl nearly thirty years younger than he is."

William guffawed and couldn't stop chuckling.

"Sorry, Lionel, now I've spilt a drop of this lovely wine. The firm is worried about Freddie's relationship with a single twenty-five-year-old school teacher? For Christ's sake, half the bloody partners are on their second or third much younger wives and others are playing away whenever they get an opportunity!"

Lionel frowned then grinned.

"OK, dear boy, point taken, but I do have one more question. Should we get yet another bottle of this Pinot Noir or a couple of glasses of port?"

CHAPTER 10

Freddie took William's advice and ordered an EVISTR mini voice activated recorder pen. It arrived on Monday and he tested it. With the pen inside his jacket it recorded very well, even when he spoke quietly. On Tuesday he got a call from Jackie Starling and on Thursday afternoon he was in a meeting room at the NCA. She hadn't told him why she wanted to talk but he was pretty sure she was going to mention Miles Bishop. And he was right.

She breezed in with a smile and sat down.

"Good morning Freddie, or should I say 'Good morning Miles'?"

Freddie returned the smile.

"I really don't know why you insist that I am somehow connected with this Miles Bishop chap. I accept that he looks pretty much like me but he isn't me."

"Fair enough, Freddie, let's have it your way. Anyway, I'm after a small favour – actually, it's not small it's rather large! But before I ask it, I'd like to tell you that, apart from me, no one has connected you to Mr Bishop. Not the NCA, not the police in Scotland – no one apart from me; however, if we can't work out a plan that benefits us both, things may change and I would have to arrest you and I doubt that would be well received at DPK."

"Arrest me! Arrest me for what?"

"The murder of Clive Lamont, of course. The man who stabbed you in the back."

"But you cannot have any evidence."

She smiled. "Of course not. But we will have evidence when we charge you. Let me explain. We have the resources to find Mr Miles Bishop's credit card details. We would expect the home address to be some sort of third party and that might lead us to you. More importantly, we will have a look at the transactions, particularly on the night of the murder. Furthermore, if Mr Bishop stayed in a hotel we can have a look at the CCTV. Who knows, we might have some decent footage of you…" she smiled once more, "sorry, footage of Mr. Bishop."

Freddie beamed although he was grimacing inside.

"Sounds all a bit thin to me, Jackie, but maybe now would be a good time for you to tell me what it is that you want."

"Well, as you know, I was transferred from running the anti-money laundering Fighting Financial Crime task force to run the Substance Abuse team, which covers everything from heroin, crack cocaine and ketamine to skunk and MDNA."

"MDNA?"

"Methyl-enedioxy-methamphetamine, usually called ecstasy, E or molly. But the thing is not just the damage done by the drugs but the deaths of the dealers as they try to eliminate the competition. Most of them nowadays are teenagers or even younger. Frankly, stopping this trade is like pushing a snowball up a snowy mountain, so I have decided to think out of the box as we get told by suits who have never seen a corpse."

"And let me guess, it's me that is out of the box."

"Of course not, Freddie. It's Miles Bishop."

CHAPTER 11

Freddie thought for a while. "OK. What is it that you want Miles Bishop to do?"

"I want him to kill a man. Simple as that. Do that for me and I promise you that Mr Bishop will be left alone. I have a note for you that I have typed with my own hands. It will tell you all you need to know. In the meantime, let me tell you this. The man is evil, he controls almost half of all the hard drugs shipped into the UK. He is responsible for many murders including a husband and wife shot in the head, and I know that he arranged for one of my officers to be tortured to death last month. I won't go into the details but they sent a video to her husband. And it gets worse. Have you heard of county lines?"

"Yes, of course!"

"This bloke owns the majority of county lines. We are talking at least a thousand kids, many of them vulnerable, most of them less than eighteen, some of them as young as thirteen. It's like slave labour and it's terrible."

"Sounds awful. But I need to think about this."

"Of course. Take your time. But if he is still alive in a month's time I'll assume our deal is off. Meanwhile, please don't contact me." She passed the paper to Freddie who glanced at it.

"Holy Christ! Edward fucking Bond! You must be joking!"

"I wish I was. But he is the man. I want him dead. And by the way, if any of his people suffer collateral damage, all the better."

Freddie read the paper in the cab home. One side documented all the crimes for which the NCA knew Bond was responsible but couldn't prove. The other side covered points that he assumed had been generated from NCA surveillance. They were comprehensive, in fact they told him everything he needed to know. By the time the cab dropped him off he had decided to go ahead. It was clear that Bond deserved to die and equally important that Freddie didn't end up being charged with the murder of Clive Lamont.

When Lesley arrived, she found Freddie on his second large gin and tonic.

"How was your day?" she asked.

"Excellent, darling. I had a swim with my coffee club pals this morning and we arranged to meet up on Saturday morning. I really enjoy their company. Then I had a couple of good meetings at the bank followed by a dry lunch. How about you?"

"Pretty good, but so far this month we have had two kids not turn up, no parental contacts and I'm told that no one answered the door when the deputy head went looking. I think it's this county lines thing where they are using kids to deal drugs outside of London, particularly vulnerable kids. Anyway, on a more positive note, what time are we meeting William and Ina tonight and where are we going?"

"The River Café, unless you are too tired to walk the two hundred yards to get there, darling."

"Wonderful!"

CHAPTER 12

In the tiny hamlet of West Hanney in the Vale of White Horse, a phone rang and rang and rang. Freddie was laid-back; he knew it could take a while for his call to be answered. And when it was, the greeting was recorded and brief.

"Say your name twice; slowly, please."

"Freddie Findlay… Freddie Findlay." Freddie knew that the voice recognition at the other end would simply close the call if his name was not recognised. But he knew it would be.

"Freddie, darling. How nice to hear from you! Is this a social call or can I be of some service?"

"Both. I would like to discuss a potential transaction and take you to The Plough for lunch."

"Done. When?"

"How about Wednesday or Thursday?"

"Thursday, please. Say about eleven o'clock?"

"Perfect," replied Freddie and he closed the line.

Kathy smiled as she put down the phone and cruised through the hall in her Invacare TDX SP2 Ultra high-tech wheelchair. She always enjoyed Freddie's company and he was a very generous and completely discreet customer. She also liked going to The Plough with him for lunch as it gave her friends and neighbours something to gossip about. Not that they needed an excuse. She had arrived in the village some years ago to live in her parents' former weekend cottage, which had been dramatically modified to cater for her needs. And she came with her carer, Sam, still the only black person in the village.

Quite early on, a farmer who tended to be blunt was in the pub one evening.

"Whatever happened to you and who is *she*?"

Kathy had laughed. "I got blown up in Afghanistan and she helps me when I can't help myself. For example, even though this wheelchair can probably take me around faster than you can walk, I can't reach my drink from the bar. Perhaps you could help? A large G&T, please!" The customers laughed and she became an adopted villager.

One evening, when Kathy was heading back home from the pub, she worried that the battery on her chair might run out and it did. She started wheeling herself and a good-looking young man called Douglas, the son of one of the villagers who was home from university, pushed her back to her house. On the way, he asked her gently what had actually happened to her.

She turned around as far as she could and told him.

"IED took off my legs, blew most of me apart. They put me back together in over a year or so, but bits of my legs were buried in the sand. Just these little stumps are left."

"IED?" he queried.

"Improvised explosive device."

He shuddered. "Of course. God, how terrible!"

"Yes, it was." She thought for a moment. "Let me ask you, Douglas; can you keep a secret?"

"Yes, I can."

"It was my fault. I was an explosive ordnance disposal operator and it was my job to make explosive devices safe. I was tired and made a mistake. Simple as that. The bosses thought the bad guys set it off and I didn't argue with them."

"Do you blame yourself?"

She shrugged. "I did for a while. But it doesn't keep me awake at night anymore. I'm just glad I'm alive, am grateful for your company and for wheeling me home."

CHAPTER 13

That night, like many other nights, it did keep Kathy awake. And she broke out in a sweat. Afghanistan. One hundred and ten degrees in the sun. On her knees, the protection gear weighing more than her own body weight. Her troop swapping rounds with ragheads. Someone screaming and dying. A bullet whizzing past her head didn't help. One of theirs or ours; it didn't really matter. Sweat pouring down her face, stinging her eyes. She had made several of these IEDs safe over the last couple of months, but each one still presented a serious challenge.

'Click'. Instantly: "Oh. Fuck!" Kathy knew she was dead. Full stop. End of story. For a moment she thought of her mother.

No pain. Just nothing. Nothing for ever. But then something: Blackness. Better than nothing. No sound at all. Complete silence. Still no pain but the blackness seemed to be real. Maybe she wasn't dead.

No noise, no blackness. Nothing. Then something. A fleeting memory, that sound – just the tiny 'click' sound from the IED. She thought of her mother again. Black became white. That was the moment when she died for the first time.

But then she seemed to be able to think about what happened. *Jesus Christ*, she thought. *I must be truly fucked up.* That was when her heart stopped for the second time. Three days later in hospital in England she found out how truly fucked up she really was.

Douglas kept the secret; he never told anyone it was an own goal. But he shared Kathy's role and her heroism with the village and now she was highly respected and every time she went to The Plough someone offered to buy her a drink.

CHAPTER 14

Thursday morning and Freddie manoeuvred his Porsche Taycan out of the parking space in the garage below his Fulham Reach penthouse and drove to the A4, then M4. At junction 13 he left the motorway and thirty minutes later he arrived at West Hanney. As usual, he had difficulty finding Kathy's cottage but when he arrived Sam was standing outside with a huge smile.

"Freddie, how good to see you. Come on in. Kathy will be along shortly!" and within seconds there she was.

Freddie ran towards her, bent down so that his head was level with hers, put his arms around her and gave her a loud lip-smacking kiss on the lips.

"Darling, you look wonderful. Wonderful! This country air must be doing you the world of good." He looked at his watch. "Business first, then lunch?"

"Sounds sensible, Freddie. Follow me."

Freddie followed Kathy along a corridor to the lift that took her upstairs. Freddie knew what was going to happen next. Instead of pressing the button pointing upwards, she pressed the button marked 'Emergency' and a few seconds later they were down in her cellar/workshop.

She wheeled herself behind her desk and put on a pair of spectacles. "So, Freddie; how can I help?"

He sat down in front of her. "I'm looking for a small device that can destroy a Mercedes EQS and all its passengers. It needs to be magnetic and activated via a smart phone. I also need a new, small, powerful handgun."

"No problem at all! As for the gun, I have a Ruger SR40c. It comes with sixteen rounds of point forty Smith and Wesson ammunition and I can let you have it today for four hundred pounds. As for the device, it depends on the size. I can manufacture one, which will do the job and be pretty small, but that will be five grand. A larger version will work out at about three. Do you mind me asking you what problem you are trying to solve?"

"Believe it or not, Kathy, I am helping the police."

"Well, there is still no discount!"

Freddie smiled. "I'll take the Ruger and I would like you to build the smaller device. How long would that take?"

"Just a few days."

"Done. How about that lunch at The Plough?"

CHAPTER 15

There were a few regulars in the pub and Kathy introduced Freddie as 'Fred'. He had spoken to a few of them before and it was clear that they liked and respected Kathy. He wondered what they would think if they knew she was using her hard-won experience in making explosives safe in order to build explosives that were deadly. But given his target, he thought they would be OK with that. As was he.

Driving back along the M4 to London, Freddie thought through his plan again. It was very simple. The paper that Jackie had given him provided him with Bond's address and photos of the house. It was in Bishop's Avenue, one of London's most expensive locations. It was protected by high cast iron gates and valued by Zoopla at about twenty million pounds. There was a live-in housekeeper and a gardener who came along five days a week. There was a well-established Monday to Friday routine that had made Freddie smile. After he had left the SBS and joined Control Risks, the first thing he had learned was that routines always expose people to danger.

Every weekday, at about seven-thirty, Bond's wife drove her Porsche 911 Carrera 4 GTS Cabriolet to The Gym in Fortune Green Road, about two miles away. She usually returned at around nine-thirty. Almost every weekday the Mercedes arrived at around eight-thirty and Bond walked out of the gates, opened the passenger door and sat in the front. The driver's name was Leroy Reid, a convicted criminal who was not just a chauffeur; he was also known to be Bond's number one man. He lived in a large house in Colville Terrace, Notting Hill, valued at about two million pounds. It didn't have a garage or drive and the car was left in the street overnight. When Freddie had read this he had smiled. *Two birds with one stone.*

The rest of the document included Bond's office address and a number of other addresses in London and beyond. The NCA knew there were dealers and crack cooks in these places but were keeping then under surveillance rather than closing them down, in the hope that Reid or Bond turned up. Freddie snorted to himself. *Good luck with that!* And, obviously, Jackie had come to the same conclusion.

CHAPTER 16

Freddie calculated that the drive to Bishop's Avenue from Colville Terrace in the morning traffic would take about twenty to thirty minutes, so he was fiddling with his bike on the pavement within sight of the Mercedes at eight o'clock. He was wearing full Lycra; sunglasses, an anti-pollution mask and a helmet, confident that no one and no camera would recognise him. He knew there was a good chance that the NCA had some watchers in the area. As he waited, he surreptitiously checked for CCTV nearby and noticed there was none to be seen on Reid's place. *Probably makes sense if you are a criminal*, he thought. And then out came Reid, locking the door with a mortice key, strolling to the car and driving away.

When the car was out of sight, Freddie pretended to have fixed something on his bike and cycled home. He knew all he needed to know and he had a client meeting in More London at eleven o'clock. When the meeting finished and he had dealt with some e-mails, he checked his calendar and then called William. They agreed to meet for supper at Brasserie Blanc in the Fulham Reach development the following evening.

It was lovely and warm and Freddie had a table outside. He poured William a glass of Sancerre as soon as he'd sat down.

"William, I'm after a small favour; actually, a large favour."

"Of course, Freddie. Just name it."

"Actually, those exact words came out of Jackie Starling's mouth when I was 'invited' to her office," he said, making quote marks in the air with his hands. "Happily, I took your advice and I recorded the whole conversation."

William was confused. "She said 'Freddie, just name it'?"

"I wish, William. She was asking for a favour! It's a big one and I need your help."

"Freddie. You saved my life. Sometimes, when I am going to sleep, I remember that moment. I was scared shitless; that crazy woman was going to torture me again. In the car she was jabbing me where she had cut my chest open and telling me how she was going to stick a cattle-prod up my arse. Then, there you were, like a knight in shining armour and with a gun! So, tell me, what do you need?"

Freddie put his hands on the table and spoke softly.

"Sometime in the not-too- distant future I want us to have dinner somewhere and I want to behave as if I am truly pissed."

"No problem there, old chap. Par for the course!"

"Agreed, but in this instance I am so pissed I end up in one of your bedrooms."

"Surprise, surprise!"

Freddie continued. "All I ask of you is for you to put my Garmin on your wrist, go to sleep and hand it back to me in the morning. If you are ever asked, you tell anybody that you put me to bed and woke me in the morning."

"I understand. No need to tell me more. Just let me know when. How about ordering some food?"

CHAPTER 17

June the twentieth. The longest day. Midnight. Freddie rolled on his Lycra and used a sanitiser to wipe his hands, wrists and face. He crept out of his room on William's third floor, walked silently past Ina's suite, crept downstairs and opened the door to the back garden. He knew exactly how to avoid William's CCTV and used the unlocked door into Neveravon Street, confident that his Garmin was on William's wrist. He put on his helmet, rucksack and gloves, got on his bike and headed for Colville Terrace. He stopped for a moment in Goldhawk Road to put on his sunglasses and face-mask and fifteen minutes later he was just one hundred yards from Reid's house. It had started to rain.

Freddie knew that this was the difficult bit. If the NCA surveillance on Reid was twenty-four-seven then the Mercedes would be in their view from the other side of the street. But it was after midnight on a Sunday and it seemed likely that their team would have been stood down. But likely wasn't enough. He put the bike in a nearby garden, grabbed the rucksack and started crawling along the pavement, shielded by all the parked cars. But then some footsteps, a couple walking fast, sheltering under an umbrella. He pretended to vomit into the gutter and they hurried on by. When he reached the Mercedes it was showtime. No more footsteps – nothing. He took Kathy's device out of his rucksack, reached under the car and felt the magnet attach, right under the passenger seat. One hour later he was fast asleep in Freddie's house. And another six hours later his Garmin was back on his wrist.

Tuesday morning, eight thirty-five, bright sunshine. Freddie, a cyclist with dark glasses, an anti-pollution face-mask and a helmet, was near Kenwood House. Far enough away from Edward Bond's house to be safe and close enough to check that there was no one near the car when Leroy Reid pulled up. As before, Edward Bond opened the car door and sat in the front seat. Freddie opened his phone and dialled the three numbers Kathy had given him.

Nothing happened. Freddie held his breath, checked he had dialled the correct numbers and frowned. Nothing. Christ, nothing! Then a massive explosion. He saw the car lift off the road and disintegrate before he heard the bang, followed by the noise of glass shattering, then burglar alarms ringing. He was tempted to take a picture of the smoking remains of the car but he knew that people would already be videoing it, so he took one last look and cycled back home. Job done.

CHAPTER 18

When Freddie sold the house he had inherited from his parents and moved into Fulham Reach, he had no idea what he should take to his new place and what he should do with what remained. Most of the furniture was pretty tired and would not suit a modern apartment. So he decided that there would be three categories: First, those things he would like to take to his new place. They included his Savoir bed and mattress and all his bedclothes and towels. From his kitchen he took Le Creuset pots and pans, his Villeroy & Boch plates and his David Mellor cutlery. His entire collection of clothes and shoes passed the test. The only furniture that made the grade was his Eames Lounge Chair and stool and there were only two pictures that he wanted to keep.

The second category contained stuff that Freddie thought might be valuable and in most cases he was correct. Some of the furniture was antique, some of the old paintings were worth quite a lot of money and some old rugs were considered 'priceless'. When everything was sold, Freddie went to Heal's and discovered that he had more than enough to finish and equip his new home. But the question remained in his head of what to do with the rest of the stuff. He decided to put it into storage using his Miles Bishop alias. He didn't know why, it was just instinctive. He chose the Big Yellow Group self-storage company in Brentford, near Chiswick Roundabout as he had driven past it many times. But today was the first time he had actually visited it. He had the number of the unit and the PIN code to open it.

Getting to the room was very straightforward, but when he opened the door he could hardly believe his eyes. It was full, almost floor to ceiling. The old microwave and cooker on top of a Formica covered kitchen unit. Curtains, carpets and the old TV. He recognised everything; some of the stuff from his childhood. He squeezed between the mountains of material, some of which smelt of his old home, and finally found what he was looking for – the old Hoover. He opened up the bag; he knew it would be empty, as he had shaken out all the dust before he left the house for the last time. Then he reached into his briefcase and removed a sealed plastic bag containing his newly acquired Ruger and rounds, plus the cleaning kit, and put it into the Hoover dust bag. Next was another bag containing a number of knives and finally, an A4 envelope containing all his Miles Bishop papers – credit cards, driving licence, passport, utility bills and a burner phone. Mr Bishop was now very well hidden but easily accessed.

CHAPTER 19

Jackie Starling called the next day.

"Freddie, could we possibly meet up for an informal chat? Perhaps in The Black Dog or maybe somewhere a little more discreet. Perhaps The Crabtree pub? I think that might be more convenient for you, given your new apartment."

"How did you know I have moved to Fulham?"

"You are, as we say 'A Person of Interest' Freddie, and you are of particular interest to me. How about Friday at one o'clock?"

"Done!"

Freddie was sitting in The Crabtree's garden when Jackie arrived. Freddie had been at a client meeting earlier and was wearing a suit but no tie. His recording pen was in his jacket pocket and he had a feeling that the afternoon might be fun. Not least because she was dressed down, to put it mildly – white loose T-shirt and, without doubt, no bra, with faded blue jeans and Converse sneakers with no socks. For a second he wondered if going bra-less was OK for a lady in her forties and in another second concluded it was more than that.

"Freddie, darling. I must say you are looking very smart!" she greeted him as she kissed his cheek.

"Straight from the office, Jackie. Would you like a glass of this white Rioja?"

"Of course! It's Friday and I deserve a drink, and so do

you. Thank you for dealing with that problem. I'm very grateful. I would like to say that my bosses and colleagues are also grateful but they believe that the incident was driven by competitor hostility and may result in reprisals." She leaned forward, smiled and put her hand on his knee under the table. "And that suits me just fine."

Freddie poured the wine and passed her a menu.

"Why don't we have a quick bite here and maybe something else at my place? It's only a five-minute walk and I think you will like it."

She glanced at the menu.

"I will go for the Chirashi bowl. What are you going to have?"

Freddie had no idea what it was but didn't want to waste time.

"I'll have the same." It turned out to be some sort of shredded raw fish and he was surprised that he liked it. Thirty minutes later they were looking at the views of the river from his terrace.

Freddie was lying on the bed in one of his spare rooms. Lesley knew their relationship was not exclusive but he drew the line at having sex with a third party in the bedroom that he shared with her so often. His jacket with the recording device was on the floor and he hoped that it was still working, but he forgot about all of that when Jackie walked into the room stark naked.

"What an amazing place you have here, Freddie. That Japanese loo. All those buttons to press. The warm water spray really hit the spot."

Freddie spent some time with that spot and it was a memorable evening for both of them.

CHAPTER 20

"So, how are we all?" asked Freddie.

The five of them were drinking coffee in Café Plum behind Fulham Reach. Adrian, as usual, was quick off the mark.

"Who was that bloke that inserted his fat fucking self into the pool when we were doing our laps this morning? Surely he knows that we own the pool at that time!"

Steve, as ever, was more reasonable.

"How could he know that?"

Adrian scowled. "Yeah, but did you see him eyeing you up when you were drying yourself, Vanessa?"

She took a sip of her espresso and glanced at Freddie. Her voice was very clear and almost seductive.

"I get used to men eyeing me up, Adrian, and if and when they are attractive men I don't mind at all. But, of course, that man did not fall into that category. I'm sure he got the message when you nudged him into the pool after he had dried himself."

"Sorry, Vanessa, that was an accident! Anyway, I'm off – people to see, places to go, bikes to ride."

After Adrian had gone, Freddie spoke up.

"Adrian doesn't suffer fools gladly and I kind of like that. And did you know that he goes to the cinema two or three times a week? Almost always on his own and at times when the cinema is as empty as possible. Strange chap."

"I like him as well," agreed Vanessa. "I'm sure he was a very caring doctor."

Steve laughed. "I wouldn't bet on it, Vanessa. He has some tales to tell. My guess is 'efficient' rather than 'caring' but, actually, I think I prefer the former to the latter. Anyway, I must be on my way. No people to see, no places to go – just a dog that needs a walk!"

"Freddie," asked Vanessa, "are you by any chance free next weekend?"

His immediate thought was *Result!* He knew that Lesley would be away at another rowing competition and the coast would be clear for some serious seduction.

"Yes, I am!"

Then his hopes were dashed when Vanessa continued.

"Sheila and I were talking here before you guys arrived and she has a small problem. Knowing you as I do, I thought you might be willing to help." She smiled charmingly at him; a smile that looked like it might contain a promise.

"Of course, Vanessa. How can I help?"

She looked embarrassed and he gave her an encouraging look.

"Well, Freddie, Sheila has a cottage near Shepperton Lock and there are some items that she wants to bring here, but using Addison Lee or a car firm like that is expensive and the journey might be a little trying. I mentioned to Sheila that you had a Range Rover and, I know it would be an imposition, but I wondered if you could drive her down there on Saturday morning, help her load up and drive her back here."

Vanessa looked Freddie in the eye and smiled. Freddie smiled back.

"Of course, Vanessa; it would be a pleasure."

CHAPTER 21

Freddie's alarm went off at seven-thirty on Saturday. He felt dreadful. It had been a busy week and on Friday he had chaired a progress update meeting at the bank followed by a team meeting. Lunch was in one of the formal dining rooms on the tenth floor of DPK and the client he was entertaining certainly liked her wine. Then at six o'clock he had arrived at Quaglino's in Bury Street, St James. It was the retirement dinner for a popular partner and Freddie felt flattered that he had been invited. Drinks were being served in a closed off area in the bar and then the guests were directed to the private room overlooking the restaurant and seated on one long table. More drinks were served and then food, then more drinks and then speeches and it was well past midnight when Freddie left.

Sheila was waiting for Freddie in the lobby as agreed and they walked downstairs to the car park. She had some difficulty with the steps, so he held her arm to steady her. It felt light as a feather as did her whole body as he helped her into the front passenger seat of the Range Rover. She started talking as soon as they left the car park and hardly stopped for the whole journey – her late husband 'a real gentleman', their house in Surrey and her grandchildren both doing well at university, then onto politicians 'all crooks', cyclists, skateboarders, scooter riders, buskers and beggars who 'should all be locked up'. Happily, her voice was very soft and didn't invade Freddie's hangover too much. He just murmured suitable responses, nodded his head and focused on the driving. When the GPS beeped she pointed to a short drive leading to a charming little cottage.

"Thank you, Freddie! That was a nice, quiet drive. I felt very safe. Come on in!" The door opened into the living room and Freddie could see the kitchen beyond. It was a nice, comfortable-looking place. "Have a seat. I'll make us some coffee and you can have a rest as I get my things together. I'll give you a shout if I need any help with anything."

Coffee cup emptied, comfortable chair, feet on a stool, the memory of Vanessa's beaming face in his head and Freddie drifted off.

CHAPTER 22

Freddie didn't dream very often, at least he didn't remember many dreams, but those he did remember were usually unpleasant and related to situations where he was in danger; more like flashbacks than actual dreams: Face to face with a tooled up terrorist and his gun jamming when he was in Aden; getting a round through the arm from a helicopter gunship and nearly drowning in the Strait of Hormuz; getting a bullet in his leg when carrying a hostage away from a firefight in Oman; a stab in the back in a large crowd and driving rain; and almost naked, facing a man with a gun who wanted to tie him to a dentist's chair and torture him. This one was different, he felt as if he couldn't move his limbs. He woke up, sighed and opened his eyes. Was he still dreaming? He blinked. This couldn't be a dream. *Oh fuck! Christ! Jesus Christ!* His hands were in his lap, tied together with duct tape. His feet were still on the stool, also tied together with duct tape. And there was Sheila, sitting on a chair nearby and smiling. *What the fuck is this all about?*

"Hope you enjoyed the coffee, Freddie. My special blend. No added colour, no smell and no strange taste. The only problem is the dose – too little and the patient doesn't sleep. Too much and the patient doesn't wake up. Lucky for me that I got it just right. I'm looking forward to having some fun with you. Unlucky for you that you woke up; there is a world of pain waiting for you."

For a moment, Freddie thought he might still be dreaming but that illusion evaporated when he found himself shouting.

"What is this, Sheila? Why am I here? Who the fuck *are* you? Is this some sort of practical joke?"

"Who am I? Good question. I am the person that you sent to suffer terrible pain."

"That can't be. I've never done anything to hurt you, Sheila. I've only known you for a few months. There must be some sort of mistake. Cut me loose and let's try and work this out!"

"You did hurt me some time ago. You hit me on the head with your shotgun and knocked me out. My name then was Sadie. Remember?"

"No! That's not possible; Sadie must still be in prison! Fuck off!"

"I never went to prison. I wish I had! My client spirited me out of hospital and then punished me. I want to show you this." She unbuttoned her blouse slowly and smiled like some sort of striptease artist and then unzipped her skirt. "Look at this, Freddie!"

He gasped. Scars – multiple, terrible scars. Calves, thighs, arms, stomach and neck. He closed his eyes. When he opened them, Sadie was dressing and working herself into Evil Incarnate.

"Now you know why I wear a full body swimsuit and now you know why you have to pay and when I say 'pay' I mean money and agony followed by death" she hissed.

"You fucked me up, Freddie. It took me almost two years to recover and I'm now going to fuck *you* up, but not until you settle my invoice. I shall be back shortly!"

Freddie was a strong man physically, mentally and intellectually. But the scars and the way Sadie was behaving had seriously shocked him. He was worried, not yet really frightened, but when she came back he pretended he was.

"Look, I'm sure we can work this out, so don't hurt me. I'll pay you. I'll pay you all I have. Anything!"

"Indeed you will, Freddie. So let me explain my invoice."

"First, one million pounds. My client left me to die in a most unpleasant and brutal way and I sensed the two colleagues tasked with finishing me off were a bit squeamish, so I persuaded them to listen to me. I offered to pay each of them five hundred thousand pounds to let me go. Of course, I killed both of them later and they suffered a bit, but I didn't recover my money, hence one million pounds.

"Second, pain and suffering; one million pounds. You have seen the evidence.

"Third, medical expenses; five hundred thousand pounds. To be specific, plastic surgery on my face and reconstruction of my breasts.

"Fourth, business continuity. I haven't been able to work. Project Freddie has kept me busy. Call that another half a million pounds.

"Fifth, sundry expenses. It was easy to find out where you worked but I needed a private detective to find your address. They are surprisingly expensive. Then I had to rent a flat in Fulham Reach; they are *un*surprisingly expensive but there were half a dozen available. Then this place, I've been renting it for two months.

Chapter 22

"So, Freddie, you are the accountant and I'm sure you can total up my invoice in your head. Three million five hundred pounds. Think on that while I freshen up."

CHAPTER 23

Freddie began thinking about his 'options'. *Maybe negotiate. But how do you negotiate with a crazy, sadistic woman when you are tied up and there is nothing you have to offer?* He shuddered when he thought back to when he went into the cottage where she had been torturing William. He had seen canes, knives, saws, pliers and pincers, hypodermic syringes, rope, a cattle prod, Tasers, some kind of plastic mask and handcuffs in a bedroom. When he entered the bathroom he had seen faeces and urine in the bath together with a severed bloody toe and what looked like the spectacles William often wore.

His thinking was interrupted when Sadie returned to the room. She was carrying a cardboard box, which she dropped on the floor by his feet. He looked at her; she looked like a quiet little lady, but he knew he was facing a stone-cold sadistic killer. She reached into the box and put a Black & Decker drill on the floor.

"So, Freddie; how are you feeling? I have to say, you *do* look a little pale."

Freddie had made his decision.

"I'm feeling fucking awful since you ask, but I am prepared to pay you. I have almost three million in the bank. But why should I? You said you were going to torture me and then kill me anyway, so let's get to it. Kiss the money goodbye and kiss my arse! Alternatively, let's go back to my apartment, let me get in front of my laptop and I will transfer all the money in my bitcoin account to wherever you want it to go."

"Oh, really. Do you take me for a fool? I have a laptop here. You can use that."

"No, I can't. Bitcoin accounts are protected with a fifty-symbol password and of course I don't carry that in my head. What's more, my account can only be accessed from my computer. If you don't believe that, then Google it now."

Five minutes later, Sadie came back.

"OK, I understand. So I will go and get your laptop and bring it here and you can transfer the money. If all goes well I promise you that you will not be hurt. But think on this, if anything goes wrong, if I get caught accessing your apartment or stopped for speeding or whatever and I can't come back, you will die in that chair. No one knows where you are. No food, nothing to drink – not a nice way to go. Now, where is the key fob for the car? Where are your flat keys and what is the code for the alarm?"

"The keys and the car fob are in my jacket over there. There is a small fob on the keyring; just touch it to the pad near the door and it will stop the alarm. But why should I trust you?"

"If I see the money in my account I promise you that I will let you get in your car and drive away."

Freddie was buying time.

"I suppose I have to trust you."

"Thank you, Freddie, that sounds sensible. By the way, have a good look at the drill on the floor. I found it in the garage. It has a range of speeds and a range of bits. If, for any reason, the money isn't transferred, I'm going to tie your hands over your head, unzip your trousers and pull out your cock and then I'm going to plug in the drill. I expect your cock will have shrunk a bit by then. That was certainly the case when I did something similar a few years ago. There was a lovely scream when I inserted the drill bit into the little hole through which you chaps pee. I can't tell you how I enjoyed his expression when I pushed it in a little further. I waited a minute or two just watching his squirming face before I pulled the trigger. I nearly wet myself! I'll do the same to you. If I pull the trigger too quickly you will faint and the fun will be over. By the way, this drill has all the attachments including the steel thingy that is designed to scrub away rust. Not ideal. But, as they say, 'Needs must when the devil drives'. See you later." And she left the room.

Chapter 24

Freddie had got bored with accountancy, joined the Royal Navy at the age of twenty-three and was selected to apply for a role in the Special Boat Service when he was twenty-six. Like most of the guys selected, he found the process very difficult. In fact, brutal. But finally, he passed and that was when the training intensified. Sitting in Sadie's armchair with his hands wrapped in duct tape and his wrapped feet lying on the stool, he wasn't worried. What he had learned within his first year in the SBS was that the bosses accepted that guys got killed and injured. But they didn't accept that guys could be captured and presented to the media. Stopping this happening required effort or, more accurately, EFRT. Escape from restraint training.

Freddie assumed that Sadie would have found it difficult to wrap his hands behind his back. Maybe she worried that she might have woken him up early. First mistake. But he would have been unconcerned anyway. Second mistake – the duct tape was not as tight as it should have been, unsurprising given her relative strength.

In one test of his EFRT, Freddie's hands were behind his back wrapped tightly by duct tape by a guy that disliked him. No favours, standard procedure: 'Wrap as tight as possible without stopping blood circulation'. He remembered it well. The room was pitch-black, music blared sporadically. Very unpleasant. It took him almost five hours to get free, talking to himself all the time, as instructed. 'Move a little, just a little; move a little more and a little more and a little more. Believe me, you can do it, Freddie. Just a bit more. A strong man can stretch this stuff. Freddie, you *are* that man. Just a bit more. Don't tell me it hurts. Of course it fucking hurts. It's supposed to hurt, but imagine the embarrassment for Queen and country if the world sees you kneeling in the middle of some square having your head hacked off by some fucking long-haired bearded old git with a blunt sword!'

Less than two hours after Sadie had left, and not the five hours he had previously endured, Freddie's hands were free. He pushed himself out of the chair, hopped into the kitchen, found a knife and cut his legs free. Always planning for the worst, he stuck the knife in his pocket, drank two glasses of water and had a good look around the place. No obvious weapons. He ate some cheese from the almost empty fridge and washed his face. He found his phone on the sideboard and had a look at his Range Rover app. His car was about forty minutes away. He checked out the door, it wasn't locked. When Sadie opened it to the left she would be exposed to his right-hand. He sat down and watched her journey on the app.

Ten minutes to go, Freddie went into the kitchen, took a pretty tea towel off a hook, damped it down and wrapped it around his right fist. He found the roll of duct tape, loosened the end and held it in his left hand together with the knife. He waited patiently. He was good at that. Then he heard the car arrive and stop. Moments later the car door slammed and he heard Sadie's footsteps on the path and he smiled – no limp, no need for a stick. She opened the door and he punched her hard in the face. She went over on her back as if being hit by a train and he kicked her in the head. Then he turned her over and knelt on her back, pulled her arms behind her and tied some tape roughly around her wrists, then taped her ankles together. Before she recovered her senses he added additional tightly wrapped duct tape around her wrists, ankles and mouth. He carried her upstairs to the bathroom, dropped her into the bath and left the room.

CHAPTER 25

Freddie walked back into the bathroom with a tumbler in his hand.

"I hope the vodka and ice have not been influenced by one of your potions or we are both in trouble." He shook his head. "You know what, Sadie, or Sheila or whatever your real name is, I don't know what to do with you. Of course, I could kill you now but Vanessa and who knows who else will be wondering if I was the last person to see you and what happened. So I need to think about that." He ripped off the tape from her mouth. "What do you think?"

She whispered something, he couldn't quite hear. He bent down to listen and she spat in his face.

"Fuck you, Freddie! I don't care what you do. You are in the shit and there is nothing you can do about it. Kill me and you will probably get arrested. Leave me alive and, sooner or later, I'll kill you," she snarled, "and it won't be a quick death."

"Yeah, it's a difficult one. I'll need to give it some thought. In the meantime I'm going to leave you in this bath and tie you to the taps, just like you tied up my pal, William. I'll be back sometime tomorrow and I hope I have a plan by then." He cut off another six inches of the tape, plastered it across her mouth and tied her hands to the taps before leaving the room.

Freddie picked up his computer from the path where it had dropped from Sadie's hands. And as he drove back to Fulham, he weighed up his options and decided he needed some help. He called William who told him Ina was golfing all Sunday morning and they agreed to meet at The Old Ship at two o'clock. The sun was shining and, as usual, William had got a table on the terrace overlooking the river with drinks lined up for them.

"So, Freddie; what's up?"

"Well, mate, you know I mentioned the sort of coffee club that has developed between a few of us residents who swim at six-thirty in the pool beneath my place?"

"Of course! The bonkers bloke with all the guitars, the sensible engineer, the actress you fancy and the little lady with the full body swimsuit – I remember."

"Correct. Now, please put your drink down, I think you might spill it when you hear what I am about to tell you."

"Christ, don't tell me you've managed to pull the actress!"

"I wish, William. The little old lady is, in fact, Sadie. The mad sadistic bitch that tortured you a couple of years ago!"

William looked at Freddie carefully. He held his eyes and tried to figure out whether his old friend had finally lost it. After all, they had both been up against it over the past few years.

He swallowed. "Freddie, she is in prison. I saw you knocking her out with the stock of your shotgun and the police put her in an ambulance. Let me go get us another drink and you can tell me more."

William came back with the drinks and wasn't at all convinced that Freddie was talking sense until he explained exactly what had happened.

Then he said, "So, as we sit here, that fucking sadistic nutcase woman who stripped me naked, tied me up in a bath, sawed off one of my toes, almost dislocated my arms, caned my arse, threatened my best friends with similar treatment and cut my chest open, is tied up in a bath near Shepperton Lock. Is that right, Freddie?"

"Yes!"

"So, why isn't she in prison?"

"She told me she was 'spirited away' from the hospital she was sent to because of her concussion."

William took a sip of his drink and frowned.

"Freddie, I think I might be missing something here. You have been conned into driving this headcase to her cottage. You have been drugged, tied up and threatened with torture and managed to escape. For God's sake, she is a fugitive from justice! Why not call the cops?"

Freddie sat back in his chair, looked at the river, stared at the blue sky and then returned his gaze to William.

"That hadn't occurred to me."

William put his hands on the table and laughed out loud.

"Freddie, you are a piece of work! Christ almighty, it didn't occur to you to speak to the police? Why not?"

"I don't know. I guess I'm a bit paranoid."

"Well, forget the paranoia and talk to your special friend in the NCA as soon as possible. I'm sure she will be appreciative, as will the plods when she informs them." He shook his head and repeated his question.

"It really hadn't occurred to you?"

"I'll call her now. Could you order the roast beef for me, please."

CHAPTER 26

Freddie came back before the roast beef arrived.

"I called her and she was pretty chuffed. The job she has now doesn't give her many opportunities to catch crooks herself. She is arranging for some plods to come here so I can pinpoint the cottage for them. I told her to tell them not to underestimate Sadie; she's fucking frightening!"

William looked at him.

"Oh really, Freddie. You surprise me. Not!"

They had finished their rare roast beef, large Yorkshire puddings, cabbage, carrots, roast potatoes and a second bottle of some decent Pinot Noir. The Old Ship was buzzing in the late afternoon sunshine and everyone seemed to be having a good time. And then two uniformed police arrived, walking along the towpath. Conversations stopped or reduced in volume as the officers approached the pub. One of them looked pretty old and weary while the other, young and enthusiastic. Most people noticed the bright yellow Tasers in their holsters. Nobody noticed Freddie waving to them from the pub. Everyone saw them striding towards William and Freddie's table. A sigh of relief when Freddie shook their hands and lots of chattering around them resumed.

The older man introduced himself.

"Good afternoon, Mr Findlay, I'm Sergeant Clive Brown and this is my colleague, Constable Carl Nicholl."

"Good afternoon officers. This is my pal, William, and he is going downstairs to get more wine and leave us in peace for a while. Show me the map and I will point out where the cottage is. Yes, this big picture of Shepperton Lock is a good place to start and, yes, that is the road and that is the little cottage. The door is not locked and the woman is tied up in the bath upstairs. Any questions?"

The older officer smiled.

"I don't think so. We have no idea what this is all about but collecting a little lady should not be too much of a challenge, sir."

Freddie stood up and responded quietly.

"This little lady is very dangerous. I have wrapped her wrists and ankles in duct tape. If I were you I would keep that tape on until you have her secure. Appearances can be very misleading."

"Thank you, sir; that's very helpful. No doubt someone from the place way above our pay grade will be in touch in due course."

As the two officers walked back to their car, the younger one, Carl, frowned.

"Boss, were those two blokes pissed?"

"No idea, mate, but our call involved the NCA so they must have some reach. Could be posh MI5 creeps. They're enjoying beef and red wine in the sunshine and we are off to fucking Shepperton to pick up a little lady and that piss artist tells us that appearances can be very misleading as if we are a couple of rookies. Put on the lights, Carl, I want to get home as soon as possible."

Chapter 27

It was about five-thirty when Carl and Clive arrived at the cottage. Everything was quiet and the door was unlocked.

Clive shouted, "Hello! Anyone here?" But no response. They had a quick look around the living room; the only thing that caught their attention was the Black & Decker drill on the floor. As they went up the narrow and steep staircase Clive shouted again but there was no response. Then Clive's phone trilled. He listened for a moment and closed it. "Fuck! That's all I need. We've been beaten by fucking Brentford!"

Two of the doors at the top of the stairs were open. Carl opened a third door that was closed and gasped.

"Jesus Christ! What is this?" A tiny lady was lying in a bath and whimpering. Her feet were bound with duct tape and it looked like her hands were tied behind her back. Her face was covered in tears and blood and it looked like someone had broken her nose. She was muttering but incoherent. It sounded as if she was mewing. She appeared to be in a great deal of pain and about to lose consciousness.

Clive reached for his phone. "This destination. Immediate ambulance required. Copy?"

"Copy."

"Carl, let's get her out of the bath. You take her shoulders and I'll take her legs. We need to be very careful. She looks very fragile. Let's take off the tape first. What were those piss artists doing to her? Look at the state of her face. She's been beaten up! What the fuck was that bloke doing with her?"

The woman was very light and it wasn't difficult to lift her out of the bath and even though her legs wobbled and her head hung down, they managed to get her on her feet and were able to remove the duct tape. She stumbled into Carl who tried to hold her up and then she opened her mouth wide and bit him in the throat, feeling his warm blood in her mouth and her energy returning. He screamed and as he put his hands to his neck she pulled his Taser out of its holster, pointed it at Clive's heart and pulled the trigger. As Carl recovered and turned towards her she reached down, grabbed Clive's Taser, pointed it at Carl's head, pulled the trigger and kept it firing until the battery failed. Both men were lying on the floor. She felt exhausted and with a broken nose too, tied for more than six hours in the bath and needing a pee. She took off her knickers, stood astride one of the officers and released the flow. Afterwards, as she walked down the stairs, she stopped. *Their car; why not steal their car? Car keys?* She almost started back up the stairs but then decided to see if they were in the car. And they were!

Sadie grinned to herself as she drove towards London although she knew there would be challenges ahead. Not least, she had to get rid of the car and get to her little house in Vauxhall. She assumed that police cars would have trackers so they would be able to trace them, and she decided to dump the vehicle in one of the short stay car parks at Heathrow and then exit the car park driving someone else's car. It all went very smoothly. She parked the police car and wandered around until the right victim came along. A woman was putting her parking ticket in her handbag and about to lock her car. It was a Golf. Sadie had hired one on several occasions and knew where the central locking button would be.

She knew she must look like a total wreck and wasn't surprised that the woman looked a bit concerned as she approached. She gasped when Sadie punched her in the stomach and screamed when Sadie hit her again, grabbed her handbag, picked up the car keys, got into the car, clicked the central locking button, ignored the woman beating on the window and drove down a couple of levels lower. She stopped, checked the parking ticket, took a contactless card from the handbag and drove carefully to the exit. An hour later she parked a few streets from her house, pulled up some dead rosemary from her front garden, retrieved her door keys from the dry soil and she was home. Time for a nice cup of hot chocolate followed by a good night's sleep.

CHAPTER 28

"Whaaat!" shouted Freddie. "You must be fucking joking!" It was ten o'clock on Saturday night when Jackie phoned and she wasn't joking.

"They are both in hospital, the Sergeant is in intensive care."

"I don't give a fuck. I told those guys to keep her tied up until they were somewhere secure. I said 'Don't take off the tape, just pick her up and chuck her in the back'. So, what actually happened?"

"Well, the Constable has tried to put the pieces together. It seems that when they went into the bathroom and saw the woman they were very concerned and called an ambulance immediately. She seemed to be having difficulty breathing, eyes rolling up in her head. Then she seemed to pass out. They ripped off the duct tape and were trying to get her to stand up when she sank her teeth into the Constable's neck and grabbed his Taser. It's clear she was familiar with the weapon. She aimed it at the Sergeant's heart, kept at it then grabbed his Taser and fired it at the Constable. Fucking plods. A complete fucking mess! The ambulance they called for *her* took *them* to hospital. A complete fuck up!"

"She even pissed on them!"

"What?" Freddie didn't know whether to laugh or cry.

Nor did Jackie. "It gets worse. The uniforms had left their car outside the house, unlocked with the fucking keys in the ignition. So she took it. We traced it to terminal three at Heathrow. It seems that she mugged some woman and took her car out of the airport, but we've had no luck at all with the ANPR so far."

"Jesus Christ, Jackie! What a cock-up. Is any of this going to cause you a problem?"

"No. I played it exactly by the rules, but someone in the Met will be up shit creek. This is the second time this Sadie woman has escaped police custody and she is a tiny little woman. It is definitely her; the prints on the car match those on file."

"So, what are we going to do?"

"What do you mean?"

"You know what I mean! What are we going to do about *me*? This crazy sadistic pensioner wants me dead, she wants to torture me and she wants all my money, for Christ's sake!"

Jackie took a while before replying.

"Well, we might be able to provide police protection, but that would be a decision for the Met. It costs a fortune so don't hold your breath. That weirdo author, Salman Rushdie, who wrote *The Satanic Curses* had a fucking fatwa issued to kill him and how much do you think it cost to protect him?"

"*Verses*, not *Curses*, Jackie."

"Whatever! It cost about nine million a year for nearly ten years. That's almost a hundred million pounds. To be candid, Freddie, I very much doubt the Home Office will push the boat out that far."

"Yeah, I get that. See you soon, I hope."

Freddie closed the call and sat back with his eyes closed. It had been a very long day and he knew he had to make some difficult decisions sooner rather than later. He called William and they agreed to meet at the Italian pop-up deli and coffee shop at Hammersmith Terrace at nine o'clock the next day. Then he took a bottle of Whispering Angel out onto the terrace, poured a glass and thought through the choices available.

CHAPTER 29

The Italian deli and coffee shop was about three minutes' walk from William's house and he was sitting in the early morning sunshine with his coffee and a double espresso waiting for Freddie when he arrived.

"So, Freddie, what's up?" he asked.

Freddie took a sip of his coffee.

"What's up is fucked up. Those two cops we met yesterday fucked it up. To cut a long story short, that mad bitch knocked them out, pissed on one of them, put both of them in hospital, stole their police car and disappeared."

William frowned. "I knew those guys weren't listening. Do you mean 'pissed on them' metaphorically or literally?"

"The latter!"

"No. Christ! But serves them right. You warned them. She's a crazy, fucking bitch."

"Yeah, but I think she will be after me as soon as she gets her act together. I need your advice. Option one is to ask for police protection. That costs about a million a year and at that price it's not really an option. Option two is to get rid of Freddie Findlay, convert to my Miles Bishop identity and start a new life, but I don't want to do that. Option three is to wait until she comes for me or I find her; either way I kill her. What do you think?"

"Ina is off playing golf as usual this morning, Freddie, and I think we should stroll twenty yards down to my garden by the river, sit at the table and demolish a couple of Bloody Marys to sharpen our minds. By the way, where is Lesley?"

It was a beautiful morning with a lot of rowers on the water. William arrived with the drinks.

"Is Lesley out on the river this morning?"

Freddie frowned. "She is away for the weekend competing somewhere on the Ouse. At least that is what she told me, but I checked on Google and couldn't find the event. To be fair, some of these events are pretty niche, but I think there is a chance she might be playing away."

William tried to come up with the right words.

"Oh, that would be a shame, she's a lovely girl and she's no idiot. My guess is that she knows she is not exclusive, so who could blame her for having her own fun, particularly with someone of her own age? I mean, some of those lads in that boat over there look pretty fit. Anyway, let's discuss your options."

Freddie sighed, picked up his drink, took a large swallow and coughed. His eyes watered and his face reddened.

"Christ, William, this is some Bloody Mary! Can I have a bit more vodka to lessen the heat?"

"Of course. Here you go," he said while he poured the liquid in. "What's the plan?"

"All the choices are terrible but I have to go with one. I think I should carry on with life and business as usual and wait for that bitch to come to me and when she does I'm going to get her locked up in a padded cell or kill her. I'm also going to ask Jackie to second someone from the

NCA to provide me with some support. Not twenty-four-seven, but just enough to mitigate some of the risks. What do you think?"

"I think you are a brave guy but not foolhardy and it makes sense to see if you can have someone looking after your back. My guess is that the bitch will want to get back at you soon so I would speak to Jackie as soon as possible. I would also suggest that you start carrying your sock knives; as I recall, it's not that long ago that they saved your life."

CHAPTER 30

Three days later, Freddie was waiting in the DPK reception when a tall, slim, very attractive black woman strode up to the desk. She was wearing jeans and a sweatshirt with a leather jacket and trainers; not the sort of clothing that was usual in the building. The receptionist pointed at Freddie who stood up to shake hands. Her grip was firm, her hand cool and she smiled, as she looked him in the eye.

"Good to meet you, Freddie, I've heard a lot about you from the boss, it sounds like you have had a few adventures. As you will have been told, I'm Barbara Hurst and I'm with the Met's Personal Protection team. Here is my ID. By the way, people call me Bea."

Freddie looked at the badge and smiled.

"Bea? Excellent, I think bees are wonderful creatures – loyal, energetic and highly intelligent. But, of course, they have a sting in their tail. Or is that wasps?"

"The boss also warned me about *you*, Freddie."

"What do you mean?"

"She said 'He will chat you up within five minutes. He's good-looking in a sort of ugly way. He is much more intelligent than he pretends to be, can be very charming and ruthless and he will be a nightmare to protect'. Is that correct?"

"Harsh, but true. Let's go and have lunch."

They walked along the river to Le Pont de la Tour and were shown to a table outside with quite a lot of space between tables.

Bea looked around. "Impressive and no doubt expensive."

Freddie explained further. "At DPK we often have lunches with clients in our dining rooms at the top of the office. Very discreet. But sometimes it's nice to be outside and we reserve this table so that we can be sure our conversations are not overheard. So, let's order and get down to business."

Freddie ordered scallops followed by Dover sole; Bea also ordered the sole but opted for a smoked salmon starter and Freddie asked for tap water and a bottle of Petit Chablis. When the wine arrived he pronounced it excellent. Bea shook her head.

"Not for me, thanks."

"Oh no. Please don't tell me you are teetotal!"

"I most certainly am not, but I never drink on duty and that brings me to explain how I operate. Like it or not, there are some rules." She reached into her bag. "Here is the manual. You need to read all of it tonight. That is compulsory. Failing to absorb this document will end your personal protection."

Freddie took the manual. It was as heavy as a hardback book.

"Christ, Bea. Is this really necessary?"

"Yes! Oh good, here are the starters. I'm starving!"

"Bea, can I ask you some questions? They may be pretty stupid."

"Of course, Freddie. We are going to know each other very well for a while, after all. Ask what you want. There are no stupid questions."

"Do you carry a gun?"

"Of course. I carry a Glock 42. It's very small and light and it's in my jacket pocket. There are three handguns available to us. I prefer the Glock 42, whereas some officers dislike it. It's all about what works for you or should I say me."

"Have you fired it at someone?"

"I'm glad you asked me that question, Freddie. It gives me an opportunity to make something clear. We never discuss operations or activities with civilians and you are a civilian. Of course, I have been fully briefed on your history and I respect it, but past operations are a locked file as far as I am concerned. Anything you do, say or think will go into that file and the only person that will ever see it is me unless, of course, you get killed in which case it will be open to the bosses so they can work out how I failed."

"That's a sobering thought," agreed Freddie as he looked around for the wine waiter to top up his glass.

CHAPTER 31

Two days later and Freddie and Bea were sitting at the table on his terrace. She was dressed casually with jeans, trainers, a blouse and jacket. As usual, she was drinking water while Freddie was on his second gin and tonic. It was about seven o'clock in the evening but still quite warm.

"OK, how did I do?" asked Freddie. "It's worse than waiting for my A level results!"

"Actually, you did very well indeed. Very impressive. Well done!"

"Good to hear. So how is this going to work in practice?"

"Well, Freddie, you are an unusual client. Normally we would be providing twenty-four-seven protection with a team of at least half a dozen people with two cars and all the other stuff that goes with it. All that you're getting is me, but rest assured I know how to do this stuff both mentally and physically. The contract for you provides sixty hours per week for six months. What you and I need is a risk assessment for each week so we can decide how best to deploy me. For example, if you are working at DPK all day then you will be in a safe environment, but if you are drunk and wandering back home along the river you will need me by your side. Needless to say, plans will change at short notice and that's OK, so long as you tell me in advance.

Freddie absorbed all this information while sipping his drink.

"Can I tell you something in confidence, Bea?"

"Of course you can. Anything. That's a given."

"I want this bitch, Sadie, to die. She tortured my best friend and she wanted to torture me. She has killed countless people and she has to go. If possible, I would really like it if you could be seen as my girlfriend, not my bodyguard. I'm pretty sure she will have eyes on me very soon and I want to look vulnerable. And here's the thing, I want to kill her – in self-defence. So you need to know that I have a handgun as well."

Bea wasn't at all shocked.

"What have you got?"

"A Ruger. I'm not carrying it now but if things look challenging it will be available."

Bea smiled. "I've already forgotten this conversation. In fact, I wasn't here or on duty, which means you can get me a drink for the first and last time. Very dry vodka martini; Grey Goose, if you have it. No olive, thanks. And don't give me that look! Our relationship will be professional and platonic, not least because I'm gay. Black and gay – the Met's diversity drive got two for the price of one. I'm virtually unsackable!"

Freddie sighed, disappeared to make the drink and when he returned he put his laptop on the table.

"I've given you access to my e-mails and calendar. I'm also going to tell a couple of people that you are helping me with a confidential project and give them the impression we are an item. A couple of people saw us at lunch the other day and that will help and the concierge here will no doubt tell his pals that I have a new girlfriend. All I have to do is square this all up with my actual girlfriend. If I still have a girlfriend!"

"OK. One more thing – your watch, it has to go."

"What? This watch? Surely not. It's a Cartier Tank MC!"

Bea smiled. "And very nice too, but as of now you will be wearing *this* watch every day, all of the time. It's a Breitling Emergency Two and look after it. It cost more than the watch you are wearing."

"Emergency Two – isn't that connected with sailing?"

"Yep, but if you have an emergency on land, it will enable us to find you, unless of course someone takes it off your wrist."

"How does it work?"

"Sit back and I'll explain. It's important. As you can see, it's not slim and elegant but I think that suits you."

Freddie frowned and Bea continued.

"The case holds a PLB Category two beacon microtransmitter. It has to work for twenty-four hours, so that means a bespoke battery that can not only punch out enough power for a satellite to pick up, but that can also be recharged regularly so that power will actually be present in an emergency. It works on two different frequencies. The first is a digital signal on 406 MHz that goes out for 0.44 seconds every 50 seconds and the second is an analogue signal on 121.5 MHz lasting 0.75 seconds every 2.25 seconds. This dual frequency ensures that the emergency signal reaches the search and rescue teams and helps them to zero in on the target – and if shit happens the target will be you."

She tapped the watch. "This is the right-hand antenna cover. It also releases the left-hand cover. From there, pulling the antennae free and extending them, activates the beacon, the signal starts going out and will be forwarded to our control room within a few minutes. By the way, it's waterproof up to fifty metres."

Chapter 32

While Freddie was swimming with Steve, Vanessa and Adrian the next day, the inevitable questions arose. 'Where is Sheila? Is she ill, is she OK?' Freddie had thought about this and had decided to come clean. Then he had changed his mind and now he had changed his mind again.

"There is something I need to tell you about Sheila, but I don't think now is the time or place. Could I invite you to lunch at Sam's Riverside restaurant sometime soon and explain?"

"I could do today," offered Vanessa. "Sounds fascinating."

"So could I!" chorused Steve and Adrian in unison. And five hours later they were all sitting outside Sam's Riverside, looking at the river with a magnum of Rock Angel rosé on the table, food ordered and waiting for Freddie to explain. Which he did, to some extent.

"Sometimes truth is stranger than fiction, so please hear me out. As you know, I'm a partner at DPK. A couple of years ago we identified some issues with a client that suggested money laundering. We took this very seriously and our investigations gave us some very important evidence that our concerns were justified. The evidence was on a data key and one of our team had asked a friend to look after it. To cut a very long story short, the money launderers arranged for our team member to be grabbed and tortured so that they could get the data key. The torturer was the woman we know as Sheila."

"What?" gasped Vanessa. "That little lady? Come on, Freddie, that can't be right!"

"I'm afraid it is. And I became involved. You can Google it if you like. You will see that she was called Sadie and you will also see that I rescued the team member and put her into custody. But, somehow, she escaped and blames me for her misfortune. When I drove her down to her cottage to help her collect some 'things' she drugged me and I was lucky to escape."

Adrian laughed. "All good, Freddie. A lovely story. Come on, what really happened?"

"Have a look at the papers about the two cops that were Tasered near Shepperton Lock the other day. That was her; and guys, please don't make a fuss, please don't look now, but that lady leaning on the wall over there is my police protection officer because they think the 'little lady' is still out to do me harm." He had indicated all quotes with his hands.

Steve looked around the table.

"Are we safe?"

Freddie replied, "You are absolutely safe and I think I am as well. Here's our food. Who wants a top-up?"

CHAPTER 33

Whilst Freddie, Adrian, Steve and Vanessa were enjoying their lunch at Sam's, Sally was eating a Mars bar in a filthy crackhouse in Newcastle. The owner had shot up an hour ago and was lying on the floor with his works on the kitchen table. He was in his forties but looked twenty years older, smelling of sweat and vomit and his clothes were as dirty as the floor. Two kids were cooking crack upstairs and the fumes had given her a serious headache. Life had been terrible since Bond and Leroy had been blown away and the Albanians had taken over. She had decided to get out of the business as soon as she could get hold of enough cash.

She was confident that none of the Albanians knew where she lived or what her surname was and that neither did any of the kids. She had taken over the county lines that Teddy Anderson had been running and was driving his car, but she didn't want to end up like him. She thought back to the killing and the funerals, the grand memorial service for Bond in St Martin-in-the-Fields and the funeral for one of her boys who was stabbed to death. The only people there were herself and the kid's mother. They didn't talk.

She grimaced, looked at her watch and waited for the boy and girl who were supposed to come back with about two thousand pounds. The Albanian boss called Tacic appeared to be able to know immediately if the moneybag was light and Sally had heard that he had beaten to death a kid who had kept back a couple of hundred pounds.

Another kid was due to arrive with product stuffed in his arse. His name was Kayne and he was thirteen years old. Sally guessed his reading and writing age was about seven and he also seemed to be autistic, but if he was caught he would be told to plead guilty and there would be an out-of-court disposal so he could walk free to offend again or end up bleeding to death in a street. *Fuck them*, thought Sally. For some reason a song by The Clash came into her mind, 'Should I Stay or Should I Go'. It was a terrifying choice and she knew the risks, but she decided to go. Just after it got dark and the kids had passed over about two thousand pounds, she stuffed the dirty notes into a plastic bag along with all her other money and some clothes and went for the car. Just as she was fastening her seatbelt, the passenger door opened, Tacic sat down beside her and he was holding a gun.

"Sally, where the fuck are you going?"

She tried to keep her voice steady.

"Just some shopping. We don't have anything to eat, we have no bog paper; we need all sorts of stuff."

Tacic reached for the plastic bag on the back seat and Sally's heart began hammering. It almost stopped when he flicked through the bank notes and slapped her in the face.

"Well, Sally, you seem to have more than enough here for provisions. Let's drive and find somewhere we can have a chat about this but, to be fair, I need to tell you now that I know you were looking to rob me and there will be serious consequences. Turn into this field, drive alongside this hedge and stop, Sally. Get out of the car."

Sally did as instructed and decided to run. She hoped for escape, but if she didn't, at least she would have a quick death. Then the bullet hit her right calf and she fell forward, smashing her face into the ground. She heard Tacic's footsteps approaching and then they stopped. She closed her eyes in anticipation of the shot but he kicked her and rolled her over. There was a wheel brace in his hand, not a gun, and he started beating her savagely. She took a very long time to die. Her mutilated remains and her hacked off head were found by a farmer within a couple of days. Just one more county lines casualty.

CHAPTER 34

Sadie was counting her blessings as she hummed quietly to herself. First, her nose wasn't broken. Her face was bruised and battered by Freddie's punch but it would heal. Second, lots of news coverage but no picture of her in the media except when she was ten years old. Third, she knew where Freddie worked and where he lived. She had even been into his flat. Fourth, she knew his routine. Fifth, she had resources. It wouldn't be difficult to kill him; the challenge would be getting hold of his money and making sure he took a long time to die. She decided it was time to clear her mind. She knew what she needed so she made the call.

The space was in the attic – white walls and bright, hot sunshine streaming in through the skylights. Her palms were damp; she was sweating even though she was wearing a thin cotton dress. She was nervous and excited. This was the first time she had visited Mercia since she had been in that cellar and she wondered how she would react when she saw the scars.

"Take off your clothes, Sadie!" she demanded and then, "Look at your scars! Please don't tell me that your tastes have become more violent. In fact, don't say a word unless it is 'the' word in which case I will stop. What is the word today?"

Sadie muttered, "Freddie," and put her hands into the ropes on the wall and prepared herself for the pain in her arms and shoulders when she was lifted off her feet. She licked the wall and waited for the first slash of the cane on her buttocks. Twenty minutes later she was strapped to a bench with her feet on the floor and Mercia was dropping hot wax on her body. Exquisite pain. Then Mercia started kissing the inside of her thighs and her tongue moved upwards very slowly. Exquisite pleasure.

When Sadie got back to her house she drank two glasses of water, slipped into her bed and slept for ten hours. Then it was time to plan.

CHAPTER 35

On Sunday evening, Freddie and Bea had a Zoom meeting to discuss the agenda for the following week. Freddie explained what he would be doing, where he would be going and what might change. Monday wasn't complicated: DPK office in More London all day, including a client lunch, drinks with William at One Lombard at six o'clock and supper with Lesley at home.

Bea said she would come along later that evening to introduce herself to Lesley and help Freddie explain the arrangements; however, when she arrived, there was no sign of Lesley. Freddie explained.

"Lesley has given me the elbow. When I told her I was under police protection she went white and then she got angry. I can't blame her, it's only eighteen months ago since I got stabbed in the back and nearly died. There's another thing, she's been 'spending some time' with one of the guys in her rowing club. To be honest, I was beginning to think that she might have been seeing someone else and I can't blame her for that either. So, there we are."

Bea was brisk. "Sorry about that. Anyway, I've been thinking about travel. It's probably where we are most vulnerable. DPK is safe and so is this place. By the way, I'm going to fix this little camera outside your door, so you can have a look outside via your laptop if someone rings your bell or knocks. I know the concierge should call you if you have a visitor, but you never know."

"So, what about travel?" asked Freddie.

"My suggestion is that you avoid public transport completely and walk as little as possible. Prebook cabs – Addison Lee, whatever. I will be available most evenings so I can collect you from DPK or wherever you are. Think of me as a chauffeur; I've done all the Met courses and I love driving. Believe it or not, our cars have bullet-proof glass and blue lights and bells for emergencies. What's more, we don't get parking tickets so I can be right outside wherever you are and if you are out on a date, there is a button you can press which raises a soundproof glass partition between the front and the back. I also have such a button!"

"Do I have to sit in the back?"

"Of course!"

Freddie frowned and Bea continued.

"Now, in places such as DPK where there is no traffic access, you inform me where you will be and I will be hanging around outside; for example, in More London I will be in that Davy's place or outside M&S."

"What if I have just agreed to have a few drinks with a pal after work or something?"

"Sorry to say this, Freddie, but spontaneous decisions have to be ruled out for the time being. You have to call me and let me know where you will be."

"Excuse me for a moment, Bea, I need to top up my drink. Can I get you something?"

"Tap water, please."

When Freddie returned, Bea put away her phone and leaned forward.

"Freddie, I've been doing this job for a number of years and I want to tell you about my primary concerns."

"That sounds ominous."

"Well, not necessarily. But here we are. You might be looking over your shoulder for Sadie but there is every chance that she might outsource your capture. Without getting paranoid, you need to consider that almost anyone could be a potential threat. You chat up some attractive lady, in a bar or wherever, and when it's closing you invite her back to your flat. She says her flat is nearer and off you go. Lots of kissing and cuddling in the cab and you're looking forward to seeing her naked, but guess what you see when she opens her flat door – Sadie and a Taser."

Bea took a sip of her water and continued.

"You are my client and I guess in your business 'the client is always right', but that's not going to be the case with our contract. I am *always* right. If I say 'jump', you jump. In my research, I discovered information about the incident when you worked for Control Risks and I spoke to the woman that accompanied you when you paid a ransom and collected a kidnapped executive in Oman on the Yemen border. She said you laid down the rules and she followed them and it all worked out pretty well. Think of you as her and me as you."

CHAPTER 36

On Tuesday morning, Freddie got a call from Caroline Brady. She was Alex Bracken's executive assistant. Alex was the senior partner responsible for DPK's Financial Services side of business and he was Freddie's boss. He wanted to have a chat so they met up at five o'clock in one of the top floor meeting rooms. It had a wonderful view of Tower Bridge and the Tower of London, but neither of them noticed it anymore.

"So, Freddie, how are things?" asked Alex.

"Pretty good; the UK bank is on track but, as you know, the clients operate in nearly a hundred countries and some of our people in some of the territories need a reminder of the deadlines. I've arranged a schedule of Microsoft Teams calls and I can update you in a couple of weeks if that would be helpful."

"Yes, please but, actually, Freddie, that's not why I wanted to have a chat. A couple of colleagues have asked me why you now have a car and driver. What's that all about?"

"Well, William West had a driver, didn't he?"

"Yes, but that was when he was no longer a partner and I'm told that your driver sometimes looks as if she is concerned about your security."

Freddie stood up and walked over to the sideboard to get a glass of water. He raised his eyebrows and beckoned to see if Alex wanted one. He shook his head, smiled and looked expectant. He trusted Freddie but his bullshit detector was on red alert.

"OK, mate, this is between the two of us. Let me repeat the question I asked you just now. How are things?"

"Truth be told, Alex, things are a bit complicated at the moment."

"Oh really! Tell me something new, Freddie! You have three ex-wives, God knows how many children and God knows how many cars. You rescued William West from some madwoman connected with that money laundering thing, you got stabbed in the back by a complete stranger outside Fulham Football Club, you got suspended from the firm for offering cocaine to a client's wife and now you are telling me 'things are a bit complicated at the moment'!"

Alex wasn't angry or even particularly worried. He was a senior partner in the largest of the Big Three firms and little was left to surprise him. His partnership income was over two million pounds and he was worth every penny. He pressed the button on the table and an immaculate-looking man in a grey suit with a bright white shirt and a grey tie arrived within thirty seconds.

"How can I help?"

"A bottle of white Rioja, please. Thank you."

CHAPTER 37

"Oh, look at that!" exclaimed Alex. "I love to see this!"

They were both standing up and looking out of the huge window. Five-thirty in London's rush hour – cars, buses, taxis, cyclists and pedestrians brought to a halt as Tower Bridge was raised to allow one solitary Thames sailing barge upriver. When they turned around the wine had arrived.

"Anyway, Freddie, where were we? Oh yes; you were about to enlighten me on your driver." Alex sipped his wine and sat back.

"Well, Alex, you mentioned that madwoman who captured William. I had assumed she would be locked up for a long time but it seems she escaped from hospital and wasn't even charged. For a number of reasons, she is trying to track me down and kill me and my 'driver', who is in fact a police protection officer on contract for the next six months."

"Fuck off, Freddie! Are you serious? What if clients find out?"

"I've been giving that a lot of thought and have a plan."

"OK."

"If anyone, anyone at all, internal or external, mentions anything about my driver we tell them the truth. The Home Office has provided her as a matter of routine for as long as my project is concerned. It's a highly confidential need-to-know project – the only person in the firm that needs to know is you."

"Cut the bullshit and humour me, mate. What is this Home Office project?"

Freddie considered Alex and lowered his voice.

"That madwoman who tortured William has escaped from custody twice; the Met police are desperate to keep the second escapade under the kimono and to capture her as soon as possible – and they want my help. The project has some complicated words and digits but I think of it as 'Project TG.'"

"Project TG? Why Project TG and is it chargeable?"

"It's not chargeable, but I'm sure it will help the public sector team when they pitch for Home Office work in the future."

"Oh, that's made my day! But you still haven't answered my question. Why have you named it Project TG?"

Freddie frowned. "As you know, I have a penchant for naming projects. I like the names to cut to the chase."

"Yes, mate, and sometimes the clients have been somewhat unimpressed. The most recent one I remember didn't go down too well with some digital bank start-up, but we won't go into that now. Come on, what does 'TG' stand for?"

"Tethered Goat."

Alex stood up, walked to the huge window and glanced over the river, then he turned around.

"Tethered Goat! Freddie, you *do* like to cut to the chase, don't you. Are you thinking that the Met is setting you up to be attacked by this woman so that they can grab her?"

"Alex, you can always read my mind."

Chapter 37

"Cut the bullshit, mate. Why would you want to do this?"

"Frankly, Alex, I don't think I have a choice."

Alex put his chin on his hands and closed his eyes for a minute or so. He stood up and went to look out of the window, then turned to Freddie and touched him on his shoulder.

"Frankly, Freddie, I agree. If there is anything – anything – we can do to help we will be here for you twenty-four-seven. I'll need to inform Partnership Protection, but apart from that, Project TG is good to go from here. Just don't do too much wining and dining on the engagement code!"

CHAPTER 38

Monday morning and Freddie was trying not to look at Vanessa as she took off her goggles and swim cap, shook her hair and started to towel herself dry.

"Freddie," she began, "I'm still feeling guilty. It was my suggestion that you helped out Sheila or Sadie or whatever she is called. You could have been killed!"

Freddie remembered the Black & Decker drill and shuddered inside.

"How could you have known? Don't give it a second's thought. I'd actually seen her before and didn't recognise her. Limping around with that stick, who could have guessed?"

"Well, I'd like to take you to lunch to put things right. What do you think?"

Freddie beamed. "Vanessa, that would be delightful. Thank you!"

The following Saturday at one o'clock, Freddie walked off Chiswick High Road into Villa di Geggiano and saw Vanessa at a table in the courtyard under the olive trees. It was the first time he had seen her with eye make-up and lipstick. She was wearing a bright yellow silk dress and looked amazing. She stood up and they air kissed.

"Don't forget lunch is on me, Freddie. Let me pour you a glass of this excellent Trebbiano. Have you been here before?"

"No. I walked past it a few times when I lived in Chiswick but I hadn't realised how lovely this space is. It's like Tuscany, not West London."

"I didn't know you'd lived in Chiswick. I lived in Bedford Park until last year, which is how I got to like this place; it was walking distance. Why did you move to Fulham Reach?"

"The house in Chiswick was my parents' place, far too big for a single bloke."

"Single? Divorced? Children?"

"Divorced three times, three children and two grandchildren. How about you?"

"Widowed, two children, three grandchildren. Now we've done that, shall we order?"

Freddie went for the burrata followed by sea bass and Vanessa ordered the scallops and chicken. They agreed to share some roast potatoes and baby spinach. After their order was taken by one of the charming waiters they sipped their wine, already comfortable with each other's company.

"Freddie, tell me about yourself. I can't really figure you out and what about this police protection? Is it real and, if so, where is she?"

"She dropped me off and will be nearby. It's really weird having her around but I'm getting used to it."

"So, tell me about yourself. No need to go into the three ex-wives!"

"I qualified as an accountant straight from university and did pretty well, but it bored me to death, so I decided to join the Royal Navy. That went well also. Then I moved to a company called Control Risks–"

Vanessa interrupted, "Why? Why leave the Navy? Who are Control Risks?"

"Well, a navy pal of mine who had been recruited by Control Risks suggested that I might want to join."

"What do they do?"

"Control Risks? They control risks! To put my cards on the table, my pal and I met when we were in the SBS and–"

"God, Freddie; please explain! What on earth is the SBS?"

"It's the Special Boat Service, the Navy's equivalent of the SAS, so when you are approaching forty you get moved to some boring job and wait for your pension. Quite a few special services guys have moved to Control Risks to get a more interesting role. Anyway, I really enjoyed my time there but then I moved to Lloyd's of London and specialised in K&R insurance. Oh good; here are our starters."

Starters finished and another bottle of Trebbiano ordered, Vanessa continued.

"What is K&R insurance?"

"Kidnap and ransom. My role at Control Risks included that area and I was headhunted by underwriters in Lloyd's that focused on that market. Between you and me, it was a bit murky because companies don't want anyone to know they have the insurance as it increases the risk of staff being kidnapped. Anyway, it was a desk job and I used my spare time to renew my chartered accountant qualifications and ended up at DPK where I am now a partner. Is the interview finished now?"

Vanessa smiled. "Of course it is. At least for the time being."

As if on cue, Freddie's phone pinged with a message from Bea:

'Vanessa is clean. I'm off. Make sure you book a cab to take you home. Speak tomorrow.'

CHAPTER 39

Freddie sighed contentedly.

"That was a wonderful lunch, Vanessa. Very generous of you and I hope you will allow me to reciprocate in due course."

"Of course, Freddie. In the meantime, would you like to finish the afternoon with a glass of Champagne on my terrace?"

"That sounds like a wonderful idea."

Vanessa's terrace was a little smaller than Freddie's and the river view a little obstructed but the décor in the apartment was incredible – Art Deco wallpaper, carpets, chairs and tables, little statues and, amazingly, a huge Art Deco print of an almost completely naked Vanessa. It stopped Freddie in his tracks. He was speechless. Tanned skin, dark nipples, a hint of pubic hair and eyes saying 'Come on and make love to me'. Highly sophisticated erotica.

"Do you like it, Freddie?" she asked, noticing that he was entranced.

"Words fail me. It's so sexy."

"I like it as well. It's my mother, a year before I was born."

"Your mother? She looks just like you."

"That's very kind of you to say but she was thirty when that print was created. I'm approaching fifty and I've had two children, but I try to keep in shape."

"You do far more than that. I can hardly keep my eyes off you when we are at the pool."

"Don't think I haven't noticed. You're pretty fit yourself, but where did you get those scars?"

"Knife fight in Afghanistan, helicopter gunship in the Strait of Hormuz, firefight in Oman, a disagreement with some people in Nigeria and a stabbing outside Fulham Football Club."

"What? Fulham? Craven Cottage?"

"Yep, mistaken identity."

They sipped their Champagne while sitting on the very comfortable sofa, waiting for each other to say what they were both thinking. Vanessa broke the silence.

"Two questions, Freddie: Would you like another glass of Champagne and would you like it here or in my bedroom?"

"I think you already know the answer to both!"

"Wow, Vanessa, that was wonderful and you are even more sexy than your mother!"

"Is that supposed to be a compliment, Freddie?"

"Well, I suppose it is, but you know what I mean. It was great and you have a lovely, wonderful body – even better than I imagined when I laid in bed thinking of you in that swimsuit."

"Oh, really? Anyway, no one could describe *your* body as wonderful but I have to confess that it is definitely fit for purpose – for the time being!"

Freddie kissed her breast and talked to her skin.

"Well, in the meantime, do you feel like doing a line?"

"Good God, yes. I hadn't had sex for ages and I haven't had coke for ages either. If the coke is as good quality as the sex, I shall be in your debt."

Freddie pulled on some clothes and was back five minutes later. It was nearly midnight when he slipped out of Vanessa's bed for the second time and stumbled back to his apartment.

CHAPTER 40

A week later, William and Ina were in his usual booth in Balthazar, celebrating two years since their first date when they had sat in the very same seats. He was drinking Sipsmith vodka on the rocks while she was enjoying a glass of Côtes de Provence.

"Cheers!" said William. "Thank you for two wonderful years. I can't believe that it's been so long since we met at dinner in Ibis Lane on the marina in Chiswick. God, time flies faster every year. Anyway, I haven't seen you since last weekend. How was your week?"

"Not easy, not fun. No time for exercise, let alone golf. My driver picks me up at seven-thirty and drops me back home anytime between seven-thirty and eight, unless of course I have a dinner to go to. Anyway, let's order and change the subject. It's the weekend!"

William ordered his usual dressed crab followed by the hamburger and Ina asked for tuna tartare, lemon sole and a bottle of Whispering Angel. She knew the wine was overrated but she didn't care.

"So, what's new with you?" she asked.

"The allotment is in great shape. I'm running or walking every day and generally pleasing myself. My non-exec role with the firm in Mayfair is going fine; I've had yet another approach from a headhunter concerning other non-exec roles, but I can't be bothered. Tell you what though, I had a drink with Freddie on Thursday evening and it was very interesting."

Ina smiled but it looked more like a frown.

"Freddie… 'interesting'? Sounds like trouble to me."

"Well, first of all, we were right. Lesley has dumped him. I don't think he was too cut up about it and guess what, he has already found a replacement, a glamorous, wealthy, middle-aged lady with a successful interior design business and a flat almost next door to his. I've never seen him so chuffed."

"What about this woman, the one who nearly killed you? The one who is supposed to be looking to attack him. Any news on that?"

William chose his words carefully.

"As you know, Freddie has police protection at the moment. DPK has put out a story that the protection is standard when working on highly sensitive Home Office projects and has explained that Freddie is working on such a project, namely Project TG."

"TG? What does TG stand for?"

"Standard DPK response – 'If I tell you I'll have to kill you!'" William lowered his voice. "In a way, it is a genuine Home Office project but, in reality, it is a Police Project. That woman who nearly killed me and recently nearly killed Freddie is a serious embarrassment to them. She has escaped custody twice and they need to catch her quickly."

"Yes, William, I understand; but what does TG stand for?"

"It stands for 'Tethered Goat'. Freddie's choice!"

"Jesus Christ! There I am complaining about my workload and there is Freddie being set up so that madwoman can get to him, no doubt despite the Met's 'best endeavours'." Ina said, using her hands to make the quote marks. "Why would he do it?"

"He said he had no choice."

"Poor Freddie. Let's ask him and his new squeeze to lunch next weekend. Saturday is best for me as I'm playing with Ginny at Royal Mid on Sunday, but if they get back to us quickly I can probably change that. By the way, is that burger too rare?"

"No. It's perfect, but I think I need something like a Pinot Noir to go with it."

The waiter arrived with the wine list before William even had a chance to glance around.

CHAPTER 41

When Freddie had a problem there were many people he could approach to see if they could help: Sky, if he needed to be cheered up; William, for common sense; Kathy, if there was a need for weapons; Alex and colleagues, if it was a business issue and Jackie if it involved the police. When it came to technology, however, it came down to Euan. He called him.

The phone connected and a Scottish voice answered.

"Motto?"

Freddie replied, "BSAGFU."

Euan asked, "Who the fuck are you? Surely not Freddie?"

"Yes, it's me, mate. Got a minute or do you want to call me later?"

"Now is fine. How can I help? How much is the budget? What is the timeline? Do I have to come to your cold, damp little island?"

"You won't even need to leave home. Let me explain how you can help me."

And one call later they both agreed that the tethered goat might need something special to get free. Freddie decided not to tell anyone but dropped a couple of clues to Bea as she was driving him from the office to the Oxo Tower restaurant for a client dinner to celebrate a merger completed. The first clue was the motto he used with Euan.

"I was talking to an old SBS buddy last night and he reminded me of the SBS motto. It was altered a bit back in the day and is now simply 'By strength and guile', but we often just used the initials 'BSAG' or sometimes 'BSAGFU'. That stood for 'By strength and guile, fuck you!' So, if anyone ever uses those acronyms, they are likely to be good guys."

"Are you OK, Freddie?"

"Sure, just making conversation."

He dropped the other clue when Bea was driving him home the next day.

"My pal, Euan, might be coming over from New York to stay with me for a few days. Do you need some information to vet him?"

"No, that won't be a problem. See you tomorrow."

Chapter 42

William loved entertaining friends and Tina, his housekeeper, was always happy to help. She arrived at nine-thirty on Saturday, before Ina was out of bed, and William was ready to explain what was required.

"We have two guests coming, neither of them has any allergies or stuff like that. If the weather stays like it is, we will have drinks by the river and lunch in the back garden. If it changes, we will eat in the dining room. I'll organise the drinks before lunch and I think we agreed that you would do the nibbles."

Tina didn't remind him that he had already explained all this the day before.

"Of course, William. We will have homemade cheese straws, the sushi and sashimi that will arrive shortly and those Twiglets that Freddie likes so much. Are we still thinking about vichyssoise being served at one-thirty?"

"Yep. There or thereabouts and the coronation chicken and salad can come out whenever you see fit. Don't let's worry about the dessert and cheese yet!"

Ina arrived in the kitchen.

"Morning Tina. Any chance of a cup of tea? I've got a hangover and it's all William's fault!"

"Unfair! It was *you* who ordered the second bottle in La Trompette. Anyway, I have already made the tea and I've been for a run!"

"Don't you just hate Mr Perfect sometimes, Tina?"

She smiled. "My lips are sealed," and put her earphones back on.

Freddie and Vanessa arrived at the house at twelve thirty-five and Ina sneaked a look at the protection officer as she parked her car. She looked very professional and rather attractive. Ina decided to have a chat with her.

"Hi, I'm Ina. Do you want to have a look around?"

"Yes, please. What a wonderful place. Is that garden over there yours?"

"Well, William's actually. There's a large garden at the back of the house where we shall be having lunch. Would you like to join us? There's plenty to go round."

"I'm fine, thanks, and anyway, I will be off soon."

When Ina returned to the house she gave Freddie a hug, looked at Vanessa and then looked at her again.

"Vanessa, Vanessa Wright – interior designer for the rich and famous. I love your programme!"

Freddie looked a bit confused but decided to keep quiet.

"Thank you, Ina! But actually, the really rich and the really famous people seldom appear on the programme; the last thing they want is people looking at where they live. There are usually confidentiality clauses in the contracts I get, but I love sharing some stories with friends on a no names basis; for example, I have a new client who has just bought a twenty-million-pound house in Chelsea and one requirement is to have an outside lavatory facing out onto his garden. My view is always 'Why not?' but just look at your house. It's amazing!"

Chapter 43

The drinks on the river garden lasted longer than planned but the vichyssoise was still nicely chilled at two o'clock and everyone demolished all their coronation chicken. Ina and Vanessa were talking nineteen to the dozen so Freddie and William excused themselves, walked around the garden, sat by the rill and enjoyed the sound of the water.

"So, Freddie; how is Project TG?"

"I'm just hoping, or should I say praying, that the bitch comes for me while I still have police protection. She's like a fucking female Houdini. You heard me speak to those uniforms and lo and behold they ended up in hospital soaked with her urine. I only have one certainty and that is that she will want me in a bath, just like she had you in a bath and I had her in a bath last month. God knows what goes on in her mind."

"Changing the subject, Freddie, I have to say that Vanessa is a very attractive woman, good-looking and very smart. God knows how you have managed to build a relationship with her."

"I've surprised even myself, old chap. She used to be an actress and I lusted after her in my youth. I shall do my best to keep her close. Fancy some weed or a little more wine?"

"Both, please!"

Tina had looked after all the washing up and as it had turned a little chilly, they were sitting in William's first-floor drawing room dinking more wine and watching REM at Glastonbury on Samsung's Frame TV. Ina was asleep, Vanessa and Freddie were cuddling up, but William was worried. It had been a wonderful lunch – food, wine, company and weather – but autumn had now arrived and for some reason it made him feel pessimistic. It didn't take long for his fears to be realised.

CHAPTER 44

It was Thursday evening and Freddie was very tired. The first three days of the week had been very challenging and it looked likely that he would be doing a lot of travelling over the next few weeks, possibly to twenty different countries. Now he was about to head to All Bar One in Cannon Street for a leaving party but he decided to go home instead. As he began to cross the street to the tube station, he saw a black cab with its light on and breathed a sigh of relief. It pulled up.

"Where to, Gov?"

"Fulham Reach, Hammersmith."

"Gotcha." Little did he know how apt that little word was.

Halfway through the e-mails on his phone, Freddie took a moment to check the cab's progress, but he didn't know where they were. He was used to cab drivers finding short cuts when traffic was heavy, but was this guy trying to rip him off? He had been in the cab for thirty minutes. He knocked on the glass partition. Normally the driver would slide it across to listen, but this driver ignored him so Freddie, who was getting irritated, shouted at him.

"Where are we and how long to Fulham Reach?" No response. *Fuck!*

He called Bea and left a breathless message.

"I think I have a big problem. I'm in a cab, the doors are locked, the driver's screen won't move. I have no idea where I am! Please call me."

Again, he tried to work out where he was but didn't recognise anything. No river, no park, no tubes, no railway stations. He wondered for a moment if he was having some sort of breakdown, then the cab stopped, the door opened and he had a glimpse of Sadie's face before a flashlight in his face closed his eyes and a Taser hit him in the chest. Seconds later, as he was recovering from the stun, he felt a sharp prick in his arm.

CHAPTER 45

The rush was just starting, accelerating; his heart was beating faster, but in a good way. There was nothing to worry about anymore, no pain – nothing – but then something. Something wonderful, filling his head, his chest, his whole body floating like an astronaut in space. *Getting better all the time* running through his mind – euphoria.

Then a voice.

"Hello Freddie; it's me."

Freddie knew where he was before he opened his eyes. He was in a bath with his hands tied behind him and his feet tied to the taps, just like William a couple of years previously. Somehow, he knew this was going to happen, and somehow, he wasn't scared. The mad bitch wanted the money and that gave him some control. He had reasoned that killing him and not getting any money was Plan B. Plan A would be getting the money, hurting him as much as possible and then killing him. He knew some pain was inevitable.

Sadie ruffled his hair and smiled at him.

"Oh, Freddie, how lovely to see you again. I'd forgotten how heavy you were. Bernie and I struggled to drag you up here. I hope it didn't hurt you when we dropped you. I think you may have a nasty bruise on your bottom. Just to let you know, we threw your phone out of the taxi a few miles away and that hi-tech watch with the emergency signal followed it. I've seen one of those before – brilliant devices. Anyway, it's nice to know we won't be disturbed. By the way, please don't do anything silly. My Pulse+ Taser is already recharged and ready to go. It has that flashlight. Rather clever, don't you think? You can buy if for self-defence on Amazon. It's about five hundred dollars plus postage if you are interested." She laughed. "Of course, you aren't. And you never will be!"

Sadie sat down on the lid of the lavatory by the bath and continued.

"Let me explain what's going to happen, Freddie. I've given your door keys and alarm fob to Bernie and he's going to collect your laptop and charger." She glanced at her watch. "It's nearly eight, he should be back by nine-thirty and then I expect you to transfer the money you owe me."

"What did you inject me with?" croaked Freddie.

"Ketamine. Do you want some more?"

"You're wasting your time. Let me explain what is actually going to happen. You are going to hurt me; that's inevitable, but you are not going to get any money. I have already transferred all my money to a very good friend in the USA and I have instructed him not to transfer it to you under any circumstances – any circumstances! I might scream, I might yell, I might cry and beg him to move the money. I might say anything and do anything, but he won't move it. If you don't believe me you can call him, e-mail him, Facebook him or whatever."

"I don't believe you!"

"Well, when my laptop arrives I will show you the transfer. In the meantime, why don't you e-mail him? It's Euan with a 'u' at 'euancdc dot com.'"

Sadie thought for a moment.

"Why not? I think I will invite him to a FaceTime."

CHAPTER 45

Sadie's laptop rang and she was looking at Euan.

"Hello, Euan, thank you for calling. Have a look at this!" She moved the laptop so that Euan could see Freddie in the bath.

"Bitch. Fucking crazy bitch! Let me tell you this. If you hurt Freddie I will find you and kill you – slowly."

Sadie tittered. "Well, I *am* going to hurt him. In fact, I am going to hurt him on camera for you. Won't be a minute." She was back in less than that.

"Have a look at this, Euan, I bought it just the other day. It's a culinary blowtorch made by SousVide and it puts out consistent reliable flames that create amazing crusts in no time. It's the Rolls-Royce of food torches and I've been dying to try it out. You just pull the trigger and there you are. Gently does it!"

Freddie shouted "Fuck!" as she moved the blue flame from his elbow to his shoulder.

She tittered again.

"Oh, do stay still, Freddie!"

On the screen, Euan tried to appear unmoved.

"You can fry his arse for as long as you like. You can cook his cock and he can beg me to make the money transfer, but it's not going to happen!"

"So, what is your proposal?"

"I need to think about that."

Euan closed the call and got busy. His business was cybersecurity. His clients included major US companies and the CIA. He knew that the Wi-Fi routers in almost every house connected to individual computers and it was those routers that then connected to the rest of the Internet using their own individual IP addresses. He was also aware that there was a tool called IP geolocation lookup, which would enable users to identify the whereabouts of an IP address. More importantly though, his company had developed a tool that used satellite technology to pinpoint a router or at least was able to identify a very specific location. Within five minutes his team had provided him with the UK postcode and an aerial view of the location of Sadie's computer.

CHAPTER 46

Bea was running her hands though her hair, her stomach was churning. She had never lost a client before and Freddie was no ordinary client. She knew it was unprofessional, but she found him very attractive and had hoped that they would get together after the assignment. That didn't look likely now though; his death looked imminent.

The local police had now searched the location where the cab had stopped and found Freddie's phone but there were no CCTV cameras anywhere nearby. In fact, they had nothing. The Met's area commander was trying to remain calm. He had put a rapid response team on standby, but Bea was getting to her wit's end, not just because of the anticipated backwash when his body was discovered but her feelings for Freddie personally. When her mobile rang her heart sank.

"Is that Bea?"

"Yes. Who is this?"

"My name is Euan, I'm a friend of Freddie's."

"Why are you calling me?"

"Because I know where he is."

"Don't be ridiculous and get off this line. We have an emergency here. Fuck off, whoever you are!"

"'BSAG' – does that ring a bell with you?"

Chapter 46

Bea remembered Freddie telling her about the guy and the acronym.

"Christ. Yes! Can you really help?"

"Yes. Give me your e-mail and I will send you a small file; stay on the line."

Bea opened the file. It had the postcode and a view of three properties by a small park in North London.

Euan spoke swiftly.

"The IP address is in one of these properties and Freddie will be there. I'm going to send you another file, which will be both helpful and horrible. Call me when it's all over."

CHAPTER 47

Sadie was looking thoughtful.

"Whilst we wait for your American friend, Freddie, something is troubling me. It's your other arm. As William might have told you, I am an artistic surgeon. I like to do the right thing for my patients, so I need to use my lovely little SousVide blowtorch to make each arm the same. But please don't worry, I'll ensure the crusts match exactly."

Freddie screamed when the torch burnt his arm and when he got his senses back he was more scared than he had ever been. She was holding a Black & Decker drill.

"I remember that look on your face when I told you how I used a drill like this on a patient's penis. You went pale! Then I referred to the little hole through which men pee." She smiled. "It's called your urethra and I shall be using the smallest drill bit so it's not too messy. And don't worry, the battery is fully charged. See you later."

Freddie's upper arms were hurting like hell and he could still smell burnt flesh. But he had hope. He was confident that Bea would have listened to Euan; he was a persuasive guy. He also knew that the location of an IP address could be quite wide. He needed to buy some time and, in spite of the pain, he decided to apply some of his sales techniques.

So, when Sadie returned to the bathroom, he asked her a question.

"Sadie, how did you learn all this stuff?"

"What stuff?"

"The tools, the drugs, the instruments and keeping people alive for interrogation. People like me. How do you get your clients?"

She sat on the side of the bath and relaxed a bit.

"In my youth I spent many years working in care homes looking after old, incontinent, stupid men and women. Most of them were vegetables and drugged up to the eyeballs. It was dirty, boring work so I amused myself by causing them pain and experimenting with drugs. On a couple of occasions my experiments were discovered, but it was easy to move on to another place. Most care homes are desperate to attract people to do the underpaid, horrible jobs and tend to be casual about references. I must have killed, I don't know, at least thirty old people and saved the local authorities a fortune. Perhaps I will get a medal at some stage!"

CHAPTER 48

Bea was trying to get the area commander to listen. He had serious reservations but, eventually, she persuaded him to speak with Euan and when he put the phone down he was excited.

"He has given us some very credible people to call. It's still the afternoon in New York and we are on that already. Good work, Bea. If we do go for this location I need you there, not least because you know the bloke."

The decision was made thirty minutes later. Three houses in a short, quiet street near Alexandra Park. The Electoral Register had not been returned for the middle property; other searches were ongoing.

Larry, the armed response team leader, carried out the briefing in the holding area.

"Heads up, all. This is not about terrorists or armed gangs or anything like that but it's very important and potentially dangerous. We have been tasked to rescue a civilian and capture the two people holding him. The civilian was, I hasten to say, under our police protection colleagues." The team shuffled in their seats.

"You will be surprised. The main suspect is a little lady, but she has evaded police custody twice, the last time putting two armed uniformed police in hospital, soaked in her urine. Do not, I stress, *do not* underestimate this woman." Some of the team looked at each other with raised eyebrows. Larry gave them his 'Don't fuck with me' stare.

"So, Team One – four people, H&K carbines, wearing full gear. Please stand up. You will be two in the front, two in the back. Understood?" They nodded.

"Team Two: four people, 9mm Glock armed. Please stand up. You will be one in the front and one in the back of the houses on each side of the middle one, if we are confident that we have the right property. Understood?" They also nodded.

"There will be an ambulance team a few streets away and it will roll on command or when any shots are heard. Any questions?"

A voice from the back pointed at Bea next to him.

"Who is she?"

"She is the protection officer and will be able to identify the civilian. Her name is Bea."

CHAPTER 49

Twenty minutes later the blue lights were flashing, the sirens were blaring and the leader of Team One was explaining something to the other three men.

"Yes, of course she's a babe, but I am the team leader and I get first dibs. As soon as this stupid exercise is over I will be after her because her arse is grass, she will be out the door and I don't want to miss out. Losing some unknown civilian? Fuck me!"

"Talking about arses, Pete, her arse looks pretty good!"

"Shut the fuck up, Simon!" someone shouted. Pete waited for the laughter to die down.

"Seriously, guys, we wouldn't be shipping out to North London with all our gear, our pals in another truck and an ambulance unless the boss thought we all needed to be tooled up. So, let me recap. We think the civilian is being held in the bathroom of the middle house. Simon and I will burst the front door when we get the command and storm the stairs. You two guys will be at the back of the house in case the targets try to exit that way... What's that smirk on your face, Brian?"

"Sorry, Larry, it just seems a big deal to catch a little woman."

"Brian, you may be right or you may be wrong. Let's talk about that afterwards. In the meantime, keep your shit together. We have no idea what we are going to encounter. The only certainty is that there will be eight of us with firearms in the dark, in the rain, in the garden and the house, and our first priority is that we don't end up shooting at each other or the fucking civilian."

CHAPTER 50

Bernie had just returned but Sadie had a problem. Freddie watched her carefully. In a way, the still very sharp pains of the burns on his arms were keeping him very much alive. He was also thinking about the time. He remembered that Sadie had estimated that Bernie would be back by nine-thirty, so that was that. Call it nine-thirty. And if Euan had managed to contact Bea and if Bea had managed to galvanise some sort of response and if that response could be assembled, say, within an hour, it could possibly be on the way.

Sadie decided something.

"Bernie, untie this stubborn idiot's hands and feet and help him stand up. If he even sneezes I'm going to shoot him in the face with this Taser and then start drilling out his urethra. Do you hear that, Freddie?" He nodded his head as energetically as he could. Five minutes later he was seated at a table in a bedroom with his feet tied to the table legs. He logged in to his laptop, the time showing as nine fifty-eight and the connection was reasonable. His hands were damp and shaking a bit but he had decided that whatever happened he was going out fighting. His voice remained unsteady but he made no effort to correct it.

"Sadie, as you can see, I am logging into my account and in a couple of minutes if you look here you will see the transfer I made to Euan's account. I can't reverse it and, as you heard from Euan, he won't transfer it to you. There it is. So why not just ship out, go and fight another day and leave me alone? It wasn't my fault that you suffered that pain and got those scars. You know that it was *your own* fault; I'll happily pay you half a million to make amends."

"How kind! As it happens, I think you might have something up your sleeve. Obviously, not literally, as you are naked."

She tittered again. "So, I've decided to tie you up again, put you back in that bath, FaceTime your pal, Euan, and see what happens when he sees me use my drill on your cock. I'll have to put something in your mouth to keep the noise down; it may be a bit uncomfortable but I think that will be the least of your concerns. By the way, after the drilling I will leave you in the bath and turn on the hot tap. I should warn you that the hot water in this house is very hot – too hot, if you ask me! So, you will either drown or be boiled. Very hot water on your testicles, that's another thing entirely. I can't tell you how much I'm looking forward to it and I'm going to video it with my phone so I can watch it over and over!"

Freddie just wanted some time. He had no idea if Euan had made contact and if Bea had been able to mobilise some help, but he remembered a US special forces veteran with a charming smile and a great sense of humour once talking to him and a few other SBS officers. 'Time, guys; try and buy time. A few seconds, a few minutes, a few hours – maybe some days. When you run out of time you have no options. The reason I am here to talk to you is that I once managed to stall the process for five more minutes. I had no idea if anyone was going to turn up. But let me tell you this – turn up they did and when my head was on a piece of rock and a guy was about to chop it off, I'll tell you what, guys, it's a wonderful world!'

CHAPTER 51

Time! "Do you know you are mad, Sadie?" Freddie asked. "I mean, mad. Really mad! Of course, you can process information – I'm not suggesting you are unintelligent – in fact, it is obvious you are *very* intelligent. The fact is that you have me here, naked, completely at your mercy, in some place that no one knows where I am. But it's still clear to me that you are completely fucking mad."

She looked at him, smiled, seemingly pleased with the compliment, and picked up the drill.

"We shall see what you have to say when I start my surgery with this."

Freddie shrugged. "No doubt I will scream and probably shit myself and that will give you some sort of perverted pleasure for God knows how long. But in the end, when you are looking at my dead body, you will have nothing. Nothing at all. You are going to be completely fucked. So, do your worst and I will see you in hell or take my half a million pounds, you crazy bitch!"

At that, Sadie smacked Freddie in the face with the Black & Decker drill. He was stunned but managed to remember 'Try and buy time'.

"There you go, Sadie, or whatever your real name is. It is obvious you are completely barking mad and, what's more, you have no idea how close you are to being shot in the head."

"Oh really, do you have an army outside? Loads of big blokes with guns? I think not, Freddie, and if you did I would piss all over them."

CHAPTER 52

The incident response ambulance team and backup police cars were in position two streets away. The rapid response teams had sight of the three houses. The one in the middle had lights on both floors and the others were dark. Team Two was deployed first, silently setting up positions at the rear and front of the houses with no lights on. Team One crept towards the middle house with two guys finding their way to the rear of the house and the other two creeping up the path to the front door. Bea was told to stay in the street. The team leader pressed a button and tiny lights on the jackets of all the team members lit up green.

Then he turned the lights red and used the pile-driver to open the door. "Armed police! Armed police!" they shouted as they checked out the ground floor and then ran upstairs. No response.

"Fuck this!" the team leader said just before spotting a small woman. Then his visor blurred and the blowtorch scorched his skin. He didn't even feel his H&K carbine plucked out of his arms but he heard the blasts and bullets hitting stuff. Sadie was pointing the gun all over the place. Pete came through the door and took two rounds, which knocked him on his back; Bernie got one round in his chest and one in his leg; Freddie had managed to get under the table but a round went into the floor just inches from his hand. Sadie then dropped the empty carbine, picked up the drill and was gone, flying down the stairs and running through the front door, running towards Bea.

Before Bea could get her gun out Sadie was on her, punching, biting, snarling and kicking, but Bea was a very strong woman and fought back until Sadie smashed the heavy drill into the side of her head. The next thing she knew was that Sadie was kneeling on her left hand, smiling, with what looked like a gun in her hand. But it wasn't a gun, it was a drill and it was pointing at Bea's eyes.

The drill looked like a gun to Brian as he came out of the house. He didn't recognise either of the people but was pretty sure they were both women and that the one on top was the criminal and the one underneath, the protection officer. But the streetlight was pretty dim and the rain didn't help.

Bea had managed to stop Sadie getting the drill any closer to her face, but it was now pointing directly at her right eye. The buzzing seemed to be getting louder. Bea saw that Sadie was grunting, with her face just inches from her cheek, the drill moving nearer, her own strength weakening. The thought of the drill entering her eye renewed her efforts and she managed to shove Sadie's arm back by an inch or two, frantically thinking to herself, *I can't let this happen!*

Brian had never prepared for killing someone. All the training was embedded, but this was real. His mind whirled. *Is it a gun? Is the woman on top the criminal? Can I make the shot? Oh fuck, their heads are almost touching! What if I miss? What if I hit the protection officer? What if that isn't a gun? Fuck, oh fuck it!* He knew he couldn't hesitate any longer. He pulled the trigger.

Blood, bone and brain hit Bea's face as the shot rang out. Sadie's body fell on top of her. The hammering in Bea's heart gradually decreased. She abruptly pulled herself away and cried with relief, her face on the pavement for a few seconds before attempting to stand up. Brian grabbed her to prevent her falling back down and stared at the body by their feet.

"Close one," he said.

"Fucking right!" Bea replied. "I think I might owe you a drink." Then she passed out.

CHAPTER 53

The time that had lapsed from the moment the team opened the front door until Sadie's death, was four-and-a-half minutes. Chaos had become calm. One ambulance had a doctor and a paramedic dealing with Bernie; he was in a bad way. Another paramedic was checking out Pete. His body armour had done what it was supposed to do but he was going to have serious bruises on his chest and back. A third paramedic was cleaning up Bea's face and attending to a cut on her forehead. He didn't know if it was the drill or a bit of bone that had done the damage, but he told Bea it was the drill and that he didn't think it would need stitches. Freddie was covered in a blanket and put in one of the two ambulances and Bea got in a few minutes later. It moved off smoothly, no blue lights or sirens. Neither of them spoke.

A little while later, Freddie looked at Bea.

"What happened to your forehead?"

"Sadie and her fucking drill. It was whirring away an inch from my eye until one of the team blew her away; I can tell you, I nearly wet myself."

"Join the club. It was mayhem up there. She managed to get hold of one of the guy's carbines and didn't stop firing until the clip ran out. She couldn't control the gun, she was just blasting away. I was under the table but I think her mate, Bernie, found himself in the firing line."

"She's tiny; how on earth did she get hold of the gun? If there's one thing I've now learnt on this job it's never to underestimate little ladies."

"She stuck a blowtorch in his face."

"You're joking!"

"I'm not. Look at this." Freddie pulled the blanket off his shoulder and showed her the burn that a medic had smothered with some painkilling protective lotion. "I've got one on the other arm as well. Christ, I'm glad she's dead. Who was it that shot her?"

"I don't know his name but you can be sure I will find out." She shivered with the memory of the fight. "What happened to the guy she torched?"

"They were working on him and the air ambulance is on its way. It doesn't look good."

The ambulance arrived at Charing Cross Hospital at about eleven-thirty and they went in different directions. Freddie was put straight into a cubicle and a doctor arrived within ten minutes.

He took a good look at the burns and frowned.

"How did you get these?"

"A madwoman with a culinary blowtorch," Freddie replied.

"Say again?" he asked for a second time, looking incredulous.

"A madwoman with a culinary blowtorch. She was trying to get me to give her a lot of money."

"Well, the lotion applied to these burns is the right stuff and I will get a nurse to dress the wounds. I'll ask her to bring some scrubs and clogs; we can't leave you here wrapped in a blanket! I'll get you a prescription for the lotion too. Just wait here."

Twenty minutes later, the doctor returned with the prescription and he was accompanied by a uniformed police officer.

"Here is the prescription. The pharmacy is closed now but it opens at seven-thirty. This gentleman would like a word; otherwise as far as I'm concerned you are free to leave."

The police officer took out a notebook.

"Mr Findlay, please tell me more about these burns."

Freddie sighed. "For the third time, a madwoman tortured me with a blowtorch!"

"Where was this?"

"I have no idea but I was rescued by a load of heavily armed police and then brought here in an ambulance."

"Armed police? Tonight?"

"Yes. It was a major incident. Please call whoever you want and let me out of here. I'm very tired."

The policeman left the cubicle and returned ten minutes later.

"All OK, you are free to leave."

It took Freddie another ten minutes to find the exit; the place was like a ghost town. Fortunately, it was just a few minutes' walk from Fulham Reach and he was in bed and fast asleep by two o'clock in the morning, but he didn't make it to the pool that day.

CHAPTER 54

"Freddie, where have you been? I've left several messages, knocked on your door and now here you are at my door. Come on in anyway."

"Thank you, Vanessa, I'll tell you all about it." He looked at his watch. "Is it too early for a drink? Believe it or not, I haven't had one for a while."

"How about some Champagne? It's never too early for Champagne and I have a bottle in the fridge."

"Wonderful. Just the ticket."

They sat opposite each other at the table on Vanessa's terrace. She stretched her long legs, put her feet on another chair, leant back and looked at him expectantly.

"OK, where have you been?" she asked him, while he looked sheepish.

"I did something very stupid the other night. Bea has told me several times to always book cabs but I was feeling completely knackered. Then I saw a cab with its light on and just jumped in. It didn't take me long to discover that I wasn't being taken home but being driven to God knows where. I managed to leave a message for Bea. The doors were locked and the glass partition wouldn't open; I was pretty worried, but what more could I do?"

"Christ!"

"Yeah! Anyway, the cab stopped. The door opened and there she was: Sheila or Sadie – whatever she calls herself, and she Tasered me! Tell you what, it really hurts, and the next thing she did was jab me with a needle and I passed out. It gets worse… I woke up naked in her fucking bath! Anyway, she had given my keys to the cab driver who went to collect my laptop and she burnt my arms with a blowtorch just for fun. She also threatened me with some other stuff."

"Your arms? She burnt your arms? Let me see!"

"Nothing to see. They are bandaged up so I have to go to my GP's nurse every other day for a week or so to have the bandages changed."

"Good God. How will you shower or have a bath with bandages?"

Freddie smirked. "Ah, that's where you might be able to help me."

"Of course, but seriously, how did you get away?"

"I showed her via my laptop that I had transferred all my money to my pal, Euan, in New York. She FaceTimed him and told him all the awful things she was going to do to me unless he transferred my money to her. He said he would get back to her. The FaceTime connection enabled him to get the IP address of her router and he has an app that's able to find the location of where I was being held. He e-mailed the stuff to Bea and the police rescued me at about eleven o'clock last night. I got home around two o'clock this morning."

"Is she safely locked up now?"

"No, she's dead. Absolutely dead. So, let's drink to that!"

CHAPTER 55

Monday morning. The area commander stood up and met the eyes of everyone in the room.

"Good morning. This is a heads-up, not an inquest. The good news is that George's eyes are OK. He will need some skin grafts on his face but he won't be any uglier than he was last week. The bad news is that the woman who grabbed his gun put two rounds into her associate, Bernie Cook, and he bled out. Bad news for his family, but not necessarily for us. The protection officer, Bea, will have a small scar on her forehead and Pete has a mighty bruise on his chest as a result of two rounds hitting his body armour. Pete, can you tell us what you saw when you entered the room?"

Pete stood up. "I could hear the shooting as I came up the stairs and saw George on his knees. There was a guy in the corner covered in blood. Turned out he was the taxi driver. Another guy, naked, with severe burns on his arms, was under the table. But the main feature was this tiny lady with George's H&K, swinging it around, bullets going everywhere. Then two of them hit me and I went backwards just at the top of the stairs. The next thing I knew she was gone. I heaved myself up. The bloke under the table seemed OK and so I picked up some clothes, which were on the floor and applied compression to the guy covered in blood in the corner. Almost immediately a medic arrived and took over."

"What happened next?"

"I heard a shot, a single shot. I guess that was Brian. The guy under the table seemed very calm. He asked 'Is that her done?' I had a look out of the window, flashlights were pointing all over the place and I saw the body. I replied 'Yes!' and he said 'Thank God, she was becoming a serious nuisance.'"

"Sorry, Pete, say again... He was naked under a table with serious burns and he said *what*?"

"'Thank God, she was becoming a serious nuisance.'"

"I assume we are talking about the *victim*, Findlay?"

"Yes, and my impression was that he is a pretty tough guy. Naked, tied up and tortured and he called her a 'nuisance'. God knows what it would take to make him angry!"

Laughter rang out in the room.

"Well, I can tell you all that Freddie Findlay has friends in high places, not spooks but the NCA. They have been on the case all night long and are very grateful. It seems he has been helpful to them a number of times."

The attention was back to the area commander.

"Now, the main reason I wanted to talk with you all this morning is not what we did last night and what we could have done differently, no. I want to talk about bravery. Many people, most civilians, think bravery is all about charging into danger; most medal citations reflect that, and of course it is correct, but there is a different sort of bravery and I am looking at you, Brian."

Everyone looked at Brian. Brian looked at the floor.

"Here was the scene: It's dark, it's raining, the streetlight isn't much help but he can see two women, one on top of the other and the woman on top looks like our criminal. She appears to have a gun close to the other woman's face and Brian thinks that woman is Bea."

Bea was at the back of the room. No one apart from the area commander had seen her come in.

"Brian was about forty feet away. You can imagine the choices he had and how little time to decide: Run forward, shout 'Drop the gun!', fire a warning shot or shoot to kill? But what if he hits Bea? Their faces are only inches apart. That's when we get to bravery, that's when the rubber meets the road. And, as you know, it was a perfect shot. Job done. A life saved. Well done, Brian!"

The room erupted with applause. Bea stood up at the back and no one clapped louder or longer than her.

Chapter 56

Bea called Freddie on his landline early on Monday evening. Her voice was a little hesitant.

"I've got your laptop, charger and phone and I've charged them. Shall I drop the stuff off later or would tomorrow be better? By the way, some of your clothes were used to stem the blood coming from Sadie's accomplice. She managed to shoot him twice; she had no idea how to hold a carbine and point it in the right direction. Sadly, he bled out. I suggest you have a look at them in the morning or just chuck the bag in the bin."

"Please come around this evening. Now I don't need protection maybe you could join me in a drink."

She turned up at seven-thirty and Freddie gave her a kiss on the cheek.

"How are you feeling?"

"A bit odd, actually. I slept well, no nightmares or anything like that but my hands were shaking a bit this morning. Possibly delayed shock. I've been in some tight situations over the past five or six years but nothing like last night. We had a good team meeting this morning and the boss said some very wise words about the guy who killed Sadie and bravery."

"Yeah, I guess it was a difficult shot. Imagine the shit he would be in if he had hit you rather than her."

"Imagine how *I* would have felt!"

"Nothing! And on that positive note, how about going out and getting something to eat?"

Fifteen minutes later they were sitting at Freddie's favourite table at Sam's Riverside restaurant with a bottle of Cortese di Gavi and menus in front of them. Freddie was looking intently at Bea's forehead.

"You know, that little piece of tape just above your eyebrow kind of suits you. I think that if you have a little scar later on that would look great."

"Oh, really. Why?"

"Perfection can be a bit boring!"

She smiled. "Christ, Freddie, is that the best you can do? By the way, I would like the sea bream followed by lobster and chips."

"Lobster and chips? That is forty-one pounds; call that fifty pounds with the service charge. Do you think I am made of money?"

"No, Freddie, I *know* you are made of money! And please top me up."

"Lovely dinner, Freddie. Thank you very much indeed."

"Are you sure you don't want to come back for a nightcap? I know you are gay so you have nothing to worry about."

"Actually, I am gay and not gay."

"What do you mean?"

"I'm bi, remember?"

"Bi?"

"Bisexual. Sometimes I might like a woman, sometimes a man or, on one or two occasions, both at the same time."

"Good Lord, the things one learns!"

"Don't pretend to be shocked, Freddie. I've been with you for about five weeks and I've got to know you pretty well."

"Well, to cut to the chase; how are you feeling tonight?"

"Actually, I'm feeling that I would like a man; in particular, the man opposite me, but, of course, I know about your relationship with Vanessa. So, when you went off to the gents I called for a cab."

Her phone pinged; she kissed Freddie on the cheek and disappeared. He asked for a glass of Fleurie, opened his phone and started work on all the e-mails, texts and voicemails.

CHAPTER 57

On Tuesday at five o'clock, Freddie was having another meeting with Alex. This time the wine was opened immediately. Alex tapped Freddie on the shoulder.

"Fucking hell, Freddie, it's only a year or so since you were stabbed in the back. Please tell me all of this is over!"

"Yes, indeed. Partnership Protection has managed to keep my name and the firm out of the press and the NCA has been very helpful given the support we gave them last year. It's a great relief that the awful woman was killed and I'm in good shape. Cheers!" and they touched glasses.

Freddie continued. "I'm sorting out a trip to meet up with some of our colleagues where the audits seem to be behind schedule. I'll do the rest online, but I *do* need to get the measure of these people, particularly those in Africa. I had lost count of the number of countries where we have offices. How many do you think?"

"Twenty?"

"Thirty-five! There are now fifty-four countries in the continent and I will need to visit about twenty-five. I haven't actually met the partners in those offices and Microsoft Teams doesn't do it for me when it cuts to the chase."

"How long do you think it will take?"

"About six weeks. Maybe two months. But if our compliance people won't let me get all the local currency

I need for the bribes you might not see me for years! It's dangerous territory and I've been thinking that I might need some protection."

"Oh, really? Who might that be? No! Fuck off, Freddie! It's time you settled down."

"Just saying, Alex. Just saying!"

CHAPTER 57

"Freddie, I have some good news and some bad news. Which would you like first?" asked Vanessa.

They were having lunch at Dinner in the Mandarin Oriental with a table overlooking Hyde Park. The view was lovely and there was a bottle of Krug in an ice bucket beside their table. The restaurant was full and, as usual, customers around them were taking pictures of their food.

He smiled. "I would like the good news, please."

"I have just signed a contract for a new series showing how I have transformed the houses of the rich and famous. My agent has been negotiating for a month and we sealed the deal yesterday when all the riders had been agreed. I didn't want to tell you earlier as these things can all fall apart at the last minute."

"Congratulations, darling. Well done!" Freddie raised his glass and clinked it with hers. "So, what's the bad news?"

Vanessa put her glass down and winced.

"The format will be a bit different, the houses will not be owned by the same sort of rich and famous, they will be owned by rich and famous stars."

"Stars?"

"Yes, film stars mainly, but that's not actually the bad news. The bad news is that the stars will be living in America, not the UK, and that's where I will be based. To be precise, I'll need to be in Los Angeles and I have to be there for six months, at least."

"At *least*?"

"Yes. If the show gets the right ratings my contract has a clause saying that if they want to have another series I will participate. Needless to say, I want the best ratings possible. We are talking serious money. Twice as much as the current UK work."

"Do you mind me asking; how much?"

"It's six episodes and I get two hundred and fifty thousand dollars for each show, plus all expenses paid. My agent has colleagues in California and they know about all of this."

"What are these 'riders' you mentioned earlier?"

"Things like if I have to travel more than two hundred miles I get a helicopter. I get suites in five-star hotels and one of these is called Shutters on the Beach, which will be my base, plus there are pages of tiny details such as costs of dry cleaning, named make-up artists, security, legal costs and on and on. I haven't read them all but my agent is pretty impressed."

Freddie dropped any idea of suggesting Vanessa reconsider, but before he could say anything the waiter arrived to take their order.

"The meat fruit followed by the halibut, please," Vanessa said. Freddie followed.

"I'll have the halibut as well but I'd like the smoked salmon starter and could we have a bottle of the Seresin Pinot Noir, slightly chilled?"

"Of course, sir."

Freddie raised his glass. "Here's to a successful six months with stars. Can I come over sometime and enjoy a bit of Hollywood glamour?"

"Of course you can, but that brings me to something else I want to tell you. As you know, LA is not a commute. It's a bloody long flight; I'll be working very hard and I doubt I'll be coming back to London in the foreseeable future. So, as I don't want to put our relationship on hold it should go without saying, but I'm going to say it anyway: Forget about me for the time being, Freddie. Have fun."

"When are you leaving?"

"Monday morning, Heathrow BA first-class and limo waiting for me at LAX, all as per my contract. Work starts on Tuesday. I need to meet the stars via Zoom or face to face as soon as possible. I'm sure some of them will be ghastly but I suppose that's what the producers want – lots of tension, lots of rows."

"I'm going to miss you."

"I'm sure you will, Freddie, but not for long, and I will miss you too. How about spending this evening together at my place?"

"Sounds like a great idea."

Chapter 58

Monday morning and the six-thirty swimming team were down to three. Freddie explained Vanessa's absence and Adrian, true to form, smiled at the news.

"Oh dear, Freddie, I thought you two were an item. Still, I suppose you have your sights set on that police protection officer. If you ask me, she will be the one that needs protection... from you!"

"Not in the immediate future, old chap. I am off to Africa in a few days visiting countries that I hadn't heard of until a few months ago."

"Why on earth are you going there?"

"For my sins, I am an audit partner for a global bank and they have companies all over the world. At DPK we have to sign off the accounts and my job is to make sure that happens, on time and accurately. As someone once said in a movie, 'Failure is not an option.'"

Adrian smiled again. "I remember someone saying that in an operating theatre and we all fell about laughing!"

Five weeks later, Freddie was in the pool again, the scars on his arms had faded but he had a large plaster on his shoulder. He got out of the water, started drying himself and glanced across at Adrian and Steve.

"Alright, before you ask, it was in Gambia and a misunderstanding. There are about a thousand languages in

Africa and my guide was fluent in all the main ones. When we were sheltering from the sun in a bar by a harbour he said something that appeared to be an insult to a couple of guys and a fight broke out. It was short and sweet; the two guys didn't know much about fighting, but one of them managed to stab me."

"What happened next?" asked Steve.

"I picked them up from the floor and bought them some beers. I couldn't understand a word they said apart from 'Manchester United', but we left on good terms and the hospital did a good job; just a few stitches and a tetanus shot in my bum required." Freddie looked at the clock. "God! Got to go to work. See you tomorrow."

In fact, Freddie didn't see them for another two weeks, he had no time for his morning swims any more; in fact, he had no time for anything but work. Twelve-hour days, working over the weekends taking calls from every time zone, dealing directly with the clients, referring the big issues to Ina and, all the time, sticking to his golden rule: 'Make it look easy'.

CHAPTER 59

Finally, Freddie had some free time and met up with William at Sam's Riverside restaurant.

"Are you still with Vanessa, Freddie?" asked William.

"Sadly, no. She is in LA. She has a six-episode Californian version of her UK series showing, focusing on famous movie stars and other famous people including 'influencers', whatever the fuck they are. It's serious money, she couldn't turn it down and there may be another six if the ratings are good. They don't do things by half over there. Before the contract was even agreed every detail was discussed and they even insisted on her having a medical."

"Why?"

"Insurance. If she gets ill and can't complete the contract there is a thirty-million dollar policy."

"Christ. That *is* serious money. Let's order."

After their orders were well and truly underway, they resumed the conversation.

"How are things otherwise, Freddie? All good?" enquired William.

"OK, I guess. I've got a date with Bea next Sunday but it was very difficult to arrange. I'm footloose and fancy-free while she is on duty most of the time."

"I thought you told me she was gay."

"Turns out she is bi. Either way she is a very attractive lady."

"What else?"

"What do you mean?"

"Freddie, I know you very well indeed and I can tell when something is distracting you. What is it?"

"I had a call from Jackie Starling the other day. It was from a burner phone so I know it's not NCA business and she wants to meet at ten o'clock tomorrow morning. I doubt it's anything intimate. My fear is that she will want to put Miles Bishop back to work again."

"I'd forgotten about that. What happened and did you get the recording pen I suggested?"

"I did get the pen and it worked."

They were both quiet as they ate their starters. As always when they were together, there was a comfortable silence and then William spoke.

"I can always tell when you are not telling the whole truth, mate, but it doesn't worry me. You will have a good reason, but if you feel like sharing or if I can be of any help I will be here for you. You know that, don't you? After all, you saved my life and all you got was pain and scars on your arms from that madwoman. Thank God she's gone."

"I'll drink to that," Freddie raised his glass, "at least I would if I actually had anything in my glass! How about another bottle of the Côtes du Rhône?"

William gestured at a waitress, smiled and pointed at the empty bottle. A replacement arrived within minutes.

CHAPTER 60

The following morning, Freddie was sitting on a bench in Bishops Park waiting for Jackie. It felt like autumn had arrived with most of the trees shedding leaves and there was a slight chill in the air. When he saw her, he switched on his recording pen and stood up. No smile or kiss on the cheek, she just sat down next to him. She was wearing a grey hoodie, dark blue jeans and Doc Martens boots. As usual, Jackie didn't waste words.

"Good morning, Freddie, I think I need Miles Bishop to help me with a project. It relates to a very dangerous man."

Freddie wasn't surprised.

"Not again, Jackie; I'm not a gun for hire, nor is Miles Bishop."

"I'm not looking for a gun for hire. I need some help and it doesn't involve killing anyone. I'm afraid it's more difficult than that."

"More difficult than killing someone?"

She frowned. "Yes; let me be specific. I've been in this new job for about six months and I need a result. Before I took over, my predecessor had managed to install an undercover cop into Edward Bond's organisation and he had been providing excellent information as to what had happened since you took Bond and his number one man off the board. I have a paper file here with what we have. I also have a photo of our undercover guy and it's not very pretty – multiple stab wounds, severe burns and his penis and testicles are rammed into his mouth."

"Jesus Christ! Bloody hell! Do you know who is in charge now?"

"Yes, we do. The guy is an Albanian called Tacic Kurti; he has all the right papers and is completely ruthless. You will see from the notes that our man witnessed him carrying out two terrible killings, one of them involved a woman having her head hacked off with a blunt machete. There is a picture of her in the file as well – before the torture. And it gets worse. A farmer found another body in his field a few weeks ago. Forensics believe she was beaten to death before her head was also hacked off and there were traces of crack cocaine on her jacket and under her nails. Looks like she was one of his dealers."

"Christ! But what is more difficult than killing him?"

"Arresting him, charging him and sending him down for a very long time."

Freddie was puzzled. "Kill him or send him down for life – what's the difference?"

"It's the optics, Freddie. My role is to round up the bad guys and put them away."

"Well, we put Bond and his pal away, didn't we!" he said, stating the fact.

"Yes and no – yes, they are off-the-board, but I get no credit. My boss assumes that they were killed by the competition and, of course, I am not going to disillusion him. So, what I need is a result. I need to put this Kurti guy away for a long time in order to advance my career. I have to have a result and I need you or Miles Bishop to help me."

"How the hell do you think I can do that?"

"I have no idea, but I'm sure you will work something out."

"No! Enough is enough, Jackie. I'm out of this. Find another sucker; fuck off out of my life."

"OK. If that's what you want, but it will be you in court as 'Mr Bishop' and I shall have all the evidence I need to get you convicted."

Freddie smiled. "And I've got all the evidence *I* need to get *you* convicted! I'll send you a file later on and when you have listened to it you might like to think again."

Freddie got a call from Jackie's burner on Monday evening.

"OK, Freddie, I've listened to the recording and I think we are in a Cuba crisis situation and we need to talk again."

"What exactly is a Cuba crisis?"

"In the 1960s, Russia began to secretly install nuclear missiles in Cuba in order to attack the United States. President Kennedy made it clear that unless they withdrew he would launch nuclear missiles at Moscow. There was a standoff for twenty days until Khrushchev backed down and removed the weapons. Both presidents understood that a war between the two nations would create MAD – mutual assured destruction. And I think that is where we are."

"So, who is going to back down?"

"I might, but I need a favour and maybe you might need one sometime."

Freddie wasn't sure whether this was a threat or a promise but made up his mind. "Tell you what, I'll look at the feasibility of getting this piece of shit banged up, but if it looks impossible or even improbable, I will tell you within a month."

As Freddie walked back to Fulham Reach he reflected on the bizarre conversation – people being murdered, drugs, plots, mutual assured destruction and God knows what else. Perhaps William might have some ideas. He called him, explained the situation and they agreed to meet up the following Saturday at William's house. Freddie chose not to mention the photographs.

CHAPTER 61

Friday night and Ina and William were sitting in his kitchen, dipping raw carrots and yellow peppers into houmous and drinking Saint-Véran with their M&S chicken Kiev and a couple of baked potatoes that had been cooked in the oven.

Ina was exhausted. "William, when you were working full-time weren't you knackered by the end of the week?"

"Once or twice I got a bit stressed out and many times I was under pressure, but nothing like the challenges you are facing at the moment."

"Why not? I know that partners in DPK can earn north of a million pounds a year and with your seniority it must have been quite a lot more. How come it was easy?"

William went to the fridge and topped up their glasses.

"Good question. First of all, I didn't have to manage people. Obviously, if I was running a project I had to manage the team but they didn't report to me. I never had anyone reporting to me. It's a very flat organisation. Second, I was always in Consulting, not Audit, so I didn't have to worry about being fined and fired if I screwed up. I focused on strategy and it's pretty difficult to screw that up."

"What do you mean? Surely strategy is key!"

"Of course it is, but it usually takes so long to implement that the client team has changed, the market has changed, regulations have changed and all sorts of stuff has happened. How do you measure success? In my experience, strategy was a pretty easy ride compared with the rest of our propositions. Project planning is also relatively light, but as the saying goes 'No plan survives contact with the enemy.'"

"The enemy? What enemy?"

William laughed. "People. Rivals of the guy who is sponsoring the strategy review and want it to fail; people lower down the organisation who don't like change; people who hate consultants and God knows who else. There's an army of them hoping the review will go tits up. But anyway, planning is a walk in the park compared with execution and implementing the strategy. Mostly, I've steered away from that. It's a fucking nightmare."

"Yeah, tell me about it! We have a finance transformation project at the moment and, to put it in your words, 'It's a fucking nightmare'!"

"Just as well DPK are your auditors and they are not allowed to do that kind of stuff with you or we would be arguing the toss instead of having a lovely evening. I promise I will do my best to make you forget about work. I've baked some of my unique cannabis cookies for dessert."

CHAPTER 62

Freddie had walked from Fulham Reach to Chiswick Mall on Saturday morning. "Sorry I'm a few minutes late, William. Any chance of a Bloody Mary?"

"Of course, old chap; it's a nice day. Go over the road and take a seat by the river and I'll bring a jug."

Half an hour later, Freddie had recounted his conversation with Jackie and summarised the undercover police notes.

William emptied the jug into their glasses.

"So, Freddie, mutual assured destruction is off the table, but you have agreed to consider doing Jackie a favour? Is that because you want more adventures or you want to put this terrible bloke in prison? Or do you think that doing so will destroy the county lines business model, which of course it won't? Perhaps you want to avenge the death of the undercover cop, do you?"

Freddie thought carefully before he replied.

"Yes. No. Oh, I don't know!"

The day was getting darker and it looked like rain so they went back over the road and into William's kitchen. William sat exactly where he had been the night before and Freddie sat where Ina had been.

"The thing is, Freddie, how on earth could you actually get the guy bang to rights? Yes, you know where he lives, at least some of the time if the undercover guy's information is correct, but this guy, Tacic Kurti, has no routine. He uses different cars, stays in different places, sometimes travels by train or plane and I imagine he never carries the product. Do you really want to get involved with this?"

While waiting for a response, William sighed, got up, took two plates of smoked salmon from the counter and some bread and butter, put them on the table and then returned with a bottle of Chablis. He sat down and asked again.

"Do you really want to do this?"

"Yes!"

Later on, when they had eaten the smoked salmon, lots of Cheddar cheese and biscuits and polished off a decent red wine, Freddie asked William further questions.

"What are you thinking? It's unlike you to be so quiet. Are you pissed off because I am sounding like Don Quixote 'tilting at windmills'? Or are you thinking of a plan?"

William looked him in the eye.

"I have an inkling of a plan, but execution will be challenging to say the least. Let's take it step by step. I'll have a think."

CHAPTER 63

After Freddie had gone, William walked out of the back door to the little cottage at the end of his garden that backed onto Neveravon Road. The ground floor contained a double garage and a wet room while upstairs stood his office with a nice view of the garden and everything he needed when he wanted to work – a table with four chairs, a desk with a 27" iMac, a fridge, an espresso machine and a black leather Eames Lounge Chair and matching footstool. He checked his e-mails, watched a bit of football and tidied up the files on his desktop. He couldn't concentrate on anything; there had been something on his mind since sitting by the river with Freddie earlier. Instead, he sat in the chair, put his feet on the footstool and closed his eyes.

When William woke up there was a name, a face, a body, a bar and a man in his mind – Norman Peters! He was in his fifties with grey hair, a little overweight, always wearing a suit, tie and waistcoat. He was a nice man but not a high-flier. And the bar – El Vino in Fleet Street. Norman had just finished a project, which involved an audit of the 'Queen's warehouses', so-called because when the UK Border Force seize illegal materials they are 'forfeited to the Crown'.

William remembered Norman being a bit tipsy and explaining how his audit report was going to identify some serious process weaknesses; for example, materials such as illegal drugs were recorded when they arrived at the warehouses, not when they were seized. So, the people transporting them could, in theory, help themselves to the goods and often the transportation was outsourced to haulage companies, albeit carefully vetted firms.

William remembered Norman being pretty concerned about the whole process.

"You know what, William; it's even worse. In the case of drug seizures, they have to be incinerated and most of the Queen's warehouses in England don't have incinerators. There are none in Scotland and guess what; there are very weak controls to ensure that all the stuff is destroyed. How about one for the road?"

William called Freddie the next day.

"Good to see you yesterday. I have an idea I'd like to discuss. Are you around?"

"Yep, I'm here all evening."

"See you in thirty minutes."

William cycled along the river to Fulham Reach and Freddie had a Sipsmith vodka and tonic waiting.

"So, what's this idea?"

William explained.

"Norman Peters! I remember him. Portly bloke, safe pair of hands and recently retired. We ribbed him quite a lot on that project. Stuff like 'How much are you putting up your nose, Norman?' and 'Have you taken up smoking?' I don't think he had much of a sense of humour, but perhaps there is a small piece of light at the end of this tunnel."

"Next step?" probed William.

"I need to do some research. First of all, do DPK audit the Queen's warehouses? It is bound to be one of the Big

Three. Second, what information relating to Norman's project is on the system? Third, how can we find out who the third-party contractors are and how does the transport get scheduled?"

"I've already got some ideas. That's really helpful, mate. Let me fix you another drink."

CHAPTER 64

DPK, in common with the other two Big Three firms, required the majority of employees to book 'hot-'desks; however, partners were entitled to a permanent desk and a couple of very senior partners had offices and executive assistants. Nigel Salter, the partner who occupied the desk next to Freddie, was fifty-five and about to retire. In the meantime, he was lunching with clients in order to explore non-executive director opportunities after he left the firm. Monday was no exception.

"I'm off to Gordon's Wine Bar to meet a few pals. See you later, Freddie, or possibly tomorrow!"

As usual, Nigel hadn't closed the lid of his laptop. Freddie took a quick look around and swapped his. The last thing he needed was a finger pointing at him should anyone suggest that someone in DPK had leaked information relating to drug seizures. Then he started searching the client database for 'Queen's warehouses' and he found a goldmine.

On Saturday, Ina was playing golf and Freddie was sitting in William's kitchen, itching to explain his plan.

"William, you have done me a great favour. So has Nigel Salter, although he will never know it. Let me explain: I got hold of Norman's audit report; needless to say it was comprehensive and meticulous. He had looked at three Queen's warehouses and I focused on the one with the most volume. It's located near Heathrow – West Drayton, to be precise – and it's a stone's throw from Polar Park police station. It doesn't have an incinerator and it uses a contractor called Crayland Carriers Limited. Norman had looked at them carefully and reported that their data security was poor. My plan is to penetrate their database and establish when they are scheduled to collect materials from the warehouse."

William frowned at this.

"'Penetrate their database'? How will you do that?"

"My pal, Euan; you know, the guy who managed to locate me when that mad bitch was going to kill me. He's had a look at the site and he's confident. Anyway, when we know when a collection is going to take place, we intercept the lorry on its way to the incinerator, grab a few kilos of heroin and plant it in Kurti's house."

William was beginning to wonder if his best friend had lost the plot.

"How will you do that? The place is bound to be alarmed and secure. He's a drug dealer, for heaven's sake and just how will you intercept the lorry?"

Freddie smiled. "I'm going to be driving a police car and I'm going to flag him down. I'm sure Jackie will be prepared to supply it. What do you think?"

"I think I need something stronger than this coffee and it's past twelve. The sun's come out so let's grab a drink and go over the road."

Chapter 65

William always relaxed when he was sitting by the river, but Freddie's plan was worrying him. It seemed flimsy to say the least. In fact, it looked crazy. He took a sip of his vodka and chose his words carefully.

"Well, mate, I like the plan but I think there are a number of risks. First of all, getting hold of the heroin. What if Euan can't access the contractor's schedule? What if the lorry is carrying other seized materials rather than drugs, for example, cigarettes or whatever? And intercepting the lorry? Surely, they will have some sort of security protocols even if a policeman approaches them. What's more, are you sure Jackie will be prepared to get involved?"

"I guess that might be an issue."

"Well, let's look on the bright side. Let's say you get a few kilos of heroin, the police car gets returned safely and both you and Jackie are safe and sound. How are you going to get the drugs into this Kurti's house? As I said before, there are bound to be alarms, maybe CCTV. Will the house be empty? How do you know he won't return when you are in there? Will Euan be able to help? All in all, a lot could go wrong. What do you think?"

Freddie sighed. "If you put it that way it does seem very high-risk. I think I need to give it some more thought." He checked his watch. "Anyway, The Old Ship is booked for one o'clock. Let's have another quick one and stroll down there."

They managed to get their favourite table on the terrace and enjoyed burgers and a bottle of Merlot, but they were both distracted, thinking about the task ahead. Then William looked at the empty bottle and smiled.

"Get another of these, mate, and I'll give you a plan."

Freddie grinned. "Good man, but you're paying for lunch if your plan has as many holes in it as mine."

Glasses filled, plates cleared away, William leant forward and spoke quietly even though the terrace was full of people having a good old, noisy time.

"My plan is a little like yours but with a couple of modifications. First off, we buy the heroin, we don't try and steal it."

"What? *Buy* it? You must be joking! How much would that be, for Christ's sake? And how *could* we buy it?"

"Well, it's a market. Prices vary, but I checked via Google when you were getting that bottle. According to an article in *The Guardian*, it was about thirty thousand pounds a kilo for uncut product a couple of months ago, maybe ten times that on the street. So we are looking at, say, a hundred and fifty thousand pounds for five kilos. And don't give me that look. I know you are rolling in it and that you have plenty of bitcoins from those terrible twins!"

"Yeah, but *where* do we buy it?"

"Your mate, Big Cam. The bloke in Glasgow. He will know. Christ, those bastard twins were dealing for years and Cam was their number one man. Actually, thinking about it, we are probably talking two hundred thousand; no doubt he will want some commission."

Freddie was still grinning, but then he frowned.

"OK, but we still have a problem. How exactly do we get the stuff into the guy's house? As you said, it's bound to be alarmed!"

"We don't."

"Isn't that the purpose of the plan?"

"Yes, but my suggestion is that we hide the stuff in his garden, maybe there is a shed there or maybe we have to dig a hole. After all, a major drug dealer would be a fool to have the product in his home. For good measure, we might be able to hide some stuff in the boot of his car. I'm sure your mate Euan will be able help us with that."

Freddie's feelings turned from concerned to relieved and then excited. He leant forward and grabbed William's shoulder.

"Lunch is on me, but not just today – any day and anywhere in the future!"

William didn't hesitate.

"La Colombe d'Or in June, of course, with Ina and Vanessa if she's back from LA."

"Not sure about Vanessa. We haven't had much contact of late. She's busy; with the time difference, my recent work schedule and other stuff, we haven't had much contact. In fact, I think it's over for us."

"That's a shame."

"Yeah, but when one door closes another opens and I have a chance with Bea."

"The protection officer?"

"Yes and I think I might need to be protected from her!"

CHAPTER 66

Freddie had known that when Vanessa started working on the new show in LA their relationship would end. He had tried to stay positive but he felt there was a vacuum in his life. He missed her humour, her anecdotes, her wonderful body and the long conversations over meals or when lying in bed. And, when he watched her first US programme live at three o'clock on Thursday morning, all the memories came back and he experienced an emotion he hadn't felt for many years – sadness.

A few minutes after the programme finished, Freddie's phone lit up. It was Bea, calling at four-fifteen in the morning!

"How are you feeling, Freddie?"

"Not great."

"How about dinner tomorrow?"

"I may not be great company."

"I'll be the judge of that."

"When? Where?"

"There's a Gaucho restaurant in Richmond that would be convenient for me as I live nearby. It is on the river though, so you will have to walk along the towpath from the bridge for a couple of minutes to get there. If the weather holds up we can eat outside, it's a lovely spot. Are you OK eating steak? Shall I book for eight o'clock?"

"Yes please, Bea. That would be great."

Friday evening and Freddie had left More London, taken the train from Waterloo to Richmond and was striding from the station down towards the towpath and still looking at all the e-mails on his phone. They were from continents, bosses, colleagues, countries, cities and clients. This was his life. He made it look easy. But it wasn't. And the date tonight with Bea, the pressure from clients and the plan to frame Tacic Kurti for the drugs was getting a bit stressful. But then, there she was, sitting at a table under a huge tree by the towpath – her dark skin gleaming in the late evening sun, her hair contained by an elegant band of sparkling stones and a wide smile on her face.

She stood up as he approached and he kissed her gently on both cheeks. Her scent was wonderful. It was the first time he had seen her in high heels and she was almost as tall as he was.

"You look lovely," he said. "I've never seen you in a dress and high heels," and he kissed the little scar by her right eye. "It makes you even more beautiful. Christ, what a night that was!"

"Yes, it was. I'll never forget it. I think we both thought we were going to die. As for the clothes; dresses and high heels are not much use when we are on protection duty and should be ready to drive or run at a moment's notice. I'm glad you like the look and I hope you like the wine I ordered," she grinned. "After all, you're paying for it!"

Freddie looked at the bottle, unsurprisingly an Argentinian Chardonnay, and had a sip.

"Very nice and no doubt reassuringly expensive. But what a great location! I've been to many Gauchos but this is in a different league. Did you say you lived near here?"

"Yeah, just over the bridge. I've got a houseboat. I inherited it from my parents when they decided to go and live in Florida. I love it."

"I'd really like to see it."

"You never stop, do you, Freddie?"

"What do you mean?"

"You know what I mean!" She looked into his eyes and tapped his foot twice. "Let's order, but don't eat and drink too much. I need you in good condition if you are going to walk over that bridge and explore my boat and other possibilities later on."

CHAPTER 67

The next morning, when Freddie and Bea were showering together in the bright wet room on the houseboat, Tacic Kurti was picking up one of his burner phones and starting to shout in his native Albanian.

"You fucking idiot! How could this happen? A fucking knife fight in Newham? I told you to get out of there. I told you to get out of that area. They're fucking savages!"

"But–"

"Don't give me any shit. We have one guy on remand and a kid at home on bail, both charged with dealing class A and carrying offensive weapons. You know the kid will call you out, so waste her."

"But–""

"No fucking 'buts'. Waste the kid or I'll get someone to waste you!"

On the tenth floor of a tower block in Tower Hamlets, Doreen was crying and looking at her thirteen-year-old daughter.

"I just can't understand it. When your dad left me I had nothing and then you arrived. I had no money, no job and nowhere to live. But I survived. *We* survived and I did two jobs and made a life for us. And where are we now? You've got involved with drug dealers, for God's sake. What are we going to do? You might go to prison!"

Her daughter gave her that sullen look that had replaced her previous sunny smile.

"Whatever."

Later, Doreen stopped crying and started shouting. The couple next door couldn't make out the words but they knew something was wrong. Later on, in the middle of the night they were woken by screaming, so they turned on the light, looked at each other and called 999. Within ten minutes there were blue lights in the car park below and a lot of noise outside their flat. They decided to get dressed; it was clear that something terrible had happened.

An hour or so later they were not surprised when their doorbell rang. They offered the police officers tea or coffee but they declined. They just wanted to know what had been seen or heard. The next evening, they were watching the *BBC London News* at six-thirty and there was their tower block and a police officer in a very smart uniform talking about the tragic death of a thirteen-year-old girl and her twenty-seven-year-old mother.

"Stabbed to death in the middle of the night; we believe that this is probably gang-related." They held each other's hands and looked at one another; there was no need to say anything.

Kurti wasn't shouting this time; he was talking calmly.

"Good work, Altin. I'm pleased that you have resolved this issue swiftly. Let's meet up tomorrow morning at the house in Hackney; we need to consider if there are any other potential problems. See you around eleven." Then he picked up another burner phone and called his solicitor.

"How was Zamier when you met him at Wandsworth yesterday? Is he cool?"

"Frankly, I'm not too sure. He was talking about a not guilty plea, which, as you will know, is crazy. He has no previous and a guilty plea will probably get him out in four or five years. The alternative is that he will be convicted at trial and do at least seven. Of course, he might be thinking about 'helping the police with their enquiries', which could be helpful to him and, of course, unhelpful to you."

Kurti thought for a few moments as he lined up some coke on his table.

"Understood. When you see him before the next hearing give him a message from me. Tell him that if he pleads not guilty and inconveniences me, he will be out of Wandsworth within twelve fucking months. In a fucking coffin and the coffin will be dropped in the same grave as his wife and child. That might do it!"

CHAPTER 68

Jackie Starling was dressing carefully; she knew she would be under pressure at the meeting with her boss and she needed to project the best possible image. She examined herself in the mirror and practised her positive smile. She loved looking at herself in the uniform, even better with the badges on her shoulders to emphasise her seniority. She felt confident; Freddie seemed to have some sort of plan to fit-up Tacic Kurti. He hadn't been specific, which was understandable, but he had suggested that the evidence would be available within two or three months.

Brian Worth, the Director of the NCA, had been in the position for many years and had been responsible for Jackie's original appointment and her promotion to Head of the Serious and Organised Crime Command team. As he waited for her to arrive he wondered if that promotion might have been a mistake. But, when she walked into his office, smiling, looking very smart and confident, his misgivings were lessened.

After some chat about general issues, he cut to the chase.

"Jackie, I am getting some serious flak from the Home Secretary's team. As you know, she is not a patient person and is very keen that we deal with the drug issue, the stabbings and the so-called 'county lines'. Have you got any good news for me; anything at all?"

Jackie composed her face to look sincere.

"I think I will have some good news for you within a few weeks. We have identified a man, an Albanian called Tacic Kurti, who appears to be the UK kingpin of an international syndicate originating from Italy and now running most of the county lines. I think we may be able to get him bang to rights in the not-too-distant future."

"Not-too-distant; what are we looking at?"

"A month or so is my guess."

"OK, schedule a meeting with me five weeks from now and don't come back empty-handed! Now, how about a spot of lunch?"

CHAPTER 69

Nine-thirty Sunday morning and Freddie was fast asleep when William called.

"What time are we kicking off? Your place at eleven?" Then Freddie remembered.

"Yep. My place at eleven." Then he closed the phone, moaned 'Gordon Bennett' to himself, but he managed to shave, shower, dress and prepare two Cîroc Bloody Marys for when William arrived for their annual Sunday river walk/pub crawl. And when another round of Bloody Marys had been demolished they strolled a hundred yards to The Blue Boat pub, took seats in the sunshine and had a glass of Champagne. Then it was time for the next pub, just five minutes away. They weren't sure whether it was going to be The Blue Anchor or The Rutland Arms next, but they settled on The Blue Anchor, which had plenty of empty seats on the towpath. William was enjoying a large glass of white Rioja while Freddie had his hands round a pint of beer.

"Are you OK, Freddie? You look a little less than your usual self," enquired William. Then he smiled. "Don't tell me, Friday night took a lot out of you and maybe Saturday morning?"

"Possibly; I had a great time with Bea. We really hit it off."

"What's she like when off duty? I've never had a proper conversation with her."

"She looks very different from when she's in her work gear; the jeans, trainers and leather jacket with no make-up makes her very attractive. But dressed up, she is beautiful – truly beautiful, and she's very strong."

William frowned.

"Strong? What do you mean by that?"

"Well, she's physically strong; I suppose that goes with the job, but she seems emotionally strong as well."

"How do you know that?"

"She told me she got divorced when her daughter was one year old, brought her up with no financial or any other support from the father and just did what she had to do. She was completely positive about the whole experience, no complaints. But there is one thing…"

"What?"

"Well, the daughter is happily married, no problems there, but she's pregnant."

"Is there some sort of complication?"

"Yes. Kind of. The thing is that after the child is born, Bea will be a grandmother. It doesn't seem right."

William laughed out loud.

"Freddie, even now you can still amaze me. Have you forgotten, *you* are a grandfather? I think that means you have *grand*children, for God's sake!"

Freddie looked sheepish.

"I guess so. Anyway, I think she is intellectually strong too."

"In that case, you are probably out of your depth, mate! Let's move on to The Dove."

CHAPTER 70

The Dove pub on the River Thames dates back to the eighteenth century and has one of the smallest bars in the UK. When Freddie and William walked down the narrow passage to the door, a group of men were leaving so there was some space on the terrace. Freddie battled his way to the bar and returned with a bottle of Chablis and two glasses.

William took a gulp.

"Wonderful. Thank you, Granddad!"

Freddie pretended to scowl.

"I'm pretty fit for someone of my age, as it happens."

"Oh, yes. Who told you that?"

"Bea."

"Before or after?"

"During."

The last stop was The Old Ship where they had just enjoyed a couple of glasses of red wine before passing The Black Cow and walking down Hammersmith Terrace. They stopped at the Mari Deli and picked up some pizza slices and salad. A few minutes later they were at William's house. The pub crawl had taken two-and-a-half hours and they had covered little more than a mile.

William placed the pizzas in the oven while Freddie examined the fridge and took out a bottle of Sauvignon

Blanc. They decided to eat at the table in William's back garden.

"OK, Freddie," began William, "where are we with fitting up Kurti?"

Freddie swallowed the last of his pizza and leant back.

"Actually, it looks like it's possible. First, Euan has sent me some really amazing photos of the guy's garden. You can see actual flowers and blades of grass. More importantly, you can see a shed with a padlock and Euan says he has never encountered a padlock that he couldn't pick. Second, it looks as if there isn't any CCTV coverage of the garden so we could get into it from the road at the back or from the garden next door. There isn't a gate but the wall is climbable with no wires on top."

"How do you know?"

"I just told you! The drone pictures are amazing. You can even see the moss on the wall!"

"Quick question, Freddie. When you say '*we* could get into it', I hope you are not suggesting I might be climbing a fucking wall?"

"No, mate; don't worry. All you will have to do is give me an alibi. It won't be a problem."

"Oh, really?"

"Yes, like we did before. Here it is: We had a long dinner here and I stayed the night. I'll be absent for a few hours but my Garmin will stay in the bed. Bear in mind it's Miles Bishop who is involved in all of this and he is not connected to me, let alone you."

William topped up their glasses and thought for a moment.

"Fair enough. Anyway, have you managed to acquire the product?"

"No problem at all, as you suggested. Five kilos. Cam has bought the stuff and will drive it down to me. He needs two hundred thousand pounds in cryptocurrency and I have all I need to pay him. The good news is that the crypto is untraceable and, also, it's coming from Mr Bishop and not me. Better safe than sorry and then we are good to go, but Euan wants to be sure about CCTV, alarms and the whereabouts of the man. He will be looking into that as soon as he arrives, which will be Wednesday. He's in Moscow at the moment."

CHAPTER 71

Euan arrived as planned. Freddie set off to the apartment he rented in Clarges Street and Euan greeted him with a wide smile.

"Freddie, if this assignment is as profitable as the last one I shall be your friend for life!"

Freddie shook his hand.

"Euan, you know that we will always be friends for life. I don't know about you but I'll never forget that fuck-up where we saved each other. I still have a hole in my arm and you still have a scar on your head – or is that just a bald patch?"

"Fuck off, Freddie. Where are you taking me to dinner? I'm starving, and then let's come back here and talk through the plan." They walked to Berkeley Square and had dinner at Sexy Fish. Euan really liked the food and Freddie also enjoyed it as well; some time ago he had stood in pouring rain outside the entrance and shot dead a truly terrible man and his bodyguard.

Back in Euan's apartment it was a glass of wine and then down to business. They had worked together in the SBS and more recently as civilians. They each knew how to plan these things. Euan began the dialogue.

"Freddie, let me give you my take on this and please interrupt me if I have got anything wrong. Is that OK?"

"Absolutely."

"For one reason or another we need to get a serious drug dealer sent to prison for a long time. The plan is to plant some drugs in his house or anywhere on his property and tell the police that we think there are drugs there. They come in, execute a search warrant and that's that. Is that it?"

Freddie nodded.

"Two questions: Why? And how come the police will believe us?"

Freddie sighed. "The thing is, the police – or more accurately, the National Crime Agency – have asked me to fit this guy up and they could embarrass me if I turn them down. To put it bluntly, they are blackmailing me and I have agreed to go along with it. That's the 'why', and the police will believe us because they will know the drugs have been planted."

"Do we trust them?"

"No. We have to keep our hands clean and our alibis solid, but we do have some cards in our hands."

"Such as?"

"I have recorded all the discussions with the person in the NCA. So, we are in a Mexican stand-off."

Euan crossed his arms, leant back and closed his eyes for a moment.

"OK, Freddie, let's have a glass of red wine and talk about the detail."

CHAPTER 72

Euan opened the wine, sniffed it and poured.

"One final question: What's in it for me?"

Freddie smiled. "I don't know. Possibly nothing, other than getting an awful guy locked up for life, but when we did that gig in Scotland you cleared around three quarters of a million in bitcoins, so do I have some leverage? Anyway, we have five kilos of uncut wholesale heroin and we think planting it in the house would be challenging. So, we plant some in the shed instead, perhaps bury a kilo in the garden somewhere and ideally hide a kilo in the guy's car. We also need to wrap the drugs in something that will ping on a metal detector."

"Agreed. How about a gun? Could you get one?" asked Euan.

"No problem! The problems are getting to the car and making sure he isn't home when we visit. There may be alarms that we can't see on the drone photos, pressure plates or similar."

Euan frowned. "If the car is there it's likely that *he* will be there. Do we need the car? We have the drugs to plant; we also need a gun to plant, night-vision equipment and pads in case there is some barbed wire around the place that isn't on camera, picks for the padlock and latex gloves. Does anything else come to mind at this stage? So, that leaves us with the car challenge. What do we do about that?"

Freddie looked thoughtful for a time.

"This guy is a major suspect. I'll talk to my contact to see if they have ANPR on his car; this will show the whereabouts of his vehicle. My contact might be able to help. Leave it to me. What's your availability?"

Euan looked relaxed. "I've got a few meetings lined up here and in Europe but I can be around for the next four weeks. My plan would be to get back home immediately this task is completed, not least as the outcome is not completely predictable."

Freddie smiled. "'Not completely predictable' – maybe an understatement, but it's good to be working with you again, Euan. Let's polish off this red and I'll get a cab home."

CHAPTER 73

Freddie had his second date with Bea on Friday. She came to his flat at six-thirty and he was pleased to see she was carrying a small case. He opened a bottle of Champagne and they discussed their week.

Bea had been looking after a diplomat.

"I can't say which country he's from but he was a pig. Fat, smelly, insisting on smoking in the car, which is not allowed, and asked me about escorts. Still, he didn't snog anyone in the back of the car, unlike somebody I know. In fact, someone I can see!"

Freddie had the good grace to look embarrassed before he kissed her. They walked to The River Café, ambled back to his flat afterwards and the sex was wonderful. He wondered about offering Bea a line of coke but decided that might spoil things. In any event, nothing could have been better and when she left the following morning he was missing her after just ten minutes. But there was work to do.

He drove to the Big Yellow Storage facility, parked and took the lift to his floor. After he keyed in his number, nothing inside had changed. He went to the old Hoover and opened the rubbish bag. First out was his Ruger hammerless revolver with a cleaning kit and, second, a burner phone. When he got home and had charged the phone he punched in a number and a recorded voice answered 'Say your name'.

"Freddie Findlay."

Kathy was immediately on the line.

"Freddie, lovely to hear from you. Are you coming to see me? It's been ages."

"I would love to come and see you and I wonder if you could help me with some items. I'm using a clean burner so I think I can be specific. Would that be OK with you?"

"Yes, indeed. Fire away. Just my little joke!"

"Very apposite, Kathy. I'm after some serious fire power and I'm thinking a Glock 19 with fifty rounds."

"Fuck me, Freddie; are you going to war? But if that's what you want I can get it for you by this time next week. What else is on your list?"

"Two sets of night-vision glasses."

"No problem. Same timing. Anything else?"

"That's it, thanks."

"Consider it done. How about The Plough next Sunday?"

"Excellent; I'll be with you at about twelve."

As Freddie was cleaning the Ruger he wondered if there was anything he had forgotten. He was aware that the Glock was probably surplus to requirements, but he also knew that Tacic Kurti would understand that he had been fitted up and would do anything to extract himself and/or punish the culprits with extreme and prolonged violence.

CHAPTER 74

Bea called Freddie a few minutes after she thought he would have arrived home. She asked if he felt like coming to her boat.

"Is the Pope Catholic?"

Freddie didn't bother to change. He charged down the stairs, got into his Taycan and was on board within twenty minutes. Five minutes later they were out of their clothes and on her bed. Another five minutes and Bea sat up and looked at him.

"It's unmistakeable."

"What?"

"The smell. It's unmistakeable!" she repeated.

Freddie was completely confused and naked, thinking Bea was talking nonsense. Could she smell the scent of another woman? That was crazy.

"Bea, there is no other woman. What are you talking about?"

She looked him in the eye.

"Gun oil, Freddie. Gun oil! There is no mistaking it. You have been cleaning a gun. What the fuck is going on?"

He tried to hug her but she pulled away and wrapped the duvet around her. She looked confused, putting as much distance as she could from him. Eyes wide, face paler, wondering if she should run and hide or stay. Thoughts were also rolling around Freddie's head. He had only been close to Bea for a few weeks but he already knew that he wanted to stay with her and he understood he had to make a choice. He decided to lie.

"Bea, relax, for Christ's sake. Give me a break! You have seen the gun case in my flat. It has been inspected in line with all the legislation. I have two Purdeys in there and I can show you my certificates if you want to see them. And, actually, I would love to see you stark naked, legs apart, knees trembling, holding a heavy shotgun worth two thousand pounds and pointing it at me."

"Christ, Freddie; I'm sorry. Perhaps I'm paranoid, but you are a pretty dangerous sort of guy. Anyway, you should have at least washed your hands before coming over here and getting into bed with me. Go and have a shower and come back quickly and note I said 'come back quickly' not 'come quickly'!"

CHAPTER 75

On Sunday morning the sun was shining and Freddie and Bea walked along the Thames towpath past Kew Gardens, over Kew Bridge, into the Bell and Crown pub and were soon seated at a table on the terrace. Freddie smiled as he looked down at the people sitting at the tables on the towpath below.

"What are you smiling at?" asked Bea.

"I'm a happy bloke about to have a decent pub lunch with a lovely lady who was indecent not so long ago. I've had some exercise, the sun is shining and the tide is coming in. I always feel positive when the tide comes in. Don't know why. Anyway, I can recommend the tomato soup and the special lunch. I used to live ten minutes from here and know it well. If we walk to my place after lunch I will show you my old house. In the meantime, we might see some theatre on the towpath."

As they finished the bottle of white and started on the red with their roast beef, the theatre began and the tourists started to take notice of the river rolling in at speed, just a few inches from the towpath. Bea looked down in amazement.

"What's happening?"

"High tide. Happens every day but some days it's higher than others. I love it. Look, it's already approaching their feet and here come a couple of paddleboarders going upstream with the tide and I know them."

Freddie grabbed his glass of wine, stood up and shouted.

"Nick! Jo! Cheers!" as they paddled alongside the towpath. Five minutes later, Freddie urged Bea to join in.

"Bea. Stand up and look at this!"

A large cruiser heading downstream was emerging from under Kew Bridge and creating quite a wake behind it; it was already rolling over the path and heading for the packed tables below them. Within a couple of minutes, the towpath was more than ankle-deep in water, glasses were falling off tables and a couple of women were screaming. Freddie was laughing. Bea wasn't.

"Freddie, that's cruel. Taking pleasure from others' misfortunes. There they were, having fun, enjoying their lunch and suddenly their feet and even their legs get soaked. What's so funny about that?"

"Well, yes; I know what you mean. It happened to me back in the day when I was trying to impress a girl." He put on his bashful look. "And I suppose I was trying to impress you with my knowledge of the river. I'm sorry."

"That's OK, but don't bother to put on that look. I'm an experienced officer and I've seen it a hundred times. Anyway, what's the plan now?"

"If you are up to it I thought we could walk all the way to my place. It's about four miles. Maybe I should call William and see if he is at home so we could have a glass of wine on the way. What do you think?"

"Done! And I'll use the facilities here while you pay the bill and call William. See you outside."

CHAPTER 76

They walked along Strand-on-the-Green and then Hartington Road where Freddie pointed to a large house set back from the road with two black cast iron gates in front of it.

"There it is, my old place."

"Tell me you are joking!"

"I'm not. It was my parents' house and they left it to me, but it's a ridiculous size. It's got five bedrooms, three bathrooms and the rear garden has a deck over the river, a gym and a terrace with a swimming pool. It's got a massive living room, dining room and kitchen. Outrageous for a single man."

"Single man?"

"Yep. I was divorced twice before my dad died and three times before my mum passed away."

"Three times!" I knew you were divorced, but *three times*? How and why?"

They walked along in silence for a while, Bea trying to take it all in, Freddie deciding how to respond. He chose to tell the truth.

"I married number one when I was in the Royal Navy and I was away a lot of the time. I have to admit that I played away some of the time as well. In the end she got fed up with me and found someone more suitable. I don't blame her and we are still on good terms. We had two boys and all is well although it did cost me a lot of money."

"Serves you right. I'm not sure I want to hear about wife number two."

Freddie shrugged. "That was a very different story. It turned out she was in it for the money. When she discovered it had all gone to my first wife she dropped me like a stone. Married and divorced within eighteen months."

Bea smiled. "Also serves you right. What about wife number three?"

Freddie frowned. "It was even more of a disaster. It was shocking and it was all my fault!"

"Again! Go on, then. Given what you have said so far I doubt it will shock me."

"OK, but I have to say it doesn't paint me in a very flattering light. My third wife was a model. Quite a famous model, but I'm not going to name her. She was about twenty years younger than me but we really bonded. Then I did something very stupid."

"Not for the first time by the sounds of it. Tell me."

"Just as my kids were getting used to having a stepmother just a few years older than them, I had a brief affair, almost a one-night stand – nothing serious but she found out and was terribly hurt."

"How did she find out?"

"The woman with whom I had the brief affair was very annoyed that I didn't want to take it further and told my wife."

"How did she even know she existed?" probed Bea.

"My wife was her daughter."

Bea was lost for words, trying to process what she had just heard.

"Freddie, just to be clear, are you telling me that you had an affair with your wife's mother? Your mother-in-law?"

"Well, not really an affair; as I said, it was more like a one-night stand, but *she* seduced *me*, not the other way round!"

Bea didn't know whether to laugh or cry, but she found herself laughing regardless.

"Jesus Christ, Freddie; you *are* a piece of work!"

CHAPTER 77

Freddie was relieved that Bea hadn't just called a cab and said goodbye. As they walked under Chiswick Bridge and along the towpath, he reached out for her hand; she didn't pull it away from him and looked at him.

"Freddie, listen: You fuck me around and I'm gone. No second chances, no one-night stands – I'm gone. Understand?"

"Yeah. I understand." And he did.

They were in a good mood when they arrived in Chiswick Mall. The road was still wet from the high tide and covered in flotsam and jetsam, some of which was on the pavement outside William's house. He came to the door within seconds, shook Freddie's hand and kissed Bea on both cheeks.

"How lovely to see you both on this fabulous day. I'm so glad you called. Ina is in the back garden; let's go through."

Freddie noticed that William was looking rather smart: blue spectacles matching the watch strap on his Cartier Roadster, which blended with his cashmere jumper. Ina was also looking very elegant, albeit casual. There was a bottle of Champagne on the table and it all felt like some sort of celebration was happening. William filled the glasses and looked as if he was going to propose a toast, but the almost imperceptible shake of Ina's head stopped him in his tracks.

But Freddie noticed.

"You guys look rather smart for a Sunday afternoon. What's up? Where did you have lunch?"

Ina smiled. "Just at La Trompette, but I think it deserves more than a shabby dress and, actually, we have been celebrating or, at least, marking a special occasion."

He knew it. Bea cut to the chase.

"So, Ina, I guess congratulations or commiserations are in order, and as my keen detective eyes observe glasses of Champagne in our hands and, as *The Times*' business pages mentioned your name yesterday as the odds-on favourite to take over as the UK CEO of the bank, I suspect congratulations are in order?"

Ina frowned. "I guess so, but I have mixed feelings. More pressure, more kissing frogs – sorry, analysts – more internal politics, more–"

"Money?" asked Freddie with a grin on his face.

"Yeah, you're right, Freddie; but who needs more money?"

Freddie was still grinning.

"'Who needs more money?' you ask – half the population of the UK. But William, more relevant to the moment, Bea and I have had a long, arid walk from the Bell and Crown and we are in desperate need of a top-up."

Later on, Freddie and Bea agreed she would get a cab back to Richmond and he would walk back to his place. As she was on duty for the next six days with twelve-hour shifts they fixed a date for Saturday night. And even later on, Ina returned to her place to make sure she would be ready and able to deal with the financial press in the morning.

CHAPTER 78

Freddie used his burner to call Jackie on Monday evening. She confirmed that it would be possible to use ANPR to provide an indication as to where Kurti's car had been and at what time.

"But let me be clear, Freddie, we are not talking real-time tracking and we won't even know who is in the car."

"I get that; I'm just looking to mitigate some risks."

"So, when will you make some progress?"

"As soon as we can; possibly two or three weeks. You need to think about how you can make the information you will be given completely credible."

Freddie could imagine her scowling when she replied.

"I don't need you to tell me what I need to think about! And anyway, who is the 'we' in 'we can'?"

"The 'we' is the person with copies of the tapes I have made of our conversations and he is five thousand miles away from your jurisdiction."

Freddie called Euan that evening.

"All good. Looks like next week, to me. Are you free on Saturday morning? I'm going to the English countryside and I think you might enjoy it."

Euan was waiting in Clarges Street when Freddie arrived. He jumped in the Taycan and it moved off almost silently.

"Nice wheels, Freddie. Where are we going?"

"West Hanney. A small village in the Vale of White Horse. I have a pal who lives there whom I know you will like. I'm going to collect some stuff from her and then we can go to the local pub. After that we have to get back to London as I have a date with a policewoman tonight."

Euan turned to Freddie and frowned.

"Sorry, mate, would that be a *real* policewoman or someone dressing up like a policewoman to fulfil some sort of fantasy? Or is it the real McCoy? Just asking; both could be dangerous in their own way, maybe to both of us."

"The real McCoy, Euan. Actually, it was her that you called with the information about the property where that madwoman was holding me. She's a protection officer, not a cop in the usual sense, and she's wonderful. I think I'm falling in love."

"Freddie. I think I may have heard you utter those words before."

They arrived at Kathy's house at around eleven-thirty and Sam opened the door to greet them. Kathy came out and Freddie bent down to hug her.

"Kathy, this is Euan, my oldest and most trusted friend. I think I told you about him and an incident which nearly got us both killed."

"Indeed, you did. Still sounds to me that you were both incompetent and lucky to get away with just scratches. Let me tell you, Euan, when I was incompetent I was *properly* incompetent and lost my fucking legs! Anyway, come on in, boys, and let's get down to business."

Kathy's chair rolled smoothly and silently along the corridor and into the lift. Freddie winked at Euan when she pressed the button marked 'Emergency' and the lift descended. When the doors opened, Euan's mouth dropped open and his eyes widened.

"Holy Christ, it's a gun shop!" Sure enough, there were handguns, rifles, carbines on the wall and a number of machine guns. He recognised an AK-47, an HK33 and a Sterling SMG. Looking around he could see all sorts of hardware and a lot of hi-tech components similar to some in his own business.

Kathy was all business.

"Right, Freddie, here is the Glock 19 with fifty rounds, here are the two pairs of night-vision goggles and the tracker. I've included a suppressor for the Glock as you requested on your phone message the other day. It reduces the bang by about fifty decibels. That all adds up to fifteen hundred pounds and you know where to send the crypto. By the way, I've added two jars of the honey from our community shop that you like. Free of charge! Now, let's put the stuff in this box and let's go to The Plough. I'm starving!"

CHAPTER 79

Freddie had decided that Saturday night would be a perfect date. Bea had been on duty all week and he wanted to do something special. Not least because of the discussions about his ex-wives last Sunday, but also because he had mentioned that the place they were going to was quite smart and he had arranged for a car to pick her up. He had also suggested that she might like to stay at his place and have lunch with him on Sunday.

Bea was really looking forward to the evening. It had been a tiring week looking after a diplomat from Qatar who wanted to stay out in nightclubs and, as a result, was late and hungover every morning. The drive from her houseboat had been relaxing and she smiled when the car entered Berkeley Square. She had spent several hours hanging around waiting for the guy to come out of Annabel's, but she frowned when the car stopped there.

"Where are we?" she asked, panicking. "Where is the restaurant?"

"Here!" replied the driver as a doorman opened her door. That was when she saw Freddie, beaming, at the top of the steps of Annabel's.

"Bea, you look beautiful," he said, before kissing her gently on the lips. "Let me give your case to this kind lady to look after."

As they walked through to Matteo's restaurant, Bea whispered to Freddie.

"I thought this was a posh club; how did you get a table?"

Freddie was a little embarrassed.

"I joined it many years ago but it was by no means as posh as this; in fact, it was in a different building almost next door, but a guy called Richard Caring bought it and spent millions to make it look like this. Actually, membership is not that expensive."

Bea looked at the menu.

"Christ, Parma ham and melon, thirty quid? No wonder the membership is not that expensive! But I'm really glad to be here; I've spent more than enough time sitting outside."

"Don't worry about the money. How about a glass of Rock Angel rosé to start?"

The dinner was good and Bea was great fun, telling Freddie about some of her more interesting protection assignments, on a no names basis of course. Freddie was captivated with her stories but was astonished when he glanced at his watch and saw it was nearly midnight. Five minutes later they were in a black cab heading for Fulham Reach; twenty minutes later they were doing a line of cocaine and ten minutes after that Freddie had his hand under Bea's chin. Warm lips, the scent of lilac and her hand on his thigh. He looked into her eyes.

"Are we good?"

She grinned. "We were the last time; hard to improve on that. But let's try."

CHAPTER 80

Middlesbrough. Monday morning: The street was shit. No rubbish collected. No parked cars on the kerbs. Houses with broken windows, houses with no front doors, and houses which had been burnt to the ground.

This house was shit. It looked like shit. It smelled like shit. But it was another county lines' cuckoo, so the door was secure. There were five kids staying there and two of the boys never even bothered to flush the filthy lavatory. The owner, a woman of about seventy, was an addict and incontinent. Her arms, scabbed with the tracks of heroin injections; her teeth, either rotten or missing; her hair filthy; her voice a hoarse whisper – her life almost gone. The only concern the kids had was what to do with her body. Until Altin turned up.

Altin was dressed in faded blue jeans, black work boots, white sweatshirt and a black leather biker's jacket. He was about thirty but he didn't know for sure. He sniffed the air and fixed his eyes on each of them.

"This is no good. The boss is angry and when the boss is angry so am I. What's happening? You are either stealing from us or being lazy. Why are you not on the streets now? It's eleven-thirty!"

No one replied.

"You," he said, pointing at a tall, thin Asian boy aged about sixteen, who was probably the eldest there, "what's the problem?"

The boy replied softly, fearfully.

"The police, the competition, the slow cooking, the supply of the product; they are all making this life difficult."

Altin frowned, looked away from the boy and eyed two girls on the floor.

"Surely difficulties can be overcome with the right attitude. How do you feel about that, girls?" Neither of them responded.

"It seems to me that we need more motivation." He reached into his backpack and extracted a whip, similar to the ones that jockeys use on their horses, and passed it to the Asian boy. "I want you to motivate the team, I want you to show them the price of failure and I want to give you a choice. I want you to choose one of these girls, pull off her jeans and pants and beat her naked arse until I say 'Stop'. If you don't hit her hard enough I shall be very disappointed with you and there will be consequences. But I will offer you another choice. You don't have to beat her, just say 'No', give me back the whip and I will beat you instead."

The boy hesitated. He knew right from wrong. His parents had drummed those things into him in Calcutta and that was one of the reasons he had left. Now both girls were crying, pleading, wrapping their arms around their chests and backing away as if that was going to make a difference. Their noses were dribbling and their eyes were red. He glanced at them again; he knew he had to make a terrible choice. His hands were shaking, his bowels were loosening; he thought he was going to faint. For a moment, he thought about running out of the open door, but Altin's driver was bound to be outside.

Altin glowered at the boy, getting impatient.

"Pick one of those fucking girls and fucking beat her!"

The boy took a firm grip of the rod, pointed it at the girl on the right, spun around and swiped Altin's face once, twice, three times before he went for the door and the driver. The driver managed to grab the rod off the boy, punch him in the face and start beating him over and over again. When the boy passed out and his clothes were soaked in his own blood, the driver passed the rod to Altin. He pushed the girl down onto the floor, pulled down her jeans and pants and began hitting her naked bottom. She screamed until she passed out, lying on the bloodstained floor in her bloodstained clothes. Nobody helped her; she was just another casualty of the county lines business.

CHAPTER 81

Freddie called Euan on his burner phone.

"Mate. I think we might be good to go tonight or tomorrow night. The ANPR caught our man in Newcastle this morning."

"Let's go tonight. Stay with the plan?"

"Yep, I'll collect you at eleven. It should take about an hour to get to where we park and twenty minutes to get to his place. Any complications, we'll have a second chance tomorrow night."

When Freddie got back from the office he put his clothes together: Dark items of trousers, shirt and jumper, socks, trainers and hoodie, then the rest of the kit: Two carrier bags – one with three bricks of the heroin – the other with two more, plus a rucksack containing their night-vision glasses, some pads to protect themselves from any barbed wire that might be at the top of walls, a first-aid kit, latex gloves and a Taser in case there was a dog. He was in two minds about bringing the Glock and decided to leave it. Finally, he included the trowel he had bought from B&Q and his beloved Ruger. He looked at his watch – eight-thirty – time for a swim before the mission kicked off.

Euan was waiting outside the building in Clarges Street and the traffic was light. It was raining but it stopped just before they arrived in Northwood. They parked the Range Rover in Copse Wood Way in the space that Euan had identified by the drone footage. Looking at the nearby houses, Range Rovers and similar vehicles were very popular and after ten minutes not another car had passed them and there were no pedestrians. Freddie looked at his watch and then at Euan. "Action stations."

"Action stations!" Euan repeated, smiling.

Euan took the heavier carrier bag while Freddie took the lighter one and placed his rucksack on his back. They had planned to walk inside the tree line rather than the pavement by the houses where the streetlights were. They knew that two men in hoodies at night in this area might well pose a risk of someone calling the police. Apart from jumping over a ditch and ploughing through some nettles, it was straightforward thanks to the night-vision goggles, but they knew the real risk would be in the next ten minutes. They needed to get into the garden of Kurti's neighbour and then over the wall into his garden.

As expected, there was no sign of a car outside the house. The first wall wasn't a problem at all but Kurti's wall was much higher, there being just a narrow, rocky gap between the two that they had to squeeze through. Euan grinned; he didn't need to speak to Freddie. He splayed his legs and arms, inched upwards and managed to get his feet on the top of Kurti's wall and disappear down the other side. Freddie followed and fifteen minutes after leaving the car they were sitting in Kurti's garden, silent, with their backs against the wall and using the night-vision goggles to check the lie of the land.

"Reminds me of Kabul but it smells better," Euan whispered.

Freddie punched his arm softly.

"And no dog. Let's rock and roll."

Chapter 82

The padlock on the shed was child's play. Euan opened the door and they had a good look around. The shed floor had planking so Freddie used the trowel to lever up a couple of planks enough to shove the bag containing two bricks of heroin underneath and then put them back neatly. Another brick was hidden behind a load of netting, plastic pots and bags of compost. All of a sudden, a dog barked and they both froze.

"Fuck. It's a dog next door," whispered Freddie.

Euan tapped him on the shoulder.

"Stay calm and quiet, mate, that's what we were good at. We have at least five hours of darkness left; relax for now, then let's find somewhere suitable to bury the last kilos and your Ruger." They sat silently for thirty minutes and then went to work.

The whole garden was overgrown, full of weeds and a complete mess. They buried the last bricks and the Ruger in what might have been a bed of roses. Then they did the hard work of smoothing any footprints they had made and checking for any signs that might suggest a third party had visited the property. Then they were sitting down with their backs to Kurti's wall and Freddie looked at his watch again: "Approaching two. Time to check."

Silence. Then an owl hooted a few times. No other noise. No dog barking, no cars, no planes. Nothing – not even the sound of them breathing. Light rain began to fall.

Ten minutes later, Freddie whispered to Euan.

"Good to go?"

Euan had been thinking about everything as well.

"Yes, Freddie; good to go. The rain will help remove any evidence although I'm sure we've left no tracks, but getting back over this wall might need that old trick."

"Yeah, but we won't have AK-47s on full-automatic and searchlights looking for us, so take the position, mate!"

Euan checked his gear, knelt down on his arms and legs and waited. Freddie ran towards him, jumped on his back and reached up to the top of the wall. A couple of minutes later, Euan saw Freddie's hand and he reached up and grabbed it. He used his feet to brush away any remaining footprints and then found himself hoisted up to the top of the wall. As they crossed the road and walked back through the trees and nettles to the car, neither of them said a word. They were both thinking about anything that they might have left behind – anything that might suggest that someone had planted the drugs and the gun.

Freddie nudged Euan as they approached the car.

"Let's give it five." Then, "Project complete?"

Euan took his time to reply.

"So far so good."

Freddie drove the Range Rover north up the M1 before taking the first exit and turning back to London via different main roads and dropping off Euan near the Hilton Hotel

Chapter 82

in Park Lane. Then Freddie drove back to Fulham Reach, parked the car, took the lift to his flat and shaved, showered and changed. Once dressed, he phoned for a cab and went to the office.

CHAPTER 83

The message on her phone was from Freddie's burner but the voice belonged to someone else – someone Scottish; someone well-educated. She listened to it again.

"Hello, Chief Superintendent Jackie Starling. I have some information for you. Very valuable information. But I do not seek any reward; I just want to see justice... Let me explain. My business involves importing recreational drugs. Recently, I acquired a new client, a chap called Tacic Kurti. He purchased five kilos of pure heroin, which I delivered, but the scoundrel has refused to pay me; in fact, he has threatened me. I would like to see him in prison and I'm sure you do as well. I know that a thorough search of his property in Northwood will enable us both to achieve our objectives. But time is of the essence."

Jackie called the boss and they agreed that they had grounds for a search warrant. But they knew there were risks; first: Kurti's solicitor and Sebastian Brown, the QC who would no doubt be representing Kurti if a prosecution went ahead. He was a complete bastard; second, the costs: Carrying out a thorough search would involve around a dozen officers, dogs, metal detectors, civilian contractors and Christ knows what else; third, public relations: They both knew that police swarming over a one-and-a-half-million-pound property in a posh neighbourhood close to other multimillion-pound properties would be fodder for the tabloids.

Brian Worth jogged to the office and back most days. Five miles each way. *Keeps me cheerful.* He looked Jackie in the eye.

"Of course, there are risks, but we can't ignore this and, anyway, I have a feeling that there might be more to this 'breakthrough' than you are telling me. So, let me promise you this. I will be supporting you all the way," he paused, "unless, of course, it threatens my career... Only joking!"

Jackie knew that Brian wasn't joking, but she kicked off the process all the same. The first step was to get one of her people to complete the relevant forms and put them in front of a magistrate who would need to be satisfied there were reasonable grounds to suspect there were controlled drugs on the premises. The second step was to put the team together. Three days later she was ready to go, but holding fire until Kurti was back in his house and when she was told that he had returned she informed the team leader to go ahead. Seven vehicles, twenty people, three dogs and a drone were on the scene at seven-thirty in the morning. Chief Inspector Claire 'Ballbreaker' Jensen was in charge and kept her finger on the bell until the door opened.

"This is an authorised warrant to search these premises. Please stand aside."

Kurti was wearing nothing other than white boxer shorts and he scratched his groin as he looked down on her.

"Fuck your warrant and fuck you, bitch! I've got fuck-all here to interest you unless you would like to suck this."

Claire smiled. "Not today, thank you. I haven't got the time. I have twenty people here, lots of arrangements to make. They need food and drink stations, screens to erect, perhaps diggers to deploy and all sorts of stuff. Nowadays the health and safety of our staff is of primary concern. So, read the fucking warrant and get out of my way!"

"I want my solicitor!"

"Of course. Feel free to call him or her. But get out of our way!"

CHAPTER 84

The house was Hollywood style as televised: A massive Samsung TV screen taking up an entire wall of the living room, white leather sofas and coffee tables, a jukebox in the corner, a wine fridge full of Champagne and a glass-door freezer loaded with Beluga vodka. The dining room had a table that could seat ten people and the kitchen looked big enough to cater for a restaurant. But Claire's experienced eye noticed that nothing seemed to have been used.

Upstairs was the same: One bedroom with clothes on the floor and one bathroom in need of a clean. Everything else pristine. Claire could see there was about four thousand feet of living space and the search was going to take several days. What a nightmare. If all of this didn't uncover some serious class A, her promotion prospects would be down the drain.

But later in the day, she heard a dog bark. Not an ordinary bark. A special bark. The bark of a trained sniffer dog finding something interesting. Then a shout from outside.

"Fuck me, two bricks! Get the photographer!"

The search teams were wearing body cameras but getting high-quality photos would be helpful in court. They brought high intensity lights into the shed and captured the space under the planks, the wrapped bricks and then the unwrapped product, almost certainly heroin. They took shots of the padlock they had removed from the shed door and then called Claire. She checked everything and signed off the evidence sheet. Then one of the dogs began barking from behind the shed; the smell of the compost had interfered with his nose but, finally, cleverly, he had located another brick. Claire rubbed his nose and patted his back.

"Good boy! Guys. Looks like we have three kilos."

The search team inside the house were getting frustrated. Traces of recreational cocaine but nothing else until they found a couple of phones hidden behind some junk in the attic. Claire congratulated them.

"Well done, guys! These might be priceless. Good job! I reckon we have done the house. Stand down for a while."

She wandered around the garden watching the two civilians with their metal detectors and one of the officers from the attic brought her a coffee. It spilled and burnt her arm when her hand shook at the shout 'Gun!'

The metal detector had found a Ruger revolver and two more bricks of heroin in a plastic bag, buried almost a foot deep in an overgrown rose bed.

Claire went into the house and found Kurti sulking in his study. He didn't get up from his chair.

"OK, bitch. All done? Clean as clean?"

"Well, actually, we found some traces of cocaine in your bedroom."

He laughed. "Might find some in your bedroom, baby." He rubbed the crotch of his boxers. "Want to do a line with me?"

"Not at this moment, Mr Kurti. What I *would* like is for you to open the safe we found in your wardrobe, please."

"Fuck you!"

"I have a warrant. If you refuse to open it I will call a specialist who will sort it."

"Fuck off!"

Twenty minutes later the safe was open and wads of cash were being recorded and packed into cases. In total, the amount was over five hundred thousand pounds.

Claire said, "Tacic Kurti, I am arresting you for possession with intent to supply class A drugs. Five kilos to be specific. You do not have to say anything, but if you do it may be used as evidence against you. I suggest you call your solicitor and tell him that you are being taken to Wood Green police station."

Kurti stood up. "What? You must be fucking joking. Five kilos of class A drugs; *what* drugs?" He poked his finger in Claire's chest. "This is some sort of set-up."

She turned to the officer standing next to her.

"You saw that assault?"

"Yes, ma'am."

"Please cuff him to prevent any more violence and put him in the van. Better get him to put on some clothes, those cells can be a bit chilly."

CHAPTER 85

Two days after his arrest, Kurti was in court seated in the dock listening to his solicitor, Julian Lowe, explain why he should be given bail and released from remand. He wasn't impressed.

The magistrates retired to consider what they had heard. Fifteen minutes later they returned. The magistrate chairman asked Kurti to stand and told him that bail was refused. She told him he would have a second bail application and that he would be remanded in custody until the next date. Then he was taken down to the cells.

Before he was moved to prison, Kurti had some time to speak with his solicitor and it wasn't a pleasant conversation for either of them. Julian Lowe was irritated to say the least.

"Why on earth didn't you come clean with me? You made me look like a fool."

"You *are* a fool. I need to speak to Sebastian."

"In due course, but in the meantime, what arrangements do we need to make and why on earth did you have those drugs on your property?"

"Fuck off! Of course I didn't have those drugs on my property. You really *are* a fucking fool! They were planted. The question is, who planted them? And the gun – just there to be discovered by the metal detectors. Let me think for a bit."

Julian was a patient man and Kurti was an important client, at least for the time being. The prison van wouldn't be leaving any time soon so he spent the next fifteen minutes looking at some of the other briefs on his MacBook. Finally, Kurti sighed.

"Let's look at the supply chain. We have the farmers growing opium in Afghanistan. They are peasants; no way could they plant five kilos of pure heroin in my garden. Next, we have the chemists, also in Afghanistan, educated peasants turning the opium into heroin. We can strike them off the list."

"Who is next?" asked Julian.

Kurti stood up. "Wait a minute; could this cell be bugged?"

"No. Not possible. Even if it was the transcript would be inadmissible."

"What about your notes?"

"No problem; they are 'privileged'. The prosecution has to show us everything they have. We have no obligation to show them anything."

Kurti sat down again. "The next link in my supply chain is the Italians. Those fuckers have no loyalty apart from to themselves. They are ruthless! But they are in the middle of a huge trial that's been going on for a year with over a hundred bosses facing serious time. I can't imagine why they would want to put me away. They have no distribution apart from us in the UK. But you never know."

"If not them, who else?"

"Well, there is a crew in Aberdeen that help bring the drugs and some illegal immigrants across, but they are just thugs with thick arms and thick heads. No way could they plant five kilos and a handgun in my property. Those fuckers wouldn't even know where I live!"

"Good point, Tacic. Who *would* know where you live?"

He thought for a few moments, then looked at the floor, looked at the ceiling and frowned.

"The cops, the fucking cops. And I bet I know exactly which fucking cop has set me up!"

CHAPTER 86

The party in The Black Dog at Vauxhall was well underway. Jackie Starling was buying drinks for the search team. It had been a long day but it was a day with one of the best results most of them had ever achieved. They were in a closed off spot outside at the back of the pub, but no one mentioned the details of the search until Jackie spoke and she spoke quietly.

"Guys, we did well today. So did the dogs and their handlers. Shame they can't be with us; the handlers that is, not the dogs! It seems to me that at last we have our man bang to rights and I see no reason why he won't be doing at least fifteen or maybe twenty if he doesn't behave. As I'm sure you will appreciate that we were working on the basis of an informant whose name is nowhere on record. But let me propose a toast: To the man or woman who got us this result." Then she walked casually to the ladies' toilet and vomited into the lavatory.

CHAPTER 87

Saturday lunchtime. Freddie, Bea, William and Ina were celebrating Ina's promotion, Freddie's bonus and the end of a difficult week for Bea.

"I had to put on the blue lights and siren to get a wanker to Downing Street and I'm sure he was pissed. Mind you, I doubt anyone in there would have noticed."

They were again at the restaurant Dinner in the Mandarin Oriental Hotel in Knightsbridge. The spring sun was shining and Hyde Park was looking great. Freddie noticed that some of the runners in their Lycra looked great as well but managed to avert his gaze. The bottle of Champagne they had ordered was almost empty and William took charge.

"I think we should all go for the tasting menu; I'll organise the wine and Ina can pay, not least because I read in *The Telegraph* this morning exactly how much her bonus was!"

"That's not fair, William. Half of that was shares, not cash."

Freddie snorted. "I remember how you complained how much us poor DPK partners got paid a couple of years ago and look at you now. William, don't hold back on the wine!"

The first course obviously had to be the meat fruit and everything afterwards was equally delicious, including the ice cream from the old-fashioned machine. William was about to order more drinks when Freddie took charge.

"Taxis back to my place, I think. See you there."

When William and Ina arrived, Champagne was flowing, music was playing and Freddie was having difficulty staying vertical. Ten minutes later, he disappeared leaving Bea with William and Ina sitting on the terrace enjoying the view of the river.

Ina smiled and looked at Bea.

"How's it going with Freddie?"

"He's a strange bloke, but I like him. How long have you known him?"

"William has known him much longer than me; I can't say I really know him. William?"

William put his glass down and looked at Bea.

"If it wasn't for Freddie, I'd be dead and, believe it or not, I'm not the only life that he has saved. Having said that, he might have accidentally damaged some innocent lives as well. But all in all, I would say he is brave, bright, honest and well-meaning. Without doubt, he's my best friend. But Ina is a bit sceptical!"

Bea turned to Ina.

"Sceptical?"

Ina took her time before replying.

"Well, by nature I'm sceptical. It goes with my job and Freddie does seem to play a little fast and loose. Having said that, on the business side he is completely professional; technically and culturally."

Bea raised an eyebrow.

"Culturally? What does that mean?"

"It means he never makes anyone uncomfortable,

he knows where to draw the line; he might flirt a bit but, believe it or not, he is pretty 'woke.'"

William topped up the glasses for the last time.

"Tell you what, girls, I've had a great lunch, a wonderful afternoon and I'm a bit pissed so I want to tell you something about Freddie. He took me to this club–"

"No, William; I'm sure that's not what Bea needs to hear at this time!" Ina interrupted, shaking her head.

There was silence for a few seconds, then William decided to recount the story.

"Like it or not, Ina, this is what happened and it's nothing like you might have anticipated, Bea, so don't worry! One evening years ago, Freddie and I met up in Motcomb's in Motcomb Street and had a few drinks. Later on, he suggested we went to a club where he was a member and which wasn't far away."

Ina frowned, but William continued.

"We were both a bit pissed and when we got to this place in Herbert Crescent, it didn't look that impressive. The guy on the door seemed to recognise Freddie, so in we stumbled. There was a staircase and, as we lurched up there, I noticed many framed photos on the wall and then we were in the bar. I was stunned. I couldn't believe my eyes. I had heard about it, I had read about it, but I had never imagined I would have actually been in it – the Special Forces Club. Turns out, our Freddie was a member and a very well-respected member indeed."

Ina looked at her watch and interrupted William.

"Freddie may well be a hero but my tee time tomorrow is at nine-thirty and I need to get some sleep, so I'm going to call a cab."

After Ina and William had left, Bea poured herself some more Champagne and put her feet up. She knew she had to make a decision about Freddie. The man was an unpredictable spendthrift and an unreliable guy, but he had some sort of magnetism. She couldn't help herself being attracted, completely attracted – sexually, emotionally, intellectually and, perhaps, lovingly. She knew that if she stayed with him there would be many bumps in the road and when she thought about it, a decision floated up into her head. *I always wanted to have a life of excitement and I can rely on Freddie to give me that if nothing else!* Looking at her watch she saw it was six-thirty. Time to see if Freddie had recovered and was ready to deliver the goods.

He was.

CHAPTER 88

Wandsworth is a Category B prison in South West London and was built in 1851. It is the most overcrowded prison in the UK and a recent investigation showed large-scale drug abuse and cannabis being smoked openly and harder drugs being dealt. There were allegations of staff corruption, including staff bringing drugs into the prison.

A recent inspection stated: 'In essence, there are too many prisoners, many with drug-related or mental health issues, and with not enough to do.'

When Tacic Kurti arrived, he found his reputation had preceded him. The prison officers were respectful and he was given a single cell on the H wing, which was relatively quiet. Two of his county line managers were at the end of eight-year stretches and he had made sure their families were looked after financially for all that time. More importantly, he had ensured that their assets were safe in the Caribbean island of Nevis and out of reach of the proceeds of crime investigators. They knocked on his door on the second day and handed him a tiny burner phone, cigarettes, a kettle, coffee and some cocaine.

He bumped their knuckles.

"Thanks, guys. Good to see you. Looks like I'm likely to be fucked. Someone planted five kilos of 'smack' in my garden; I'm sure it was the pigs, but my brief has told me

there's no chance of convincing a jury, so I might be putting my hands up for it. A guilty plea might get me nine and I could be out in five. In the meantime, I might need some help from you two."

The younger one, Matteo, didn't hesitate.

"Of course, Tacic; whatever you want."

The older one, Roel, was a little more cautious.

"How can we help you, boss?"

Tacic frowned. "If I am going to be stuck in here for five years someone has to pay and I have a source in the police that has identified who that person is. So, when you get out, I want you to sort this. And I will pay what it takes to deal with the bitch!"

"Bitch?" asked Roel. "Who is that?"

"That will be Chief Superintendent Jackie Starling. She is a senior officer in the National Crime Agency and I want her to die – painfully!"

After a couple of weeks, Tacic was transferred to the E wing and invited by some very serious influential and wealthy prisoners to join them in The Annex. This was a very special area in the basement with its own entrance from the landing. The cells were larger and they had one each and they had what could be called a common room with a flat-screen TV, Sky, a sandwich toaster, a George Foreman Grill and duvets rather than the standard thin, coarse blankets. They all had phones and their well-paid prison officers took care of them when searches were scheduled. From this annex, Tacic was pretty much able to continue running his business. At his birthday party there was Belvedere vodka, excellent cocaine and the new James Bond movie on the TV.

CHAPTER 89

The arrest of Tacic Kurti had some wider implications. A number of sources were now helping the NCA unravel hundreds of county line operations and rescue thousands of vulnerable children. This was achieved as the NCA and GCHQ had managed to penetrate the cell phones that the gangs had thought were completely secure. Within one month, nearly two million pounds' worth of cash had been seized, together with forty kilos of heroin, over fifty kilos of cocaine and nearly a hundred guns, zombie knives, machetes and other weapons. Jackpot! But Jackie Starling was up to her neck with the bureaucracy surrounding the successes – meetings with the CPS lawyers, the boss and the media relations team. She had never worked so hard and when she wasn't in meetings she was staring at screens from the time she woke until she went to bed and tried to sleep. Her husband was away, working in Australia, and appeared to have found a new partner with a less hectic career. Her meals now came from Deliveroo, the washing was mounting up and pressure was turning to stress. The only time she had to herself was the walk to her office and back.

Monday morning and it began to rain, just as predicted on last night's forecast, and Jackie was furious with herself for not bringing her umbrella. She had yet another team meeting at ten and she knew she was going to look like a drowned rat. She looked at her watch and increased her stride; maybe there would be plenty of time to fix her hair after all and at least her skirt was still dry. Things could be worse. And then they were. Much worse. A man grabbed her right arm and as she tried to pull away another man snatched her left arm and she found herself lifted off the ground and propelled forward. She screamed as the doors at the back of a white van in front of her burst open and she carried on screaming and shouting as she was thrown into the van, hearing the doors slam behind her. Someone slapped her hard in the face. A foreign accent.

"Shut the fuck up, lady!" then he punched into her stomach, punched into her breasts, another punch in the face and then blackness.

Jackie didn't know if it had been a few seconds or a few minutes but she finally felt able to focus. Her hands were tied behind her back and she was lying facedown on something like a mattress. The van was dark; she couldn't see anything. It sounded as if they were in heavy traffic, certainly not speeding. Two men were talking calmly but she couldn't understand a word they were saying and they seemed oblivious to her presence. She groaned as one of the men rolled her over so she was on her back. She moaned again as her weight descended on her tied arms.

"Sorry, lady. Didn't mean to hurt you. The hurt comes later. Let me explain. We are just doing a favour for a friend who we met in prison. Nothing personal. We are being sent back home next week and the money will be useful."

"What money?" croaked Jackie. "I don't have much on me but you can have it all." She began to think more clearly and looked around. The van had a couple of tiny windows;

perhaps she could break one and call for help, but she could see that the two guys were large, very large – little chance of fighting them. Their body odour was making her feel sick, but her fear was retreating. When there was no response to her question, she asked, "What do you want? Where are you taking me?"

The man to her right took out a piece of paper from his pocket, studied it for a few moments and then read it slowly.

"We know you arranged for some heroin to be planted in Mr Kurti's garden. We want to know who actually planted the stuff. Give us a name and we will not harm you but we will require some cooperation from you from time to time in the future."

Jackie's voice trembled.

"I have no idea what you are talking about. Let me go!"

The other man smiled.

"I'm really pleased to hear you say that, lady," he said as he straddled her legs, pushed her skirt up to her waist, seized the top of her tights and panties and pulled them down to her knees.

"So, I'm now going to fuck you. And when I have finished, my friend will do the same, but he likes the anal. You know what I mean? And if you still talk stupid, we will really hurt you. So, who planted the drugs? If you tell us the truth I promise you we will not harm you. I guarantee that."

Jackie could feel the man's hands pull her underwear further downwards and gasped.

"OK, OK! The man's name is Miles Bishop. I have a burner phone with him on speed dial. I don't know where he lives but I also have an e-mail address. The phone is in my bag."

CHAPTER 90

It seemed at least an hour later when the van finally came to a halt. There was no traffic noise, just a dog barking very loudly. The men got out and Jackie heard the van's doors lock. She was more scared than she had ever felt in her life and had no idea what was going to happen next. Then the door opened and she was looking at a large, derelict lorry park. The men untied her hands and legs, pulled her out of the van and she stumbled and fell as her underwear trapped her ankles. One of them kicked her in the face. They pulled her to her feet and she saw a large, rusty container with an open door. A vicious-looking guard dog was chained up nearby, foaming at the mouth and snarling. It was jumping up and down excitedly as they dragged her along. It looked like a Doberman Pinscher and she prayed the chain was strong enough to restrain it if it tried to attack her. They lifted her up a couple of steps and pointed to a table in the middle of the container, which had a lit torch and a wooden chair in front of it.

One of the men shouted orders at her.

"Sit down! Read that piece of paper."

She staggered across to the desk and began reading.

'Hello Chief Superintendent Jackie Starling. I hope your journey has not been too uncomfortable. I assume you have provided the information we needed and, as promised, we will not harm you. My situation is reasonably comfortable in Wandsworth – three meals a day, convivial company and plenty of banter – but I have to say that being locked up is unpleasant, to say the least. But at least it's not a life sentence – as yours is.'

Jackie was confused, trying to work out what the letter meant. Then the men picked up the torch and the two of them walked out of the container. The door slammed. Absolute blackness. She couldn't even see her hands in front of her face. No sound other than the dog outside barking. Then she knew what was going to happen to her; she was going to die in that container. No water, no food. Just certain death. She bellowed. A long bellow, which tailed off to a whimper when she lost control of her bladder.

Minutes later, perhaps an hour later – hope! Hearing the door open, witnessing light appear, even the sound of the angry, barking guard dogs, was music to Jackie's ears. Then the voice with a foreign accent again.

"Maybe we have been a little unkind leaving you here. No water, no food, no phone; facing a lonely and painful death. It doesn't seem fair."

Jackie was quick to speak.

"I will do anything you want. Anything at all. Just let me out of this place and I promise I will make you very happy."

The man, Matteo, looked at her thoughtfully, holding on firmly to the dog's chain The animal seemed to sense the tension and its yelping got louder and more frenetic, jumping up with front legs extended, back legs ready to power the dog forward. The man shook his head, grabbed the dog's chain, pointed him towards the doorway and looked at Jackie. He grinned.

Chapter 90

"Sorry, lady. This is it." And he let go of the chain. The dog leapt into the container and headed straight for Jackie with its jaws wide open. The door slammed and that was the last thing she saw.

Then total blackness. Silence for a few seconds followed by the dog's furious snarling and her terrified screams.

CHAPTER 91

At three-thirty that afternoon, Freddie was in a black cab heading for Canary Wharf and it was still raining, but that was the least of his problems. He knew the meeting with the client was going to be tricky as there were several important technical issues that needed to be resolved by the end of the week, but he felt confident that those arguments could be settled. His big problem was one of promotion: He was looking forward to retiring from DPK and replacing himself over the next twelve months. Human Resources, Human Capital, Talent Management, Employment Architecture or whoever and whatever had sent him a list of potential candidates and all of them were women or at least people who had identified as such. He decided he was fucked. The firm had targets for high-level women so he had to toe the line; however, some solid male candidates might have felt that they had been left out of the process because they were male. He thought again. Yes. He was *truly* fucked, but when his burner phone trilled, the DPK promotion challenge went straight into his mental bin.

The call was from Jackie's phone but she was not on the line.

A man's heavily accented voice spoke.

"Is that Miles Bishop?"

"Might be. Perhaps not. It depends on who you are and what you want," responded Freddie.

"Let's talk about the drugs you dropped in Mr Kurti's garden."

"I have no idea what you are talking about. You must have the wrong number." Freddie closed the phone but knew he was just buying some time. And the next call nearly stopped his heart.

"Take a look at the photo and show some respect. Keep on the line!" The photo was Jackie Starling on her back; face frozen with fear, clothes dishevelled, underwear pulled down to her knees.

Freddie swallowed and put his mind in gear. In his head he could see a pinball machine and ideas came and went – most of them went. There were lights flashing, but there was a message on the top of the screen getting brighter and brighter. 'Sound nonchalant!' it said. He waited a while.

The man spoke first and sounded a bit worried.

"Are you there?"

"Of course, but I don't really care about this woman. Why are you calling me? Would it be sensible if we met up and talked about this?"

After a few seconds the man replied.

"Why not? Battersea Park tomorrow morning, eight-thirty in the car park between the Lemon Tree Café and the tennis courts. Don't even think about doing anything stupid like speaking to the police. If we suspect anything, the lady dies."

Freddie called his assistant and asked her to cancel the client meeting.

CHAPTER 92

Battersea Park. Sun glittering on the River Thames. A little chilly but quite a few people around. Roel and Matteo were close to the car park checking out everyone. There was a singles' game in action on one tennis court and a couple of doubles' games on the other courts, which seemed highly energetic and well-humoured from Roel's perspective. There were also a couple of fit-looking girls in matching leggings powering along the path, an old, hunched over bloke with a stick and a dog which seemed to be pulling him along, a couple of ladies who stared at them suspiciously, a woman with a pram and also a couple of men in high visibility jackets.

"How about him?" asked Roel, pointing at a man on a bicycle. He was wearing Lycra, a mask and was speeding straight at them. Matteo opened his jacket and put his hand on his SIG Sauer. The bike flashed past them then a black cab arrived and a smart-looking man stepped out. Roel nudged Matteo and pointed.

"Keep your eyes on him!"

On the other side of the park were two more cyclists in full Lycra. Something about them worried Matteo this time, and he alerted their presence to Roel.

"See those guys? This place is full of fucking people. How will we recognise this Bishop motherfucker? And what about that black guy? And what about those guys in the high-viz jackets?"

Roel smiled.

"Relax. Here he comes, the guy from the cab. Looks pretty fit and is staring at us as if we are a couple of targets."

"He's not going to look so confident when he sees your gun pointed at his head!"

The man strolled up to them, noticed their worn leather jackets, faded jeans and cheap trainers and frowned.

"Good morning gentlemen. How might I help you?"

Matteo pulled out his SIG Sauer and laughed.

"How can you help *us*, you pathetic pussy?" But before he got an answer he was hit hard on the right side of his head by something heavy and sharp. He collapsed, banging the left-hand side of his head onto the gravel of the car park and dropping the gun. When he recovered his senses, he was on his back looking up at the stooped old man with the stick and the dog… except there was no dog, no stoop, no grey hair and no stick. Just a tall man with a gun.

"Good morning. I'm Miles Bishop. No need to get up, in fact, better remain on the ground if you want to stay alive. The gun in my hand is the one that I smashed into your head. It is a Glock 19 and I guess you know it's got serious stopping power. If you look carefully it has a suppressor. My pal is going to check your colleague and you can see he has your SIG." He glanced at his partner. "All good?"

William nodded.

"All good!"

Matteo was a big guy, confident, experienced and ready to put this old man down. Even though he was unarmed and lying on the ground, he squared off to Freddie.

"Fuck you, old man! Do you know who you are dealing with?"

Freddie looked around. No one was close.

"Correct. I don't know, but do *you* know where the woman is?"

"No. And if I did I wouldn't tell you!"

"Are you sure?"

"Fuck off!"

Freddie scanned around once more and shot the guy in the face. Blood, bones and brain spattered across the gravel, his legs twitched for a few seconds and then he was still. Freddie then turned the gun on Roel.

"I hope you know where the woman is or you will be joining your pal shortly."

Roel started trembling, his arms were outstretched and his hands were open, pleading with him.

"I know, I know!"

Freddie's voice was calm.

"That's good. Now, you can take us to your car. We are going to walk briskly – not too fast, not too slow. In spite of the suppressor, that shot will have woken up a few people and we don't want to look suspicious. But understand this: If you mess us around you will die and it will take a lot longer than it took for your pathetic pal." Freddie turned to look at William. "Do me a favour and get any phones from the guy on the ground and from our friend here."

CHAPTER 93

As the three of them walked to the car, William took a look at Freddie.

"Where did you get that dog and how was it I didn't even recognise you until you came up behind that chap?"

"Well, there was a homeless bloke on a bench over there, just inside the park, and so I gave him a twenty quid note in return for taking his dog for a walk. It will have found its way back to him by now. I'm sorry for the shock it would have witnessed though. As for the clothes and stick, I got them from a charity shop in Fulham Palace Road last night. No big deal. These guys are amateurs; presumably nowhere near the top of the county lines food chain. Anyway, this prick will drive, you can sit in the front and I will be behind him with my Glock with the safety off."

Freddie poked the barrel into Roel's back.

"Hope you understood what I've said. We don't fuck around. Tell me where you are going to take us."

"What about Matteo?"

"He's dead, mate. And no doubt the cops will be swarming all over Battersea Park soon and maybe checking out this car. Anyway," he turned his attention back to the situation, "where is the woman? Is she alive?"

"She is in a container. She might be dead, she might be alive."

Freddie nearly lost it.

"What! She's in a container? What do you mean? Did you harm her? Why did you say she might be dead?"

"I'm not sure if she is dead. I didn't kill her. We just did what we were told to do."

Freddie smacked Roel in the face making him momentarily lose control of the car.

"She is in a fucking container? How long has she been in there? Does she have food and water?"

"I don't know."

"How long until we get there?"

"It's in Mill Hill. Maybe another thirty minutes."

"What sort of container? How big is it? Are there other containers there? Is there any security? How do we open it? How long has she been in there? Is she safe?" Freddie was consumed with rage and shouted the torrent of questions at the driver.

Roel didn't know what to say. He swallowed, trying to find a way to lessen the danger he knew he was facing.

"I don't know if she is safe; there was a dog."

William stared at him.

"A dog. What's that got to do with it?"

"Matteo had told me to let the dog into the container before I closed the door!"

William had known Freddie for a very long time and he was surprised that Freddie seemed so relaxed in taking this news and in his response.

"OK, Roel; seems like this is mostly all down to Matteo. All we need to do is see if we can rescue the woman and go our separate ways and you can tell your boss that I am a fair opponent – if he leaves *me* alone I will leave *him* alone. Are we clear on that?"

Roel breathed out a relieved reply.

"Thank you! Whoever you are! We'll be there in about twenty minutes."

CHAPTER 94

The road leading to the container park was very quiet, no other traffic, and the morning sunshine was filtering through the trees as they drove in. There were about twenty containers stored there, most neglected-looking.

"Which one, Roel?" asked Freddie.

Roel pointed to one, drew up in front of it and stopped the car. Freddie told Roel to get out of the car and the three of them looked at the container. Birds singing and hardly a cloud in the sky with no one else around. Peaceful. William was shaking, having no idea what scene would be before them when they opened the door. Freddie was steadfast.

"William, if this guy does anything other than stand still, please shoot him in the knee with the SIG, but please don't kill him."

Freddie walked up the steps and unlatched the door of the container. The first thing that hit him was the smell. Blood, faeces, urine, vomit. He had an immediate flashback from a firefight that he had survived. But this was even worse. Jackie: Pale as a sheet, almost naked, unconscious or dead – he didn't know. Something bloody was wrapped around her thigh. There were bruises and blood on both her arms.

He shouted, "Jackie!" There was no response. He rushed towards her, carefully picked her up and carried her to the door, almost tripping over a dead dog on his way.

William blanched when he saw what Freddie was carrying, but kept the SIG pointed at Roel. Freddie passed him one of his phones.

"Call 999; don't use our names. They will get the location. Tell them loss of blood, unconscious, shock and dehydration, imminent possibility of death. And tell them she is a senior police officer. Probably the woman who was reported as missing a few days ago."

Freddie took a bottle of water from his jacket and managed to wake Jackie sufficiently to get her to sip.

"Drink this, drink this. You are safe now. An ambulance is on its way. You are safe. One of the guys that did this to you is dead. The other is going into the container. You are going into the ambulance. Call me when you feel ready." He held her hand as she lost consciousness and then let her go.

"William, could you pass me that SIG? The ambulance should be here shortly and I guess we should depart before we have to explain our presence. But there is a small matter I need to address and it involves our friend, Roel."

Freddie's voice remained relaxed.

"Roel, I think we are finished in here. Could you just check if there is anything we need from the container, please?"

Roel came back with a couple of sheets of paper.

"This is all."

Freddie smiled and said "Thank you", then he knocked the thug onto the ground, picked him up, carried him up the steps to the container's door, threw him on the floor, stepped back, closed the door and dropped the latch. Then they carried Jackie to a container some distance away and laid her down in front of it.

Ambulance sirens were getting louder. William was at the wheel, Freddie was in the passenger seat and they drove sedately out of the container park.

Freddie didn't say a word until William spoke.

"What do you think about Jackie?"

"Don't know, mate. Really can't say. From the state of her clothing, she might have been raped; she was certainly bitten badly by a fucking dog, probably nearly killed by the dog. No water, no food – nowhere but the floor to crap and pee on – pitch-black, fucking pitch-black with no watch and no phone... and no chance of rescue!"

William took his time to respond.

"Can't argue with any of that, apart from the last bit."

"What last bit?"

"'No chance of rescue'. I bet she didn't give up on that and nor would I if I were in her place – and, of course, I have been."

Freddie laughed.

"Point taken! Any idea where we might get a drink around here at this time of day?"

They found a pub in Finchley. Freddie had a pint and William had a double vodka – no tonic, just ice.

He asked, "Freddie, why did you move Jackie in front of a different container?"

"Well, the police will look inside that one and may not even open the one where we found her. If they do, that bloke will have some explaining to do. If they don't, he's fucked."

"You're going to leave him to die in there?"

"Yep, unless you and Jackie outvote me. Let's have another round and get back home. I've got some Zoom meetings later on."

CHAPTER 95

"What the fuck?" Tacic Kurti was shouting into one of his tiny burners and the man opposite him was frowning. Given that the man was doing life for murdering several serious villains, including a cellmate, Kurti nodded, waved his hand to apologise and spoke more softly. "Altin, you're telling me that Roel has been arrested but not charged and that Matteo has been shot dead, in daylight, in fucking Battersea Park?"

"That's what I understand. Also, the policewoman has been extracted alive from the container; your note to her is in the hands of the police and it's all down to this Bishop bloke."

"Oh, for fuck's sake. So, he's the man that planted the product. But what's his angle?"

"Fuck knows! Could be a new competitor, but we did get some information on Bishop from the woman and we have her phone with his number. Roel will be able to identify him. His name is Miles Bishop and he lives in a flat in Fulham close to The Hurlingham Club. It's an upmarket area on the river. We have his home's building name but it's a mansion block and we don't know the number of his flat. Maybe he is helping the police because they have something on him?"

"Whatever. I want the motherfucker dead and I don't care how much it costs. Speak to Julian Lowe. He will be able to help with any funding required."

The man had been listening to every word and said "I like the sound of that, mate: 'I don't care how much it costs'. Sweet. Perhaps I might be able to help if you need extra resources."

Tacic didn't hesitate.

"That's very generous. This project might need some extra manpower. If you'd be so good as to provide me with a contact I will arrange for my team leader to get in touch and make a down payment to show good faith. Would that be acceptable?"

"Yes, my son; that would be just what the doctor ordered!"

CHAPTER 96

Jackie was emerging from sleep with what seemed like the worst hangover of her entire life, but the moment she opened her eyes and saw the nurse's uniform it all came flooding back. She felt the vomit rising and the nurse grabbed a dish to catch it. When it was over she handed her a glass of water and smiled.

"How are you feeling?"

"Terrible. Everything hurts; my throat, my head, my legs and my head, just for starters. Where am I?"

"You are in Guy's and St Thomas' Hospital near Waterloo Station and, believe it or not, you are in pretty good shape. You have a drip in your arm, which is hydrating you and also providing you with some stuff to boost your immune system. You also have a catheter. We have stitched up a serious dog bite in your thigh and there are two other smaller bites which just required plasters. You also have some bruises, which look much worse than they are. There are no internal injuries and we have given you a tetanus injection and something for the pain. I understand that you had a fight with a dog?"

"Yeah. Fucking awful. One moment I thought I was going to be raped by two men, the next that I was going to be killed by a vicious-looking dog and then I knew I was going to die in that container. I *knew* I was going to die."

Jackie started crying. The nurse held her hand until she stopped.

"Is there anyone you want to contact?"

"Yes. My husband. Peter. He is working in Australia."

"No problem there. I understand he has been contacted and will be here as soon as he can. You must have friends in high places!"

"What do you mean?" Jackie asked, looking puzzled.

"Well, you have a side room, there is an armed police officer outside the door and I have a number to call when the doctor feels you are up for it. Is it OK with you if I page the doctor now?"

"I guess so. What day is it?"

"Wednesday."

"Christ! Wednesday? What time is it?"

"Six o'clock in the evening."

"It was Monday morning when those men grabbed me. I thought they were going to rape me. Oh God, I think I told them something important. I can't remember!"

Jackie fell asleep again and woke when a doctor put his hand on her forehead.

"Hi Jackie, I'm Dr Bharat. How are you feeling?"

"Not too good, actually."

"Well, the first thing I need to do is remove your catheter, then you might feel a bit more comfortable. Then I need to check you over. The thing on your finger tells me that your oxygen saturation is good and your heart rate is normal. I think I can also remove the drip in your arm now, as you seem well hydrated. My only concern is the risk of infection. You have one large animal bite on your thigh, which required twenty-two stitches, though I say it myself, they are pretty neat stitches! But they will have to stay in for a couple of weeks and you will need to keep them dry. Everything else is superficial. I expect the nurse has told you that we've given you a tetanus jab. Unless there are any complications tonight you should be able to leave the day after tomorrow."

Jackie relaxed but then everything went downhill in seconds. She started shaking violently, was sobbing and she couldn't get her breath. She was panicking, on the verge of fainting, when the doctor took hold of her hands and held them tight.

"Don't worry, Jackie; don't worry. What you are experiencing is aftershock. This is perfectly normal. You have been through a terrible experience and your body and mind need to adjust. Please swallow these pills, then hold onto my hands and all will be well."

Ten minutes later she was fast asleep.

CHAPTER 97

When Jackie woke up the following morning she felt much better and her mood improved even more when Carol, her executive assistant, arrived with some news and a new iPhone.

"Well, boss, you look better than I imagined. How do you feel?"

"Fed up with people asking me that. What have you got?"

"First, here is a new phone, which I've synched with your personal phone. The office one will be synched over the weekend. There's lots of security protocols that need to be followed; I gather it takes ages. Second, Pete has been collected from Heathrow and wants to know what he should bring you this afternoon. Third, the plods found a bloke inside a container. It was close to where you were found and they guess it was where you were locked up. He's not being co-operative but if you can ID him as one of the bastards that picked you off the street, he's fucked."

"I'm not sure if I will be able to ID him, but I'll give it my best shot. Any news on the other bastards?"

"Well, a bloke was shot in Battersea Park yesterday morning. At close range. Headshot. No witnesses, but I gather the team think there may be a connection. It's looking as if you were rescued from that container and no doubt someone will be coming to get a statement as soon as you're able to talk about what happened. Is there anything I can do?"

"Well, yes. I'll write down all the stuff I need Pete to bring; that would be very helpful. Also, speak to Ellie. If this incident gets out, and I bet it does, we need to liaise with her Media Relations team as soon as possible."

"It's out. Several people saw you hoisted up and shoved in a white van. It's just a question of time for someone in the office to leak that the victim was a senior officer in the NCA and possibly provide your name in return for a few hundred quid."

Jackie shuddered.

"I thought they were going to rape me and I was sure they were going to leave me in that container to die."

"How did you get out?"

Jackie started practising her story.

"I'm not really sure. I had passed out and I remember lying on the ground outside with someone holding a plastic water bottle to my mouth. And I think I passed out again. Then I heard a siren and two medics were kneeling beside me. That's when I realised I was almost naked, with my tights wrapped around my thighs and cuts on my arms. The next thing I remember was waking up in the ambulance and then waking up in this bed. Christ, I really thought I was going to die in that fucking container!"

"Bloody hell!" exclaimed Carol. "Why? Why you? Do you think it has anything to do with the job?"

"No idea. To be honest, I'm trying not to remember it."

"Of course. Sorry. I'll speak to Ellie. Is there anything else I can do? Please give me a call anytime. You look like you need a rest now. I'll go now; take care."

As soon as Carol left, Jackie swallowed about half the water on her bedside table and opened the phone. She was relieved to find her old password still worked and she pressed the contact named 'Fred'. The call was answered by a recorded message and she recognised his voice immediately.

"Leave a message."

And she did: "It's me. I'm good. Well, almost good."

CHAPTER 98

Pete had come and gone. A kiss on the cheek and genuine concern for Jackie, but their relationship was now history and he was keen to get the divorce sorted as soon as possible so he could marry the woman in Sydney with whom he had been living for the past six months. That suited Jackie fine, she had plenty of options when it came to men.

Later on, Dr Bharat arrived. Jackie had just struggled through the awful lunch of tepid soup and a dry sandwich and was delighted to hear that she could be discharged the next morning unless any complications emerged. As soon as he had gone, a woman walked into the room. She was wearing jeans, trainers and sweatshirt and looked a little uncertain.

"Chief Superintendent Jackie Starling?" she asked.

"That's me. Who are you?" Jackie smiled.

"I'm DS Linda Peterson and I've been tasked to take a statement from you."

"Which nick?"

"Victoria."

"So, your boss is Simon?"

"Yes." Jackie smiled again.

"What did you do to piss him off that ended up with you having to take my statement? And if you don't tell me the truth you won't be taking my statement, but after you tell *me* the truth, I will tell *you* the truth!"

"We were in the pub celebrating a good result a couple of weeks ago. It was quite late when he put his hand inside the back of my trousers. I turned around and kneed him in the balls. Discreetly, but firmly!"

"Excellent! Do me a favour and get me a black coffee from wherever the machine is and we will have a good chat. I need to get some things off my chest."

Five minutes later, Jackie was inhaling the caffeine and Linda had begun taking her statement.

"Chief Superintendent Jackie Starling, I am DS Linda Peterson and I would like to ask you some questions relating to when you were assaulted on Monday morning. All of the information will be written down and may be used in court. Do you understand?"

"Yes, Linda, I do understand and I want to describe exactly what happened, but I need to agree a couple of things with you. First, please call me Jackie as if I am a civilian. Second, I would like you to record our conversation, transcribe it and send it to me before taking it any further. Third, don't interrupt or ask questions unless they can't wait until I have finished. I know it sounds crazy, but I want to get stuff off my chest. Some of it will be pretty harrowing. Is that OK with you?"

"Of course, ma'am. Sorry; Jackie."

"OK, here goes. I was walking to work on Monday thinking about the team meeting planned for eleven o'clock, when two men attacked me from behind. Each of them lifted me up by one of my arms and walked me forward with my feet hardly touching the pavement. The rear doors of a parked white van opened, they chucked me in, got in themselves and then drove me off in the van. The van was pretty dark but I could see the men staring at me at intervals; my immediate thought was that they were going to rape me. A bit later, when they forced down my knickers and tights, I screamed. One of them slapped me in the face, the other punched me. I think I passed out, but they didn't touch me again. I don't know how long I was in the van, probably about an hour."

"Would you recognise them again?"

"Maybe, but it was dark in the van. They spoke to me in English but when they spoke to each other it sounded like some Eastern European language. I was still frightened they were going to rape me. Why else would they have grabbed me? Anyway, the van stopped, the doors opened and I was in an industrial park where there were some old containers. Close by I saw a dog on a chain and it was barking like mad; the whole scene was horrible and I realised that this wasn't about rape, it was something much worse."

"What happened then?" she urged.

Jackie leant forward and ran her hands through her hair.

"I'll tell you what happened. Shit happened. One of the men lifted the latch on the nearest container, opened the door and ordered me to get in. I looked around to see if I could make a run for it but he lifted me up and threw me in."

"Christ!"

"Yeah. Look, do me a favour, Linda. Switch off the recorder."

"Really?" Linda frowned.

"Yes please!"

"Done."

"Thanks. Now pop outside, find a pub and bring me two double gins with ice and a bottle of tonic. I need something to help me explain what happened next."

CHAPTER 99

When Linda had left, Jackie went into the shower room and looked in the mirror. It was the first time she had seen herself since she had arrived and no one had spent much time cleaning her up. Her hair hadn't been brushed since Monday morning, her lips were chapped, her eyes were red, her cheek had a bruise and there was another on her forehead. She took off the hospital gown, looked at her body and gasped when she saw the stitches in her thigh.

And then, "Fuck. Fuck!" Bite marks on her arms, one on her shoulder and another on her breast. It all came flooding back. And when Linda returned with the drinks, she found Jackie weeping.

"Boss, should I come back later?"

"No, Linda. I need to get this out and you can turn on the recorder again, but remember, I need to see the transcript."

Jackie poured the two double gins and the ice into her water tumbler, added a bit of tonic and looked straight at Linda.

"It was a fucking nightmare. I knew I was going to die," she repeated.

"But you didn't."

"Yeah, but I didn't know that then. Imagine you are in a plane on your way to New York and there is a loud bang. The next thing you know, everyone is hollering, the plane is upside down and falling from the sky. You *know* you are going to die. But you are lucky. It probably takes just a few minutes and you are dead. Probably no pain. I knew they were going to lock me in the container and it would take me days to die!" Jackie swallowed some of her drink. "There was an old table and a chair – looked like a dining room chair – in that container. Some garbage and other stuff on the floor. It smelt horrible, cold and filthy. The bloke who shoved me in pointed to the table and chair and said 'Read'. There was a piece of paper on the table and I think I can remember some of what it said."

"What do you mean?" asked Linda. "Some sort of document?"

"Yes. Some sort of explanation as to how I was going to die. They were going to lock me in the container until I did. They thought I was responsible for their boss being in prison. Something about drugs being planted. I didn't really understand; I was terrified."

"Fucking hell. What did you do?"

That question brought everything back – everything. Jackie could recall every detail. The door slamming shut and the noise of the latch dropping down to close it. No light. No light at all. Silence, apart from the loud barking of the dog outside and the occasional mumbled words from the men outside. Not a chink of light, just a disgusting smell, dampness and despair. They had taken her phone and watch. She had slid to the damp floor with her back to the wall. No water, no food. She couldn't see anything in front of her face. She was shivering from the cold and the fear, even beginning to wonder if there was some way she could kill herself to get it all over with. She had cried and cried. Then it got worse.

"Jackie, do you want to tell me about it now?" Linda asked.

"Later, I have no idea how much later, the door opened and light flooded in. 'Thank Christ', I thought, as I saw a bloke in the doorway, but maybe they were just trying to frighten me. I managed to stand up and smile. That was when I noticed he was holding onto the dog's chain. It was snarling, barking and foaming at the mouth. Lunging around as if it was rabid. I assumed that he was holding on to it to keep me safe, but then he smiled and let go of the chain."

CHAPTER 100

Jackie's words and emotions exploded into the room and her eyes filled with tears. She hugged herself as she spoke disjointedly, as that's all she could manage.

"That fucking dog leapt at me, but when the bloke closed the door all was blackness; it just knocked me in passing. It couldn't see anything either. For a moment it stopped its frantic yelping and all I could hear was it grunting and panting. I had no idea what to do! Then it began barking again, the sound bouncing off the steel walls of the container – really loud, and it was impossible to know whereabouts it was. I guess it was also terrified with the situation it found itself in. I backed away from where I had last seen it and felt the chair behind me. I held on to the back and stood up on it. It wasn't too bad for a couple of minutes, but I was completely petrified when I could hear the animal sniffing around my feet, then barking again and, at one point, trying to bite my ankle. I could feel its nose on my foot! So I stepped up further and stood on the table. And that's when I completely lost it and became feral."

"Feral?" Linda asked.

"Yeah; feral. A feral dog was attacking me and somehow my mind chose to become feral too. Like a wild beast or something! The fucking dog seemed to know exactly where I was and I could hear its fucking feet rattling on the table.

So, I grabbed the chair and started swinging it where I thought its head might be, but my swinging and the dog's weight caused the table to overturn and, before I knew it, I was on the floor and the fucking dog was biting me. I could feel and smell its breath and the stink of its body. I tried punching it, I tried sticking my fingers into where I thought its eyes might be, but nothing had any impact. It bit me once, then bit me again and again and then I felt a massive, agonising bite in my thigh. I tried to pull the fucker away; all I got was more pain. The more I tried, the more pain I got. I was close to fainting. It was fucking agony, but when my fingers touched the dog's chain I knew I had a chance. Just a chance!"

Jackie took another big swallow and composed herself for the next part.

"As soon as I touched that chain I knew there was a chance. I managed to get hold of it, but then it slipped through my fingers; I guess it was slippery with my blood. And then I couldn't find the fucking thing. The dog's teeth were buried in my thigh; the more I tried to push it away the more it hurt. I was hyperventilating and thought I was going to pass out again. And the pain; the pain was just awful. And the noise with the dog grunting. Oh, fuck me; it was terrible. Terrible!"

"What did you do then?" probed Linda.

"I realised that the dog's head must be very close to where I was experiencing the pain, so I ran my hand over it, fed the chain around its neck twice and pulled it tight, then tighter. I gave it all I had and then some more. The fucking thing snarled and tried to bite my hands, but I was choking the fucking animal and shouting 'Die, you fucking

TERRIBLE CHOICES

dog; die!' And after two minutes or maybe ten minutes, it did die. And there I was, dog shit on my body, blood coming out of my thigh, no water, no food, with dog bites on my arms, ankles and chest in complete darkness with no idea how much blood I was losing, no chance of rescue. Completely fucked."

"What happened next?" whispered Linda.

Jackie finished her drink and grimaced.

"I pulled the dead dog off me and could feel my thigh was bleeding quite a lot so I managed to pull off my tights and wrap them around the area where I thought the blood was coming from. It didn't seem to make much difference. And, you know what, Linda? I asked myself why I was trying to stop the blood. Why did I care? I'd read something, somewhere, that dying from dehydration was very painful, so I stopped worrying. Bleeding to death might be a better way to die. I got a bit sleepy from time to time and when I was awake I banged on the side of the container just in case someone might be around. Actually, my mind was all over the place.

"Remember, Linda, I get to see and edit the transcript! I found myself thinking about relationships and saying goodbye to people who meant a great deal to me. I didn't think at all about The Job."

"Don't blame you for that!" Linda said, who was totally absorbed in her recall of the awful events.

"Anyway, days or hours later I heard the container latch being lifted and expected that one of those bastards would be checking to see if I was dead yet. But it wasn't. I couldn't see anything as the light was so bright and I'd been in the dark for ages, but I knew that two people were there to help me. One of them gave me some water and the next thing I remember was the sound of a siren, then being in an ambulance and then being in this room."

"Could you recognise the two people who helped you?"

"I don't think so."

"Would you recognise the man with the dog?"

"I don't know, but I'm feeling very tired, DS Peterson. Thank you very much for your patience. I look forward to receiving the transcript of my statement, as we agreed."

"Of course, Chief Superintendent; I mean, Jackie."

"Goodbye," and then Jackie fell asleep.

CHAPTER 101

Two weeks later, early on a Friday evening, William and Freddie were sitting at a window table in The Glasshouse restaurant in Kew. The sun was shining and they were enjoying a bottle of Beaujolais Blanc and looking forward to seeing Ina and Bea. But William was worried.

"Freddie, it seems that the Battersea Park and container thing is now done and dusted, but I'm really not keen on this derring-do stuff."

"Fair enough, old pal. I'm looking forward to settling down too, so let's shake hands on less exciting futures; after all, you are retired and I'm on the glide path out of DPK and into some boring non-executive director roles. Having said that though, who knows what the future holds? And look, there's Ina stepping out of her car. I wish I had a job with a car and driver twenty-four-seven!"

"Don't mention it, Freddie. It's a sensitive issue."

"Of course I won't!"

Freddie leapt to his feet as Ina got nearer.

"Ina, you look wonderful. Hope the traffic from your office wasn't too bad. Anyway, just as well that the bank provides the transport!"

Ina smiled.

"Fuck off, Freddie. I seem to recollect that you have six cars including a very late Aston Martin, a Chevrolet

Corvette Stingray, a Bentley Coupe and an old E-Type Jaguar. Would that be correct?"

Freddie leant forward and kissed Ina on the cheek.

"I'll be happy to take you for a ride any time."

"No chance! Double Bell's on the rocks, please."

Bea arrived ten minutes later, having walked from her houseboat in Richmond looking very elegant. Freddie stood up, kissed her and put his hand on her knee as soon as she sat down. When he was sure that no one would notice, he moved it up her thigh, but she clenched her knees together and stuck her elbow into his ribs. Ina gave her a wink and all was well.

Ina was on a roll.

"NatWest have just been fined about two hundred and fifty million quid for allowing bin bags of cash to be deposited in their branches. It would have been three hundred million if they hadn't pleaded guilty. So much dosh that the bags were splitting and the branch safes overwhelmed. My options are down a bit, but the NatWest boys are weeping! And that minnow, remind me; yes, Metro Bank, is also up shit creek with their money laundering processes, or at least the lack of them! What *is* that German word – schadenfreude?"

"Yes!" confirmed William. "It means something like getting joy from someone else's problems or failures."

Freddie laughed.

"Just as well I'm looking after the bank's audit, Ina. Just imagine the mischief you guys might get up to if some firm other than DPK was holding you to account!"

"Yeah, just imagine," agreed Ina, "and imagine if we weren't paying you guys thirty-two million in fees just in the UK. What would *that* do to your bonus, Freddie? Might you have to sell one of your cars?"

Bea lifted her glass and touched it to Ina's.

"Please don't do anything that reduces his bonus, Ina. I might have to find a new man that could treat me in the way I am used to nowadays. I might even have to get a proper job."

"Proper job?" asked William. "I thought you were employed as a personal protection officer. What could be more proper than that?"

Bea shrugged.

"It's OK; usually a bit boring, but even with overtime it doesn't pay very well and promotion would be to a desk job and that doesn't appeal."

"Are we ready to order?" asked Freddie. "And William, don't go mad on the wine list; the dinner is seventy pounds a pop, plus service, and if Ina gets any more fractious I might be losing my bonus."

CHAPTER 102

Tacic Kurti was on his way to Court 6 at the Central Criminal Court, otherwise known as the Old Bailey. It was the third day of the trial and his barrister, Sebastian, had told him that his defence summary would be quite short and the jury would probably have lunch and then continue with their deliberations. Tacic had continually refused to plead guilty to the 'Possession with intent to supply' charge, as he knew that the drugs had been planted. Sebastian had warned him repeatedly that, if found guilty, he was facing at least fifteen years.

He had told him, "It's the cash, Tacic. The jury might *possibly* agree that the drugs had been planted, but it's the cash. Nearly half a million in the house, most of it in your safe! No one else knew the combination. And where did the cash come from? You claimed to be a businessman but you have no accounts, no staff and no national insurance or tax records. If I may use an elegant legal phrase: 'You're fucked!'"

The barrister did his best but the jury took less than two hours to reach a verdict: Guilty! When he arrived back at Wandsworth he was facing fifteen years and was even more determined that Miles Bishop should pay for it. The warden brought his phone to the cell and Tacic called Altin and demanded an update.

"Where are we with Bishop?"

"We have progress. We have been staking out the address we were given using different people and different cars. We are certain the man doesn't live there but he has visited twice, each time in the evening. Roel is completely confident it is Bish–"

"If he's wrong, he's fucked!" Tacic interrupted.

Altin continued.

"The team followed him home last week and are now following him around during the day. He doesn't have much of a routine but seems to work for a company called DPK, which has a huge office near London Bridge. Sometimes he drives there and sometimes he takes the tube. He goes out quite a lot with people in the evening, spends a lot of money and he lives in a place called Fulham Reach, which is expensive, two million pounds upwards. We are pretty sure he is not a competitor. DPK is an accountancy firm."

"OK, Altin. Whatever he does, whoever he is, he has to go and we need to make him an example. So, hurt him hard, first. I know you are good at that; I know you like doing that! Then deal with his family – wife, parents, children – whoever and whenever is convenient. I'm not in any hurry. Just do it when it's safe."

CHAPTER 103

Jackie called Freddie and they arranged to meet at The Avenue restaurant in St James's Street for an early dinner. For some reason, Freddie wanted to get there early. He didn't know why and he also asked for a table in the alcove towards the back of the restaurant. It was the first time they had met or spoken since the incident and, at the back of his mind, concern was lurking that someone seeing them together tonight might somehow lead back to the shooting in Battersea Park. Anyway, a large gin and tonic settled any nerves and he was on his second when Jackie arrived.

Freddie stood up and they air kissed.

"Sorry to be late, Freddie. Work!"

"No problem, you look great. What would you like to drink?"

"Glass of Champagne, please, and I'm paying. I owe you for the rescue and I owe you an apology. I'm starving; no time for lunch today, so let's order."

Jackie ordered smoked salmon followed by sea bass. Freddie went for beef tartare and venison and ordered a bottle of Viognier.

Freddie didn't beat about the bush.

"So, Jackie; why do you need to apologise?"

"Those men, the ones who shoved me in the van and threatened me unless I told them who planted the drugs in

Kurti's garden – I was so scared that I told them it was Miles Bishop and gave them your address in Fulham and Miles Bishop's phone number. I'm so sorry!"

Freddie wasn't surprised. How else would they have had the number of his Miles Bishop burner? And he wasn't disappointed.

"I understand, I really understand!" He put his hand on Jackie's and looked her straight in the face. "There are times in our lives when we have to make decisions, make choices, sometimes terrible choices. You chose to give those thugs some information, which may or may not have repercussions for me. Who knows? But being raped, that seemed like a certainty. So, I think you chose the best option available, so please forget about it. No apology required!"

"Thank you, Freddie. Thank you!" Jackie's eyes welled up and Freddie looked around nervously.

"No need for the waterworks, Jackie. People might think I have just called off our wedding! And anyway, I have some good news for you if you promise to stop weeping and forget what I am about to tell you. Promise?"

"Promise."

"Well, here are our starters and the wine. Let's get stuck in!"

"Well, Jackie, how was your healthy option?" Freddie asked once their plates were cleared. "My cholesterol treat was superb."

"Lovely, thank you. Can you give me the good news now?" Freddie smiled.

"Of course; it won't take long. The two men in the white van were called Matteo and Roel. They chose to do what they did to you. No one forced them."

"And?"

Freddie grinned, leant forward and whispered.

"I shot Matteo full in the face and locked Roel in the container with the dead dog."

"You *what*?"

"You heard, and remember what you promised a few minutes ago? You promised to forget! And just to be clear, Matteo was carrying a SIG and I have no doubt he would have killed me given the chance."

"Is that the guy who was shot in Battersea Park?"

"Yep. He chose not to tell me where they were holding you. Wrong decision! Wow, look at this venison. I think I will have some red with this and you can finish the white wine."

Later on, with most of the wine finished and coffee on the table, Freddie and Jackie were talking some more.

"Jackie, you mentioned that you owe me and, frankly, given the last twelve months, I think that's a bit of an understatement."

"Yeah, I think that's true."

"Well, if something seems to threaten my Miles Bishop alias, if these drug dealers come after him and, by definition, me, can I depend on your support? The reason I ask is that I think it's a possibility."

"Yes, of course. Do you actually think it's a possibility?"

"No. I think it's a *prob*ability!"

Chapter 104

It took a few weeks after the dinner with Jackie for Freddie to be sure that he was being tracked. He had been using all of his experience to check whether or not he was being followed and he now knew he was dealing with a high-quality team, one with very substantial resources. He was certain that the followers were unaware that he knew they were there. He had checked that the UK Special Service hadn't tracked him when he had to fly to Edinburgh, and all was clear, so he knew it was criminals – probably the county lines crew who were looking to find a way to deal with him. He guessed they would not be looking for a simple headshot to remove him from the board; they could have done that already. He made a call and the answer was brief.

"Yes?"

"Have you learnt to swim yet?" Freddie asked. He heard a laugh.

"Freddie, what sort of shit are you going to get me involved in this time?"

"Easy shit. When can you get to London?"

"I will book myself on the BA flight from Berlin on Saturday morning. It gets in at nine-thirty. Pick me up?" he asked.

"Sure. Thanks, Euan!"

"OK, Freddie, spill the beans. Is this about the drugs we planted in that guy's garden or have you found some other reasons to spoil my weekend?"

They were in Freddie's Taycan driving away from Heathrow and joining the M25 motorway. Euan, as ever, was looking unremarkable; medium height, medium weight, ordinary clothes; a man that simply faded into the background of any situation.

Freddie kept his eyes on the road.

"I'm afraid it might take longer than your weekend, mate, but no hard feelings if you don't have the time or don't want to get involved. What I suggest is that you come to my place now and I lay it out for you. If you are up for it, great; if not, no problem. In any event, I will buy you lunch and get you a cab to that apartment you keep in Clarges Street. Whatever happens, it's your choice."

As they turned onto the M4 motorway to London, Freddie couldn't resist setting the scene, which he hoped might encourage Euan to get involved.

"Anyway, mate, the Scotland project worked out well for both of us financially and those terrible brothers got what they deserved, and you also saved my bacon when that madwoman was about to kill me. As for us planting the heroin in that county lines guy's garden, that turned out very well. He got fifteen years."

"Fifteen years? Christ!"

"Yeah. Trouble is, he managed to find out that I was involved. But don't worry, he has no idea anyone else was."

"How did he find out you were involved?"

"It's a long story and it can wait until we get to my place."

The motorway turned into the two-lane Chiswick flyover and, as the traffic slowed and then stalled, Euan chuckled.

"Freddie, fuck off! You are lining me up for something, setting some sort of bait. Spit it out!"

"That bloke, the bloke doing fifteen years, has got a team following me and I need someone to follow them."

"Just follow them?"

"Well, maybe a bit more, but we can discuss that over a drink at my place."

CHAPTER 105

"First question," Euan began as he sipped the excellent Sancerre, "how did that drug dealer find out you were responsible for planting the heroin?"

"He arranged for the woman at the NCA to be kidnapped, threatened with rape and worse and she gave me up. Not actually *me* because I was using the Miles Bishop alias and, by the way, after they had finished with her they locked her in a container. No food, no water, no light."

"Christ!"

"And then, Euan, and you won't believe this, they opened the door a while later and set loose a huge, fucking big dog on her and slammed the door shut. She is still recovering."

"Fucking hell! How did she get out?"

Freddie shrugged.

"I arranged a meeting with two of the kidnappers on the basis I wanted to do a deal and one of them drove me to where she was being held. I took her out of the container, locked him in there, called an ambulance and left them to it."

"Just like that! How come the guy co-operated?"

"I had a Glock 19 pointed at his head. Do you remember when we went down to that village to get our supplies?"

"Yeah! Of course. But where was the other kidnapper? Why wasn't he stopping you?"

"Well, when I arrived at the meeting, that guy had a SIG. I disarmed him and asked him to co-operate but he more or less told me to fuck off, so I had no option but to shoot him. That's when the other guy became *very* co-operative!"

Euan decided he needed some time to get his head around this information.

"Wow; Christ, Freddie. You killed one man and locked another in a container and prior to that you planted heroin in their boss's garden, no wonder you are being followed. I think I need another glass of that wine and where is the men's room..?" he asked while pointing towards the terrace, and then, "Is it out there?"

"No, the loo, as we call it here, is down there," Freddie pointed towards the hallway, "and I'll take the wine and glasses out there" pointing to the terrace.

"What a view," said Euan when he stepped outside. "Christ, what is that green building over there on the other side of the river? It says 'Harrods'!"

"Yep. As you know, Harrods is in Knightsbridge, but that building is like a replica of the store and it used to be where they stored stuff. It's now apartments; pretty expensive, I guess."

"And this place is cheap?"

"Not exactly."

"Show me the spare rooms!"

"What? Why?"

"Because if I am going to follow the people who are following you, Clarges Street will not be a useful place to start. Let me be clear... I'm not agreeing to do anything other than follow these guys and I may need some help just to do that, but if the spare room and facilities are not the usual British Victorian standard I'm prepared to give it a go. Let's go to lunch. Do we need to call a cab?"

"No, there is a café just ten minutes along the river from here and I think you will like it."

CHAPTER 106

"Fuck me, Freddie. This is The River Café. I've read about this place; some people say it's the best restaurant in London and it's right on your doorstep!"

"Yeah, but here's the thing – will we get a table outside?"

They did get a table outside. After they had ordered and Euan had recovered from the prices on the menu and wine list, Freddie explained the situation.

"In the UK, back in the 1960s, the most common drugs were pretty much harmless – uppers and downers in the form of tablets, plus cannabis and cocaine. Nowadays, the cannabis is very, very much stronger. It's cultivated in UK warehouses and called skunk. It's not addictive but it can truly fuck up users' minds. What's more, the pills have become more sophisticated and dangerous. But more dangerous by far is crack cocaine, which is a blend of cocaine and, usually, baking powder or something similar and heated in water to create rocks. The product is so highly concentrated, it is extremely addictive. Some people say you can be addicted the first time you use it."

Euan finished his calamari and nodded.

"Yeah, tell me about it. It's an epidemic back home; people turning into zombies, falling over dead in the street. No one knows what to do. Why's it called crack cocaine?"

"I'm not an expert, but I understand that when the mix is heated it breaks into rocks and as it does so it sounds like a crack."

"And what are the county lines? You mentioned that before."

"Here come our main courses. Shall we get another bottle of this Verdicchio? Eat up and then I'll tell you. I don't want to spoil your appetite!"

Later, Euan sat back and smiled. "Freddie, that Dover sole was the best ever. Thank you!"

"A pleasure. And trust me, you deserve it because we are going to be dealing with some very ruthless people and some very fucked up children."

"Children?"

"Yes, the drug dealers in the UK tend to use teenagers and children, maybe as young as ten or even younger, to distribute the product. We are talking about thousands, literally thousands, of kids. And they are almost always members of a gang and the gangs compete with each other in specific areas. The problem is that the supply of the drugs exceeds the demand so there is too much competition and they are fighting each other for territory all the time. In London last year, thirty teenagers were killed; mostly stabbed to death but some shot. Hundreds have been wounded and most of these kids are victims. Kids as young as ten or eleven. As I said, the men are ruthless."

"Jesus! But what are the 'county lines'?"

"Given the gang warfare that has broken out in some parts of London, the bosses have set up in towns and cities outside the capital where there is less competition and 'county lines' relates to the mobile phones used to manage the kids' activities. The men identify a property in a city where the owner is an addict or has mental issues and they move in and start cooking."

Euan frowned.

"What, just like that?"

"Just like that. They call it cuckooing." Freddie looked at his watch. "Let's get the bill and I'll stroll back to my place. How about you walk in the opposite direction and come to my place in about thirty minutes? If you see a spotter, all well and good, but no worries either way."

"Sounds like a plan. I'll explore the river for a while."

Euan knocked on Freddie's door an hour later.

"Sorry, Freddie, I visited The Crabtree pub further downriver and back to the one called The Blue Boat near your development. I noticed two guys that looked suspicious, mainly because their clothes looked pretty down-market for the area. I could be wrong but, of course, I will recognise them again. To be fair to them, setting up surveillance on your property isn't easy – nowhere to park, no café nearby. I guess their role is just to watch when you come out and then call another team to follow you.

"Of course, my role is to follow the followers and for that I won't be charging for my time, but I'll expect expenses to be reimbursed. These could possibly include buying a motorbike and hiring black cabs at fixed prices and perhaps car hire."

"What do you mean 'fixed prices'?"

"I mean I might have to hire a black cab for a day, or a half-day, like I have people back home using yellow cabs in New York. Much less risk. Cabs are ubiquitous, virtually invisible and the drivers know their way around a city. I will also need a gun and another burner phone."

"A gun?"

"Sure. You know and I know that it's best to hope for the best and prepare for the worst, Freddie. Remember that sock knife that saved your bacon in Scotland?"

"Christ, yes! The mad guy, the dentist chair with straps. It was pretty scary. Anyway, I've got a SIG Sauer, a Ruger or a Glock. They are all safe and secure in a storage facility in Chiswick with plenty of ammunition. I also have two Purdey shotguns in my gun cabinet."

"You have a gun cabinet here?"

"Yep, and a wine room. Come and have a look; it's about time for something refreshing."

CHAPTER 107

Freddie and Bea were due to go to dinner with William and Ina on Saturday evening, Euan decided to stay in Fulham Reach and Freddie had booked him a table at the Brasserie Blanc, just a few minutes away. Freddie had enjoyed a thirty-minute snooze in the afternoon and decided to walk to Chiswick Mall. Euan changed his clothes, waited for Freddie to leave and then, there they were – two new guys following Freddie, on their phones almost all the time. Far too close, never looking behind. Amateurs! He kept well back and when he saw Freddie walk into Chiswick Mall, walk up the steps of a large house and knock on the door, he turned around and walked back towards Fulham Reach. On his way he passed another two men, both on their phones, walking with the pimp roll and noticing nothing. The amateur night-shift. Now he had six faces firmly in his head.

"Hello Freddie, good to see you!" greeted William as he opened the door. "Where is Bea?"

"She called me. She'll be here soon. What a lovely evening. Summer's coming and all's well. I had lunch at The River Café followed by forty winks and I'm in the mood for… Ina! How are you? You look wonderful!"

At that moment, Ina walked into the hall and kissed Freddie on the cheek.

She laughed.

"Same old line, Freddie. Surely it's time to update it, but since you ask I am in a very good mood. I had a great game with my pal, Ginny, at Royal Mid this morning and a very relaxing afternoon."

Freddie raised his eyebrows.

"Relaxing, Ina? How relaxing?"

"Fuck off, Freddie. We are having dinner in the back garden. Pick up this tray and come on through."

Bea arrived ten minutes later. As her car pulled up to the kerb she noticed the two guys. She wasn't even looking, but in a road like Chiswick Mall where the average house price was over three million pounds, they stuck out like sore thumbs, but she decided that she wouldn't mention them until later on or maybe she wouldn't mention them at all. After all, in her job, she knew paranoia was not unusual.

Ina answered the door when Bea rang the bell. In the hall, Freddie glanced back – two beautiful women. A thought crossed his mind.

He grinned, dismissed it and instead spoke to Bea.

"Bea, I haven't seen you for a whole week. Come here and give me a hug!"

Bea gasped.

"Freddie, that was a nice hug, but I have been on duty for ten hours, six to six today, so what I really need is a drink."

William was working hard to keep the drinks flowing; his Sipsmith vodka, Gordon's gin for Freddie, Bell's whisky for Ina and Sancerre for Bea. He was also getting the food together. He had set the table in the back garden, made sure the lighting and music were exactly right and all was ready to go. After the food was finished, Ina disappeared and came back with a bottle of Champagne.

"What are we celebrating?" asked Freddie. "Don't tell me you two guys are getting married!"

"No!" exclaimed Ina.

"Surely you're not pregnant, Ina!"

"No, Freddie, I'm not and I'm not sure if your question was flattering or a bit of an insult! What we are celebrating is that I have sold my place in Kingston and I'm moving in with William, subject to some conditions."

"Conditions? What sort of conditions?" asked Bea.

William smiled ruefully.

"I've happily agreed that Ina can have my library on the ground floor as her private room and I've agreed she can have whatever she wants in terms of furniture, decoration, technology or whatever."

"And Sky TV and a Samsung Frame for the golf," Ina reminded him chirpily.

"I've also agreed that Ina can redecorate her bedroom and bathroom however she wishes and a few other little requests, which I won't go into at the moment. Anyway, I propose a toast to 'partners'. I think I will go and get the cookies I have prepared, they will go well with the Champagne."

As soon as William had left the table, Freddie's eyes lit up as he glanced at Ina.

"What are the 'other little requests', if I may ask?"

Ina gave him her cool stare.

"Well, Freddie, you *can* ask but don't expect many answers. But, to satisfy your curiosity, I can confirm the requests do not cover who fills the dishwater and when we have sex. I think those things kind of take care of themselves. What do you think, Bea?"

"Too early to tell, Ina."

Freddie and Bea decided to walk home. William and Ina felt like some exercise and so the four of them set off. After a while, Freddie and William were striding a little way ahead of Bea and Ina when Bea asked Ina a question.

"I hope you don't mind, but what made you decide to move in now? I gather you have been with William for quite some time."

Ina took a while to reply.

"I'm a bit pissed and those cookies aren't helping, so bear with me. Actually, and I know it's not very romantic, but it's practical. Going backwards and forwards from Kingston is a pain. And anyway, I've finally got around to putting up with William's foibles and I get to have my en suite and private room downstairs."

"Foibles? What foibles?" asked Bea. "And don't worry about being a bit pissed; I'm having trouble putting one foot in front of the other!"

Ina smiled.

"Just little things. William insists that Tina irons his socks and folds them up to ensure the little Pringle logos are always on the outside and he always wears blue socks with his blue suits and grey socks with his grey suits, and the same goes for his ties and spectacles. Everything must match every day when he is working."

They walked companionably alongside the river approaching Hammersmith Bridge in silence; Ina thinking she had said too much, Bea wondering who Tina was.

"Who is Tina?"

Ina chuckled.

"Tina is William's housekeeper!"

Bea was puzzled.

"Housekeeper? What housekeeper? What does she do?"

Ina explained.

"Tina looks after William. She keeps the house clean, does the laundry, buys the food, irons the clothes and sometimes she cooks – she is an excellent cook! She works Monday to Friday, so I don't see her very often. When she is in the house she tends to be in the utility room downstairs. Her son helps out with the gardening and the allotment, cleans the windows and fixes stuff that needs fixing in the old house."

As they approached Fulham Reach, Bea asked Ina another question.

"So, those are all the foibles?"

Ina laughed out loud at this and then whispered to her just as they were catching up with the guys.

"Good God; no, Bea. I'll give you another example. William uses Acqua di Parma cologne, Acqua di Parma shampoo, face wash, hair wash, deodorant and hand wash every day. When I give him anything else he just sticks it in a cupboard. And as for his dressing room!"

"What?"

"Everything's organised – blue section, grey section, sports section. Ties, shirts, belts, spectacles and watch straps."

"Watch straps?" Bea asked, incredulous.

"Didn't I tell you? He has different watch straps to match everything else, including his spectacles! But I think I love the bloke and, seeing as I am still a bit pissed, I'll tell you one more thing. In his immaculately organised dressing room there are two pictures…" Ina stopped walking before they reached their men and looked at Bea, "…and William touches both of those pictures every morning."

Bea knew she was going to hear something important and leant forward to hear Ina speak in a low tone.

"Two pictures; black and white photos, to be accurate. One is a lovely shot of Ryoko, William's late wife who died about seven years ago. It really fucked him up."

"And the other?"

"Bea, the other is a photo of Freddie."

"Freddie? Why would William have his photo?"

"Because Freddie saved his life not so long ago."

CHAPTER 108

A week later at about eleven o'clock at night, Freddie and Euan were sitting on Freddie's terrace and going over the plan.

Euan began.

"OK, when you leave here I will already be in position outside The Blue Boat pub and will watch you walk past. I expect to see someone following you. If there are two people or more the mission will be aborted. If it is just one person I will follow your follower, but if I even *sense* that there is someone behind *me*, the mission will also be aborted. Agreed?"

"Agreed!"

"Excellent! So, if all goes well, you will have just one follower and I will be following him. When the moment is right I will sweep up the guy and ping you. You will then turn around and meet me and we will take the guy to some place nearby where we can chat to him.

"And the reason I haven't given you the details of the 'place nearby' is that, if push comes to shove, you won't be able to identify it, but trust me; it'll be safe and soundproof."

In the end it was quite straightforward. Freddie left Fulham Reach and walked westwards with the River Thames on his left. He passed The Blue Boat but didn't see Euan. He would have been disappointed if he had. As he passed by, Euan recognised just one follower and took position behind him. To be sure no one was following *him*, Euan turned right down Crisp Walk, an alley by Sam's Riverside restaurant, and waited across the road. No one appeared so he walked swiftly back to the towpath and continued to follow the follower at a safe distance, then he called Freddie from his burner.

"I'm in position."

Ten minutes later, Euan was about fifty yards behind the follower as they walked along the river. He knew there was the possibility that the man in front might sense someone was behind him and look, but who would he see? An unremarkable-looking grey-haired man in a suit with a pot belly, stumbling a little; probably a bit worse for wear after too many drinks on a Saturday night. In reality, Euan's hair had been dyed grey, he was completely sober, he had a Ruger in his back pocket and the pot belly was, in fact, the result of two ropes tied around his waist underneath his shirt. If the follower had looked and listened carefully he would have realised that the unremarkable man in the suit was wearing trainers that made no noise whatsoever.

It was about twelve-thirty when Euan looked behind to ensure no one was around and, as he silently closed the gap between them, he unwound one of the ropes and checked the Ruger in his jacket pocket, safety cap on – just in case. He could now see Freddie as well as the follower and closed the gap a little more. Then Freddie turned right and walked through a small, modern development into a street Euan noticed was called Neveravon Road. Time to put the hammer down. He sent the text to Freddie and went for it. The crude lasso he had created from the rope went over the man's shoulders and trapped his arms. Euan pulled the rope tight, moved in, and the man shouted something incomprehensible. Euan was right up against the man now and held onto him, tightening the lasso but wincing as the man rammed his heels into his legs. Then Freddie arrived, smacked the man in the face, put a blindfold over his eyes, kicked him in the crutch and, as he crumpled, dragged him a few yards into a doorway.

CHAPTER 109

When the blindfold was ripped off the man's face, the man realised he was sitting on a wooden chair, his arms still trapped by the lasso, his legs strapped to the chair by another rope. The masked man that was kneeling in front of him had his hands on the zip of his jeans. He yanked them down over his knees and pulled his penis out of his boxer shorts. The target, the man called Bishop, was standing nearby drinking what looked like whisky and holding a revolver.

"What's your name? Do you speak English? Do you want to live?" asked Freddie.

"Fuck you, Bishop; you're dead!"

Freddie laughed.

"Doesn't look that way to me. Have a look around!" It was then that the man saw he was in a large room with a shower above his head; there was a bath in one corner, a lavatory in another corner and he would have also seen that the other man was holding an old-fashioned razor.

Freddie continued.

"We are not after you, we are after Kurti's senior team, but if you don't co-operate you will be dead before it's light tomorrow morning, but you'll be begging for death before that, so at least tell us your name so that if you have any friends or family we can send them the videos."

The man croaked in shock at the suggestion.

"Videos? What videos?"

"Yes, of course!" said Euan. "We think it's important that they see how you died and how much you suffered and, trust me, we will make sure that they see every detail – the cuts, the screams, the begging, the suffering – everything. We will also make sure that your county line colleagues see the videos as well. Might put them off the job. Anyway, I think it looks like you are not circumcised, so please tell us your name or I will carry out the procedure. I haven't tried it before so bear with me."

"No! Stop! My name is Besnik! I don't have much English. All I do was following Bishop and tell boss where he went."

"Who is your boss?" asked Freddie.

"I don't tell you!"

"OK. I understand," said Freddie. "I admire your bravery, Besnik. What we are going to do now is wrap this scarf around your mouth so that your screams can't be heard. Then I'm going to check that the rope is tight enough. But, first, I'm putting on these rubber gloves. We can't afford to have any of my DNA on your body now, can we? And, to be honest, I don't want to touch your cock with my bare hands. When all that's done, my colleague will set about the circumcision. If you don't co-operate then we will get serious. Understand?"

"I can't; I can't tell you!" shouted the man before the scarf was wrapped around his head. And he screamed when the scalpel touched him. But they both heard him say a name – "Elira" – and so they stood back.

"Elira?" quizzed Freddie. "Is that a man or a woman?"

"It's a woman. And she would kill me if she knew I told you! You must not tell her!"

"We shall decide that," said Euan. "How can we find her? What is her surname?"

"I can't tell you!"

Euan made his voice sound casual.

"That's fine. Please stop wriggling, as your circumcision might not be as I would like it to be." He held the scalpel up to the light, saw the terror in Besnik's eyes and tapped his penis with the cold metal. This time the shriek was even louder.

"Harlesden! Harlesden. We have a house there! Her surname is Shkodra!"

"So, will we find Elira Shkodra in this house? What is the address?" Euan asked, glancing behind the terrified man to check that Freddie was filming with his phone.

"It's 23 Acton Road!" he shouted and the man was crying now – defeated and broken. He had made his choice and he knew he was going to have to face the consequences of telling on her, one way or another.

Freddie and Euan needed to discuss the next steps so they stepped outside.

"Let's start with the basics," began Euan. "The bad guys now know what you look like and where you live. Besnik or whoever he is won't have a clue who I am or where we are; in fact, *I* don't even know where we are! So, if we let him go, it doesn't put us in any more danger than we are in now and, anyway, he won't be keen to let this Elira Shkodra know that he told us anything. If he does then she might ship out or get ready to deal with us if we go there."

Freddie sighed.

"You've nailed it, mate, but I'm not after the fucking foot-soldiers, I'm after the officers and I'm certainly not after the unfortunate kids who find themselves cooking crack, stabbing other kids or getting murdered themselves. How about we tell this Besnik guy to fuck off out of the UK? Maybe give him some money? And tell him that if he raises his head anywhere we will send the video showing that he tipped us off to Elira?"

"OK, not bad; sounds like a plan. Let's do it and point him in the direction of the tube."

CHAPTER 110

Freddie and Euan were going to meet Bea for lunch at the Gaucho restaurant on the river in Richmond at two o'clock. The challenge was how Freddie could lose his followers without it being obvious that he knew he was still being followed. Euan, meanwhile, was enjoying a riverside Bloody Mary and enjoying the view of Hammersmith Bridge.

"Why isn't any traffic going across that bridge?" Euan asked Freddie.

"Believe it or not, that bridge needs major work to make it safe, but the people this side think the people on the other side should be paying for it and vice versa. So, nothing has happened for ages and God knows when work will start and… Euan, you are a genius; you've solved our little problem!"

"Have I? How so?"

"I have a bike in the garage. I'll simply get it out, ride over the bridge, turn right onto the towpath and cycle to Richmond. It's only about nine miles. The guys outside will have a car nearby, but that will be of no use to them at all and, even if they manage to get hold of a bike, there is no way they could catch me. What's more, there are a couple of bridges and many turn offs, so when they look at the map on their phones they will see loads of options including the possibility that I rode straight on when I crossed the bridge. Job done?"

"Yep; job done, Freddie, but don't give yourself a heart attack!"

Freddie looked at his watch.

"It's nearly twelve-thirty. It will take me less than an hour to get to the restaurant, so I guess we have time for a sharpener or maybe two. You might want to book a cab for one-thirty; they can drop you off in Richmond and you can walk down to the restaurant, the table's in my name. G&T?"

"No thanks, Freddie; I think I'll have a beer. I want to be sober when I meet the new love of your life. But changing the subject, where is that Harlesden place that the Besnik boy shouted out and when are we going to check it out?"

"Good thinking! It's in West London. I've never been there but I gather some parts of it are pretty rough. I'm working tomorrow, so how about Wednesday?"

Euan Frowned.

"I think the sooner the better. How about early tomorrow morning? It's light by five and I guess these guys are not early risers and there won't be any followers, but if they are then I'm sure we could lose them. Depending on the situation, I might hang around the location and you could go off to work."

"Done!"

Freddie set off as planned and Euan watched him cross the bridge. No sign of anyone following him, but no one on the Fulham Reach side of the river would be able to trace where he went once he reached the other side. Euan helped himself to another beer, opened his laptop and started checking out 23 Acton Road via his VPN.

Meanwhile, Freddie had passed Barnes Railway Bridge and was enjoying the ride.

Euan gathered as much information as he could about the Acton Road property and then he e-mailed Pam Keeler, the location team leader in the New York office.

'Please contact Joe Imholtz at Langley and remind him that he owes us a big one. Please explain we would be very grateful if he could arrange for a small re-configuration of some of their satellite observation facilities to provide us with a download of activity for the next 48 hours relating to the London address (attached). The request relates to the UK National Crime Agency and a major narcotics organisation, but no contact should be made with the NCA at this time. Thank you and have a good day.'

Then his phone pinged and he went down to the car that was waiting for him.

CHAPTER 111

Euan glanced at his watch as the driver checked out his satnav to find the Gaucho restaurant in Richmond. Finally, he stopped and turned around.

"Sorry, sir, but I think you'll need to walk down this path and I think you will find the Gaucho at the bottom by the river."

And there it was; tables in the dappled shade and then Freddie beaming and waving. The time was precisely two o'clock and Euan relaxed. He hated being late for anything.

"What ho! Euan," cried Freddie, lifting himself out of his chair at the same time he lifted a bottle from an ice bucket. "I made great time along the towpath and no sign at all of the enemy. And on that point, I'm not sure we need to share the situation with Bea. It's a lovely Sunday and it would be a shame to spoil it. And here she comes!"

Euan stood up as Bea approached. He was astonished. She looked like a famous model: tall, slim, dark skin, jet-black hair, a huge smile and a confident, sexy walk. He wondered how on earth Freddie had managed to capture her. She kissed Freddie briefly and turned to him.

"Euan, how lovely to meet you. Freddie has told me all about you; seems like you guys have had some very interesting experiences!"

Euan grinned in response while Freddie poured the wine.

"This white Chardonnay is from Mendoza; I hope you like it. I've already had a couple of glasses. Don't give me that look, Bea. I cycled here and I was thirsty!"

Bea laughed.

"Why on earth did you cycle here?"

Freddie took a moment to reply.

"I don't really know, I just felt I needed some exercise; the last thing I need to do is put on weight."

"Well, darling, reducing the booze will be more effective, but let's not worry about that this afternoon. Anyway, Euan, what brings you to London? And I hope Freddie didn't force you to cycle here as well!"

"No, I came by cab as it happens. I'm here on business; I have some clients in the UK." "What sort of business?" enquired Bea. "Freddie mentioned your business involved security or something like that."

Euan smiled modestly.

"Yeah, I provide technology security for large organisations, institutions, governments and, in some cases, individuals."

"Do you have a team or do you work on your own?" Bea probed further.

Euan grinned again.

"Sometimes I work on my own, especially when talking to clients, but I have a team approaching a thousand people to do the heavy lifting. Anyway, Bea, it's good to meet you. That was a pretty dramatic call while we were getting this ugly bloke out of trouble; not for the first time in my experience and probably not the last!"

Another bottle of Chardonnay and a magnum of Unus Malbec later and the sun was slipping below the hill overlooking the river. The lunch had been excellent but Bea had become uncharacteristically quiet.

"Are you OK?" Freddie asked.

"I'm not sure," she replied. "Let's have some coffee and you can tell me what's going on."

Freddie ordered the coffee and leant forward.

"What do you mean, 'what's going on'?"

Bea smiled and looked at Freddie and Euan, noticing their concerned expressions.

"First of all, Freddie, the bullshit about you cycling here. You could go for a bike ride any time, any place, so why set off and leave your mate to travel here by taxi? It doesn't make sense!"

Freddie tried to stay calm.

"It just seemed a good idea at the time."

But Bea wasn't convinced.

"Fuck off, Freddie, and stop smirking, Euan! You guys are up to something! I'm a cop. I can smell bullshit from a mile away and you two are just inches away. What's more, I'm less drunk than you two, so spill the beans and tell me why you are both glancing at the towpath again! Who are you expecting?"

There was silence for a few moments. Freddie was about to say something to try and change the subject, but Bea suddenly put down her coffee cup.

"Share!"

Freddie looked at Euan, Euan looked at Freddie. They both looked at Bea as if they had no idea what she meant. No one spoke until Bea did, in monosyllabic tones so there was no misunderstanding.

"Lunch at William's and Ina's, Freddie. A couple of weeks ago. Saturday. Lovely food. Champagne and cannabis cookies. Do you remember?"

"Of course. And later when–"

"Forget later, Freddie. Think *earlier*. I'm pretty sure there were two men following you or watching you in Chiswick Mall. I'm trained to spot these situations just like I'm trained to spot bullshit. So, let's share or I'm out of here."

Euan stepped in to try and take care of the situation.

"Yep, you're right, but I think if you could give us a few days we would be in a better position to share. Everything is a bit uncertain at the moment; could you bear with us? Maybe we could fix a date and time now. When are you next free?"

Bea took a moment to think about this proposition. She didn't feel threatened in any way but she wasn't happy about the situation and she knew she had two choices: 1) Walk away and forget about Freddie; or, 2) Give it a few more days.

"OK, guys; but Freddie, sooner or later you are going to have to come clean or you and I won't be spending any more time together. And that's not an idle threat!"

"That's kind, Bea, but in the meantime, can I suggest one more drink?"

"Thanks, but no thanks, Freddie. I think I've had enough and I ought to be going. Be careful how you cycle back. We don't want you falling into the river!"

As Bea walked out of Gaucho and along the towpath, Euan sighed.

"Well, mate; that went well, didn't it?"

CHAPTER 112

Monday morning and Freddie's phone alarm woke him up at four o'clock. As he walked to his bathroom, he heard the TV news and saw that Euan was already dressed with a cup of coffee and some toast on the kitchen table.

They were in Freddie's Range Rover, out of Fulham Reach before five, and driving down Acton Road by five-thirty. No one was following them. The house numbered 23 was unremarkable. It was a large, scruffy building, which had obviously been converted into flats, with rubbish in the tiny front garden overflowing onto the pavement. Euan took a couple of quick photos including some of the two dirty, but relatively new cars.

"Tell you what, Freddie, drop me off at the end of the road. I'll have a good look around and if you come back to where you drop me in fifteen minutes' time I guess I'll have got as much info as possible."

Fifteen minutes later when Euan got back in the car, he sighed.

"I'm pretty sure it's the right address. All the windows and curtains closed at the front. Several windows at the back wide open. The back garden is a tip. Trouble is, I can't see anywhere suitable for observation unless we take a risk and speak to some of the people opposite."

"No way," said Freddie, "but I'm no more surprised than you. Let's head home and I'll tell you what I think."

Euan smiled.

"If you think the solution is me becoming a homeless person sleeping on the pavement opposite that house, you need to think again, mate!"

Freddie took his left hand off the wheel and patted Euan's leg.

"Don't worry. I've a suggestion. It's a bit outrageous, but I think it's worth considering. Let's tell the police about the property."

"What? How is that going to help you get this Kurti killer off your back?"

Freddie was silent for a moment as he navigated the Range Rover through the three lanes, leaving the Hanger Lane junction.

"As you know, I've got a pal in the National Crime Agency and I think that she would be very grateful if we gave her the Acton Road address."

"Yeah… but how does that help us?"

"I think she may be able to help us. We give her the address. She gives us Elira!"

"How's that going to work?"

"Let's think about that tonight," replied Freddie. "I bet the two of us can figure that out. In the meantime, unlike you, I have people to meet and a crust to earn."

"Done," said Euan as he looked at his watch. He knew he would be looking at some footage of Acton Lane later on.

Freddie called Euan at lunchtime and left a message.

"How about meeting up in town this evening? I have a meeting that should finish around six."

When Euan picked up the message he called Freddie straight back.

"Where and when?"

"The Avenue at six-thirty. You take the Piccadilly line from Hammersmith to Green Park, walk down St James's Street and it's at the bottom on the left-hand side. Call me if you have any problems."

Chapter 113

When Euan arrived at the restaurant he could see why Freddie had chosen the place. He had a table in an alcove where no one else could possibly be within earshot and the atmosphere was cool. It was only six-fifteen, so he wasn't surprised that Freddie wasn't there. He ordered a carafe of Minuty and relaxed. He knew there were difficult decisions ahead, but he was sure the two of them would be up to the challenges.

"Hey, Euan, you're looking great!" Freddie said as he approached the table. "Where did you get that gear; Carnaby Street, Harvey Nicks or Paul Smith? Wherever, it looks great! What's that you're drinking? You can pour me a smidgen, I've had a long, dry day!"

Euan poured before replying.

"It's a Minuty and you are very welcome. Looks like you have had a good day."

"Not too bad; not too bad at all. I've managed to win some work unconnected with my audit responsibilities and it's worth some serious fees. Should be really interesting; much more fun than the audit's bean counting stuff and much less risk for DPK. Anyway, what's the plan? I know this place and the menu, so I'm having the cured salmon and the beef tartare."

Half an hour later, Euan and Freddie were enjoying the remains of a Cloudy Bay Pinot Noir and getting down to their options. Euan asked the first question.

"Freddie; why don't we walk away from this?"

Freddie thought for a few moments.

"Good question. First, some people seem to be organising themselves to kill me and I suspect they are not planning to make my demise painless. Second, if we don't deal with these people they could deal with my friends and family for revenge," Freddie smiled, "and I think that might include you, mate! And third, these cheapskate motherfuckers are taking advantage of kids with all sorts of problems and we are in a position to dial the dialogue down."

Euan thought very carefully about what Freddie had said. And when the waiter came to the table he ordered a double espresso. As he sipped it, as he gazed at Freddie, he remembered his thirties. Terrible choices. Nearly dying in a sinking RIB in the Strait of Hormuz with Freddie, deciding whether to chuck the new guy out of the boat to keep it afloat; after all, he was bleeding out and already half-dead, but they kept him alive and they received medals.

Euan remembered another year. Dawn, lying flat in a depression on a pebbled beach with warm rain pouring down, pushing themselves into the ground. Tracer rounds inches above their heads, screams behind them and then the boss at the back shouting 'Up and at 'em!' And Freddie, punching him on the neck and shouting at him and the rest of his team, 'Kneel up! Up! Fucking kneel up! Select single fire! Don't blast away! Pick your targets. If we stay down they will just walk towards us and fuck us up! They're firing way above us. Stick behind me and we will fuck them up!' Then Freddie kneeled up, picked his targets, killed two men instantly and most of the enemy immediately ducked down. Then he stood up straight and shouted 'Follow me!' and the team just walked forward and wasted them all. No medal that time; just survival.

Euan looked over the table.

"Freddie, if your pal in the NCA can find a way to give us this Elira woman, that would be ideal, but I can't see how she'd manage it. If we decide to fuck them up it will be very high-risk. We have no idea how many people will be in the house, where they are and what weapons they will have. If this was the US we would probably do a deal with the woman, some sort of clemency in exchange for names and addresses."

"Yeah, what sort of clemency?"

"Well, in the States, not all prisons are the same. Some of them are very hard, violent places with terrible food and so on. Others can be very soft, in particular, women's prisons, which are a bit similar to the open prisons we have here and you can request a particular location so you can be near your family. Actually, thinking about it, the NCA might want to think about offering Elira a stay in a US prison."

"How would that work?"

"I have a very good friend in the US Embassy here in London. They might be able to fix the documentation, passport, social security and so on."

"Sounds like a plan, Euan. Could you call your pal tomorrow? No names, no pack drill at this stage." Freddie checked his watch. "It's only eight o'clock. How about another glass or two of Cloudy Bay?"

Freddie called Jackie on her burner the next day and she agreed with the plan.

"But no guarantees, Freddie. When push comes to shove I will need my boss to agree. By the way, your friend must have some clout if he has some recent videos from a US satellite; please ping them to me asap. Given the way these people move around we need to invade the premises as soon as possible, probably early tomorrow morning, and I'll let you know how we get on with this Elira if, of course, she is in the house. As I just said, no guarantees."

CHAPTER 114

Euan had flown to Edinburgh for some client meetings and expected to be back on Saturday evening, so Freddie invited Bea to dinner in his apartment on Friday with the promise that he would explain all. She was very clear that if she didn't get a full and honest explanation she would not be staying the night and so he knew it might be a difficult conversation. And it was.

The dinner went well. Smoked salmon with a few capers and Chablis followed by Freddie's lasagne with salad and Rioja and some raspberries and cream to finish. Then it was time for Freddie to tell all. He cleared away the plates and sat back down at the dinner table looking Bea in the eye. He spoke softly, hesitatingly.

"Darling, this is going to be difficult for both of us. So please bear with me. I'll be as brief as possible and promise to tell you the truth."

"Christ, Freddie, this sounds ominous, but just go ahead!"

"As you know, when I was in the Royal Navy I was selected for the SBS and years ago, a number of us were sent to the Middle East to help replace the existing Soviet-influenced ruler with his Eton and Sandhurst son. We flew in like civilians, helped the son's troops remove his dad and that was that. Mission accomplished. No casualties on our side."

Bea scowled.

"Bravo, Freddie! But what's that got to do with you and me?"

Freddie took a gulp of his wine.

"Well, the thing is is that we were given passports to get into the country as civilians and back into the UK. False names, completely genuine. I kept mine and built a new identity."

Bea shook her head.

"What? Why? Why did you need a new identity, for Christ's sake?"

Freddie looked embarrassed.

"Just in case… Just in case I might need it. A couple of other guys did the same, and I built on mine – driver's licence, bank account, credit cards – all that stuff. And I fixed an address courtesy of a pal. It's all watertight."

"Why are you telling me all of this, Freddie? What's going on? What's it got to do with the creeps you think are following you?"

"It's complicated."

"I should *think* it's fucking complicated. I assume it's connected with that madwoman who nearly killed me!" She touched the scar above her eye. "The woman who nearly blinded me and seared your arms with a fucking blowtorch!"

Freddie's face took on a pink tinge.

"Actually, no. This is quite different and it's not about me. Well, maybe it is, but it's really about Miles Bishop."

"Miles Bishop? Who the hell is he? Wait; don't tell me. He's your other identity."

"How did you guess?" asked Freddie.

Chapter 114

Bea shook her head slowly and stared at him.

"Who else could he be? Sometimes I wonder about you, Freddie. Anyway, I need a brandy. You can sort out the drinks and then you can continue with this tale of death, disaster and potential destruction."

CHAPTER 115

Freddie poured Bea's brandy into a tumbler and emptied the remains of the Rioja into his glass. He managed a faint smile.

"This is where it gets quite complicated and I need an assurance from you; after all, you are a police officer."

"Get on with it, Freddie. I'm on your side, at least I think I am so far, but it's fucking unbelievable!"

"OK... Back in the day I had some dealings with Jackie Starling of the NCA and then she found out about my other identity and associated it with a chap that was murdered in Glasgow. Actually, I did kill the guy; it was self-defence, but she threatened to expose Miles Bishop and possibly charge me unless I helped her with her county lines campai–"

"*Help her* with her campaign? What sort of help?" Bea interrupted.

"I'd rather not go into the details, but it involved planting some bricks of heroin in a guy named Kurti's property, which is why he is now banged up in Wandsworth for God knows how long."

"What! Jesus Christ, Freddie, I know about that case. You and Starling stitched this Kurti guy up?"

"It was that or I would have been in Wandsworth instead. But just to be clear, it wasn't me that planted the drugs, it was Miles Bishop, and it's Miles Bishop that is being followed, not Freddie Findlay!"

Bea was quiet as she worked through Freddie's words, then she took a sip of her brandy.

"Freddie, how come these scumbags know that you, or more accurately, Miles Bishop, stitched up Kurti?"

"Do you remember that Chief Superintendent Jackie Starling was captured in that white van a while ago?"

"Yeah, how could I forget?"

"The reason she is alive is that she absolutely had to give me up, but we are all square now. In fact, I think she will be rounding up these county lines leaders very soon, including those looking for me or should I say, Miles Bishop!"

"But wasn't she rescued from a container or something?" Freddie nodded.

"I believe so."

"And was that the same day the drug dealer was shot dead in Battersea Park by a couple of old men?"

"Who knows? Old men. Obviously nothing to do with me!"

Bea took a long, hard look at Freddie and he gave her his come-to-bed eyes. But they didn't work. She sat back, finished her brandy and moved her chair back from the table. The music playing earlier had stopped; the room was in silence. Freddie had nothing more to say and he knew that even if he said anything it wouldn't make any difference.

Then Bea stood up, walked to the door and turned to Freddie.

"I'm going to have a bath and then I expect to see you showered and on the bed with some Champagne and a couple of lines. I know you haven't told me everything but it's good enough for me for the time being... provided..."

Freddie gave a huge sigh of relief.

"It will be. Promise!"

CHAPTER 116

Saturday morning and Freddie was making scrambled eggs. They were in their dressing gowns and Bea was in charge of the toast. The sun was shining and all was well, but Freddie was under pressure. He liked his eggs runny; Bea liked her eggs firm. She liked the toast light brown while he liked his almost burnt. But in the end, it all came together… just like the previous night.

"Lovely eggs, Freddie. Thanks. Could you pour me a little more coffee?" asked Bea. "And what's the plan?" Freddie placed his foot lightly on Bea's slipper and stroked her shin with his toe. "Well, seeing as you have the weekend off, I have some suggestio–"

"Forget your 'suggestions', Freddie! I know there is something going on and I won't be comfortable until I know what it is. Take Euan, for example; where and when did he fit into your life? What the fuck is he doing here? I'm not naïve; it's obvious you guys are involved in more stuff than you told me about last night!"

"OK. This is more confession time." Freddie swallowed, reached across the table, put his hands on the back of her hands and tried to explain. "Bea, my suggestion is this: We get dressed and ready to go, we get into my Taycan, lose anybody that might be following us and go to meet a very close friend of mine. And as we drive there I'll tell you stuff that I've never shared with anyone else – and about a terrible decision I have to take. OK?"

Bea frowned.

"Alright, Freddie, but it sounds very dramatic. If you are good to go, so am I." She paused. "But is this trip taking us somewhere dangerous?"

"Absolutely not! In fact, I can't think of anywhere *less* dangerous. We will be going to a small village in the back of beyond."

"That's OK with me, then. Leave about ten?"

Shortly after ten o'clock they drove out of the car park below Fulham Reach and, after entering and leaving Hammersmith Broadway, they were confident that they were not being followed. Bea soon relaxed and decided now was the time to probe.

"What is it you are ready to share? Is it about Euan?"

"Yes; most of it. But it's mainly about what happens to you when you are involved in military action, when you are in a place where you kill people or get killed. Seeing comrades with terrible injuries and comrades who are dead and when I say 'comrades', I'm referring to people who are very special. I'm not talking about special friends or even close relations. I'm not talking about 'brotherly love'. I'm talking about men who would put themselves in harm's way to help you without a second thought. Men like Euan and others. Sadly, there are not that many 'others' left, but those that remain are extra-special. We have literally saved each other's lives and we love each other."

Bea waited a moment, wondering if now was also the time for a different question.

"Freddie, talking about love, how do you feel about me?"

"I think I do love you. But not like I love Euan!" he added, chuckling. "Anyway, when I tell you what might happen in the next few weeks you might feel differently about me. So, let me explain. I'm not some sort of knight in shining armour or a Don Quixote tilting at windmills. I'm a guy that hates criminals who ruin peoples' lives or kill people for personal gain. I particularly hate the county lines gangs that exploit thousands of vulnerable kids and I think I have an opportunity to destroy or at least disrupt the largest gang in the UK."

"How could you do that? It sounds like a pipe dream."

Freddie didn't reply as they left the M4 motorway and joined the A34 dual carriageway. Bea didn't want to ask the question but she knew that she had to.

"Freddie, are you thinking about taking the matter into your own hands?"

"Yes. Possibly. But in any case, I need to be prepared."

"What do you mean 'prepared'?"

"I'll leave that as a surprise for you. But I *will* make a promise: I won't do anything unless you agree with me. In the meantime, relax. You are going to meet a remarkable lady who lives in this tiny village, and enjoy a pub lunch."

"Why is she remarkable?"

"Well, she is always cheerful, she is a war heroine and an expert in ordnance."

"Ordnance?"

"Yeah. Weapons and stuff."

Bea gasped, knowing that Freddie never ceased to amaze her.

"Jesus Christ, Freddie! Weapons? In a tiny village? You must be joking!"

"Not at all. And, by the way, she lost both her legs from an IED in Afghanistan, but she has a high-tech wheelchair, which is almost as fast as this Taycan. You'll like her, I know!"

CHAPTER 117

It was about eleven-thirty when they arrived in West Hanney and pulled up in front of Kathy's house. Her carer, Sam, was waiting outside with her usual huge smile.

She opened Bea's door.

"You must be Bea. Lovely to meet you. It's good to see a beautiful black face; you won't see many of us in this village."

Then Kathy rolled up and, as usual, Freddie bent down and gave her a huge kiss on each cheek.

Freddie and Bea had to walk very swiftly to keep up with Kathy as they entered the house and along a wide corridor before arriving at the lift. Bea was confused when Kathy pressed the button marked 'Emergency' and the lift descended. And she couldn't believe her eyes when the doors opened and she saw Kathy's shop.

"Fucking hell!" she whispered when she turned to Freddie. "What is this? What are all these weapons?"

Kathy answered on his behalf.

"This is my shop and I'd like to explain, but can I trust you, Bea?"

Bea continued to gaze around the room in amazement.

"Trust me for what?"

"For forgetting you have ever been here."

"Well, of course I won't ever forget what I am looking at, but I can promise you that I will never tell anyone. And anyway, who would believe it? How would I ever identify this place? Freddie drove around several little villages, past two churches and God knows where, so there is no way I could find it again."

Kathy smiled, appearing to be satisfied with her answer.

"Alright, Bea; have a seat. I'll explain what we have here and then deal with Freddie's order."

Order? Bea wondered.

Kathy wheeled her chair to face Bea.

"My shop is available to a very small number of individuals and organisations and my criteria for entry is very simple: 'Do the right thing'. Sometimes, but rarely, the police, sometimes special forces, sometimes The Increment and, occasionally, individuals who need untraceable, reliable ordnance approach me for the goods and I provide them, at a price. Freddie meets my criteria and has ordered some stuff on a sale or return basis. This is a deal where if the customer ends up not using it he can bring it back and I will refund half the original fee," she explained, looking at Freddie and Bea, "provided, of course, that the customer is still alive!"

"What is The Increment?" asked Bea.

"Freddie would be better placed to explain," replied Kathy. "Anyway, let's get down to business. I have everything that was on your list, Freddie, and the sooner we deal with it, the sooner we can go to the pub. Please put on these latex gloves, just in case you inadvertently touch something you shouldn't."

Kathy sped over to a large cabinet and opened it.

"Your order is here, Freddie. First, I have four stun grenades or flashbangs as some people call them. As requested, they will do no permanent damage as you told me there might be innocent people in the room. Second, two Beretta 93R machine pistols with ten rounds for each; are you sure that's enough?"

"Well, let's put it this way; if it *isn't* enough, we will be fucked. Actually, I will take another ten."

Bea couldn't believe what she was hearing. First, The Increment, whatever that was, and now stun grenades and guns. She was about to intervene but managed to hold back.

Kathy continued. "Third, two A-TEC silencers. I've used them on a Beretta and they reduce the noise by more than fifty percent and I've included two cleaning kits free of charge. Last, but by no means least, you have two Kevlar ballistic vests. All good?"

"All good, Kathy," confirmed Freddie. "By the way, I transferred the dosh yesterday and if all goes well I shall be bringing some of this stuff back in due course and will be looking for some of my money back."

Bea tried to sound calm when she finally spoke.

"Freddie, can you tell me what the fuck is going on?"

"Can it wait until we are going back? There is no reason why Kathy needs to hear. In fact, I'm sure she doesn't want to hear anything. It's a sensible protocol, but I guarantee I will tell you everything; but just so you don't worry I fully expect to be returning all this gear to Kathy unused. Can we go to the pub now, please?"

The Plough was pretty empty but the few locals who were sitting inside happily moved chairs and tables around so that Kathy had plenty of space. Of course, they knew Kathy and Sam, but it was Bea that took all their attention and throughout the lunch she could spot them staring at her from time to time. Freddie seemed amused but Bea was not in the mood and just toyed with her food and a small glass of wine. By the time they had returned to the cottage, stowed the gear in the Taycan and said their goodbyes, she was about to boil over.

Then Freddie said, "Would you mind driving? I've had a bit to drink."

CHAPTER 118

Bea loved driving; it was one of the reasons she enjoyed her job and she loved driving fast, but she had said "OK" as if she was doing him a favour. After they left the narrow lanes and joined the wide highway with wonderful bends and some dual carriageways, she was thrilled with the performance of the car, so Bea was a bit disappointed when Freddie asked her to turn right and they encountered narrow lanes once again.

"Don't worry, Bea. This is just a small diversion. You will be able put your foot down again shortly. Could you drive into the little car park ahead, please?"

"OK, Freddie, but where are we?"

"We are on the Berkshire Downs near a path called the Ridgeway. I thought it would be a good idea to explain about the guns and stuff when we were parked rather than going at eighty miles an hour."

"So, please explain," Bea asked, when they were parked and settled.

"I'll bring you up to date. You know that I was being followed by some guys who worked for the kingpin of the county lines business who I stitched up, well, it seems to me that sooner or later those guys are going to try and kill me and so I will always be looking over my shoulder. Of course, they might also try to kill you, by accident or design, so I had to do something about it."

Bea just frowned.

"Last week, I left Fulham Reach and walked towards William's house. Needless to say, a guy followed me. What *he* didn't know was that Euan was following *him*. To cut a long story short, we gathered him up and had a chat with him. He was kind enough to tell us where the county lines HQ was in London and we've provided the NCA with the location and the name of the London boss."

"Why did he do that?"

"We persuaded him. We didn't harm him at all!"

Bea wasn't convinced.

"Just how did you 'persuade' him? Tell me the truth, Freddie."

"We took down his trousers and exposed his penis. As you can imagine, it had shrunk a bit. He was uncircumcised. Euan told him that we would circumcise him if he didn't tell us what we wanted. I'm not sure he understood the term but he certainly got the message. Unsurprisingly, he complied. The London boss is called Elira Shkodra. And before you ask, we let him go when he told us. He was only a scared teenager."

"Where did you do this?"

Freddie smiled.

"In William's wet room at the bottom of his garden, but please don't tell him!"

"Bloody hell, Freddie. You never cease to amaze me!"

"Thank you," said Freddie. "The plan is that the NCS round up the London team and get this Elira woman to give up the man or the men who have taken over from Kurti, then find them and arrest them and their top people."

"Why would she do that?"

"They will promise her that they will ship her out to the States with a new name and all the documentation required and ensure she goes to a soft prison for a few years. So, if that goes well then all is good. But Jackie will need to convince her boss to offer Elira the deal and she will have to go for it, but that's not the only problem. By the time the police raid the property there may be no evidence, so…"

"So, what?" asked Bea.

"So, that's the reason for calling on Kathy. We can't let these guys continue to destroy lives; kids stabbing each other, murdering each other, inflicting dreadful wounds on each other, leaving home and never going back. Thousands of kids! Cooking coke in terrible places, setting up in houses belonging to the most vulnerable people in society and making millions as they create more and more crack addicts. It has to stop… and I'm going to do something about it."

"On your own, Don Quixote?"

"Nope. If we need to take the fight to them I have a pal who I'm sure will come down from Scotland to help and Euan is happy to be our driver. We shall be a very strong team."

They sat in silence for a few moments and Freddie feared the worst, but Bea reached over and put her hand on his.

"Freddie, you're a fucking idiot but I still *think* I love you."

He grabbed her face and kissed her hard on the lips.

"That's wonderful to hear. We must be off in a moment."

Bea grimaced.

"I'm really sorry, but I need to find somewhere to have a pee."

"No problem, there are trees and bushes galore over there."

Bea found a suitable spot and then felt much better, but as she was pulling up her jeans she heard several shots of gunfire. Her heart beat fast as she threw herself to the ground, moving to her right and keeping down low before she heard another shot. All the sounds were coming from the direction of the car. Her heart was beating furiously; she was panicking, but then she saw Freddie standing calmly with a gun in his hand.

"What's happened?" she shouted as she ran towards him.

He looked startled.

"What do you mean, 'what's happened?'"

"The gun shots!"

"Oh, Christ. I'm so sorry. I was just test-firing the guns. Not many places in London where you can do that."

CHAPTER 119

The traffic was light on the way back and Bea had recovered from her shock as she carefully parked the Taycan in the space next to Freddie's Range Rover. But there was something at the back of her mind as she poured herself a glass of Chablis on his terrace. And then it came to her.

"Freddie, when we were in Kathy's cellar she mentioned something called The Increment and said you could tell me about it. What is it?"

"It's a small group of people who served in UK special services like the SAS, the SBS and the Special Reconnaissance Regiment. I know it sounds like a James Bond adventure, but the grapevine suggests that The Increment carries out tasks for MI6 and other more specialised UK intelligence services. Officially, it doesn't exist, but you can find it if you Google it."

Bea did just that and raised her eyebrows.

"Christ, is all of this true?"

Freddie smiled.

"How on earth would I know? You would have to ask Miles Bishop!"

Tuesday morning. Bea had just started a six-day shift and Freddie was in the More London office trying to concentrate on a substantial document entitled 'Terms of Reference for the Independent Governance Committee (version 5)' and feeling sorry for himself as he amended it and tracked his changes. Then his burner vibrated; he saw the call was from Jackie and clicked to accept.

"Hi Freddie. Do you want the good news or the *very* good news?"

"Yes, both!"

"First, the boss agreed the proposal for Elira Shkodra. Second, our teams went into her place in Acton Road at three o'clock this morning and they are still there. We've hauled away several guns, loads of knives – some of them machetes – bin liners full of cash, twenty-two kilos of pure heroin, half a dozen laptops and God knows how many phones; it's a fucking gold mine. Oh, and we've arrested eighteen people; some of them very young, some of them claimed not to know how old they were, whereas others were not able to speak any English. The youngsters have all been safeguarded. Our guys have seen a load of shit in their time but they were truly shocked when they went into that house, and to make matters worse they found an old lady upstairs who seemed to have severe dementia. They think the house is hers. You may see some footage of the team breaking through the front door on the six o'clock news."

"How about Elira? Is she talking?"

"No idea," replied Jackie, "but I'm pretty sure we'll make her an offer she won't want to refuse. I'll keep you updated. Bye for now!"

Freddie sat at his apartment desk amending 'Terms of Reference for the Steering Committee Project Jupiter (version 5)' and didn't lift his head until he sent version 6 to his team leader. Then he made a call on his burner.

"Cameron, how are you?"

"Freddie. Please don't tell me you want to buy some more drugs! You know we are not in that business anymore. In fact, our partnership with Diana Hamilton is working out very well, thanks to you. So, what is it that you want?"

"I'm not sure, Cameron. I know I need a good friend; a very tall, fit, bald, black friend with a shiny head, a heart of gold and a very heavy right hook, which broke my fucking nose before I took him out on the count, back in the championship."

"Well, that's not me, honkey!" and the call was closed.

Two minutes later, another call.

"Freddie, will this friend get paid? Will he be put in danger? Will he have to come to London?"

"No. Yes. Yes."

"Let me think about this," said Cameron. Then, "When?"

"Soon!"

CHAPTER 120

Thursday evening. Freddie and William were having dinner at High Road Brasserie in Chiswick, sitting at their favourite corner table deciding what to eat. Ina, meanwhile, was having dinner at Royal Mid-Surrey Golf Club and Bea was still on her six-day shift. It was about eight-thirty, the restaurant was crowded but the service was efficient.

"Another G&T, Freddie, or some wine to keep us going?" asked William as he swallowed the last of his second large Sipsmith vodka.

"The latter, please; maybe the Cortese di Gavi?"

"Excellent," said William. "I'm going to have the cod with beans." He looked at the menu, "And I'll have tuna nicosia as a starter."

After they had ordered, Freddie leant forward.

"William, old friend; I'm after a favour."

"Of course – anything, unless it involves danger; you have a habit of attracting it!"

Freddie laughed.

"No danger at all. It's just that my solicitor has been banging on about my will and the need for an executor. Of course, she *is* an executor, but she says it's important that there is another one, someone that has a personal relationship with me, and I wondered if you could possibly be that person."

William didn't give it a second thought.

"Of course, old chap. It would be my privilege. I was an executor for both my parents, so I know the form. Just ping me your solicitor's details and I'll get in touch. Here's the wine, let's drink to that. By the way, the chances are that I will pop off before you do, so you might like to line up someone else as I near my dotage."

"Freddie, how long have we known each other?" asked William.

"Must be six or seven years, I guess. Why do you ask?"

"Because you seem distracted. I think you have something going on which might be dangerous. Is it to do with this county lines business? Have you been connected to the man you shot that morning in Battersea Park? Or is it something else?"

"Well, did you see that drugs bust video on the news the other night?"

"Yeah."

"I gave the location to Jackie!"

"How did you do that? How did you even know the location?"

"Colleagues of the guy I shot have been following me, looking for an opportunity to get some revenge. One evening, my pal, Euan, followed the follower, we had a chat with him and he gave us the address. And before you ask me, he wasn't hurt; frightened, yes; very frightened, but not harmed at all."

"Sounds like you did well, Freddie. So, what's the problem?"

"There isn't one, actually, but there *is* a plan… The NCA are after the big bosses and hoping to offer a deal to anyone in that house that can tell them where to find them – and I'm waiting to hear if they have been successful."

"But haven't you done your bit, mate?"

"Well, I guess so, but if the big bosses stay in place they might still be looking for revenge. You know me well; I'm not the sort of guy that hangs around waiting to be killed. I will have to take affirmative action and I'm already prepared!"

What he *didn't* say was that sorting out his will and executor was part of the preparation: 'Plan for the worst, hope for the best'.

CHAPTER 121

Freddie was in the office when Jackie called, so he found an empty study booth.

"Fuck, fuck, fuck!" she shouted.

"Hello Jackie," greeted Freddie. "I imagine that things haven't gone as planned."

"Well, we did the deal with Elira. She couldn't have been more helpful. She gave us the names of the senior UK team and some of the county lines locations outside of London. Most important, she gave us a location where the bosses are staying and we went for it like a shoal of sharks after a child in the wrong place on Bondi Beach. I've been told that, unlike the Acton Road property, this one was in a posh street in Chelsea and there was a Ferrari and a McLaren parked outside. So, instead of breaking down the door, they knocked and when it was opened a well-dressed middle-aged man wearing jeans and a cashmere sweater greeted them politely. They presented him with a search warrant; he looked surprised but not worried. And then an awful thought entered the team leader's brain: 'Could we have the wrong house?'"

"Oh, fuck me; no!" Freddie groaned.

"No! It was the *right* house and they were the *right* people. Names correct, passports to prove it. All four have criminal records – Possession of class A drugs with intent to supply, Possession of an unauthorised firearm, Assault and Grievous Bodily Harm – you name it, they've done it. Add their sentences together and they have done about thirty years."

"Christ."

"Yeah. Initial checks have discovered that they have no declared income and the house they are renting is worth five million plus. There are expensive pictures, top-of-the-range everything, but no drugs. No drugs at all! Not even cannabis or ecstasy. Not even statins or fucking Viagra! Forty-eight hours searching – sniffer dogs, metal detectors to look for containers in the back, floorboards up – apparently, they were all polite but none of them asked why the search was happening, which just about says it all! The only time there was any concern was when the team found nearly one hundred grand in cash, but the chap using the bedroom where it was found just said 'Lucky streak at the tables', so, basically, we got fuck all."

"Where exactly was the house, Jackie?" Freddie asked.

"Who cares? What difference does it make? We are fucked!"

Freddie was calm.

"I'm just interested, is all. So, please send me the address as soon as possible."

Jackie felt a little flutter in her heart, a glimmer of hope.

"Of course, Freddie. You will have it in five minutes."

Freddie called Big Cam.

"*Soon* has become *now*. Can you get down here tomorrow?"

"Yes."

Then he called Euan.

"Where are you?"

"New York."

"Could you get a night flight tonight and come to Fulham Reach by tomorrow morning?"

"Yes, I think so. Do you want me to ask what's up?"

"No! But I am going to send you the location of a house that we might visit tomorrow night and any information or photos that might prove useful."

"Done."

Freddie always thought of Eisenhower when he was planning. He remembered that when the man was overall Commander of the Allied Forces in WWII, he famously said, 'In preparing for battle I have always found that plans are useless, but planning is indispensable'. So, Freddie stayed in the study booth and made a plan. It wasn't complicated. The only uncertainties were whether or not the men were in the house, whereabouts in the house they might be and how many of them there were. But unlike previous, similar situations, he thought it unlikely that these guys would have guns in their hands. In fact, there were probably no guns in the house given the possibility of another visit from the police.

CHAPTER 122

The first thing that went wrong with Freddie's plan was in New York. Euan's executive assistant, Bonnie, was truly pissed off.

"I've been at it all morning. I still can't find a flight to the UK this evening, let alone to London. The best I can do is a flight at ten-thirty tomorrow morning, which lands at six their time."

Euan's heart sank.

"OK, please book it." He sent a text to Freddie with the bad news. The response came within five minutes.

```
'Should be OK. Please update me as
and when. And thanks mate. I really
appreciate it.'
```

When Freddie got home he made himself a strong gin and tonic and decided, *No more drinks after tonight until after tomorrow evening's action*. Then he called Bea and suggested she come over to his place for a late dinner the next evening. Next, he used his burner to call Jackie.

"Hi. Time and safe to talk?"

"Yeah," she replied, understanding his abbreviated question.

"I've got a couple of questions about the raid on the house in Chelsea. First, are your guys' eyes on the property in case there is a development? Second, is there CCTV on the property? And third, are there any photos of the property?"

Jackie was delighted to hear these questions and Freddie realised this when she replied.

"I don't know the answers yet, but I'll get back to you as soon as possible. Is there a deadline?"

"Yeah, tomorrow lunchtime!"

"Done. And good luck, babe!"

Freddie thought for a moment. *'Babe'? 'Good luck'? She must be under serious pressure, but if all goes to plan she will be in my debt.* He put a frozen pizza in the microwave and poured himself another G&T to celebrate.

After dinner, Freddie opened his safe, took out the iPad with his VPN and opened up the file Euan had sent. The address was in Cheyne Walk and there were some properties in the street valued at over fifteen million pounds. The house that was currently being used by the county lines crooks was last valued at three million pounds. More important, there was a small garden at the back, which could be reached from a lane leading down to the main road alongside the River Thames. There was also a posh pub near the property. Freddie frowned, then he smiled. Even posh pubs were usually noisy.

The next thing that went wrong sounded like a showstopper. Euan called at eleven o'clock.

"Freddie, I'm fucked! There's dense fog and chaos here at JFK and I haven't even got an estimated takeoff time."

Freddie's heart sank.

"Well, it's not your fault, mate. I'll just have to revert to Plan B."

"Thank God you've got a Plan B. What is it?"

"Find another driver or defer. In any event, I suggest you don't waste your time coming over here today; I'll update you as and when. Thanks again for trying, mate; really appreciate it."

CHAPTER 123

Could he, should he? Was it fair to ask? Freddie couldn't make up his mind, but then he decided: 'Nothing ventured, nothing gained'.

He called Bea.

"Darling, would it be possible for you to come over earlier, maybe around four? I have a favour to ask."

"What sort of favour?"

"A big one and I'd like to ask face to face, if that's OK."

"Not sure I like the sound of that, but yes, I can get there by four, but I will be in uniform as I have been driving a very special visitor this morning. As that's now done, I just have to return the car and brief the lucky lady who is taking over from me."

Freddie resisted making a comment regarding how her uniform turned him on.

"That would be great. Thank you, thank you!"

"I haven't agreed to do the favour yet…"

Cameron arrived at midday.

"Freddie! Good to see you. Last time I was here was at your lovely party."

Freddie smiled.

"Yes, and I remember you met a lovely young man and the two of you left quite early. Still together?"

"Yep. Going strong and we are about to adopt a baby. Anyway; what's the plan?"

"Blimey, that's good! Have a seat, Cam, and I'll give you a heads-up."

"Do you remember the Lamont brothers?"

Cam laughed.

"Do I remember those terrible twins? Of course I do. Don't tell me, they were actually triplets and the surviving one is looking for vengeance! No, seriously; what have they got to do with this plan?"

"The NCA have evidence that could convict me for the murder of Clive or, at the very least, get me charged, which would finish my career. And they know that Miles Bishop is actually me. When I say 'the NCA' I'm actually talking about one very senior officer. Let's call her Jackie. And it was Jackie that asked me to plant those bricks of heroin in return for her silence."

"What! Plant them? Where?"

"In the garden of the guy running about fifty percent of the county lines in the UK. A guy called Kurti."

"Bloody hell, Freddie! I read about him. He got fifteen years and you framed him?"

"Yeah, but it gets worse… Kurti got his guys to grab Jackie and she gave Miles Bishop up. So, they came after me. I retaliated as you might expect, but they are still out there as a threat and my plan is to remove that threat."

"When?" asked Cam.

"Tonight!"

Cam stood up and paced around the room for a couple of minutes before speaking.

"Freddie, if I didn't know you so well I would tell you to fuck off, but just in case you are not out of your mind, I will carry on listening."

"The four most senior guys in Kurti's operation are staying in a house in Chelsea. The police raided it the other day but found nothing incriminating – nothing at all. But these guys have all served time and there is no doubt they are the county lines ringleaders and, in all probability, they will be looking to kill me, so the plan is to kill them first."

"Yeah, Freddie; but how?"

"The two of us and the driver steal a car and drive down to the house in Chelsea. The driver rings the bell, someone looks at him, he poses no threat and the door is opened. We push the guy back and throw in a stun grenade. We have another to use if necessary. I kill the guys on the ground floor; you go upstairs. We only kill adults. If there are any kids or teenagers we leave them alone or punch them out if we really have to. Then we leave and get back in the car. If leaving via the front door is impossible, we go out the back, through the garden and over the wall."

Cam couldn't believe what he had just heard.

"Freddie; stun grenades, guns! How do you expect to acquire them?"

"Already done, mate. We have stun grenades, Ingram machine pistols, ten-round magazines with spares and suppressors, Kevlar vests and other stuff that will come in useful. I've test-fired each Ingram. We are good to go."

"Jesus Christ, Freddie; you're serious, aren't you? But are you sure these guys are as bad as you say? If so, will they be tooled up?"

"Very unlikely given the possibility of another police visit, but, of course, they might be. They might not even be home. They might be in different rooms, who knows? But the stun grenades will disorientate them."

Cam carried on poking at the plan.

"Sounds like a noisy event. If it's a posh street I guess it will be quiet outside and those stun grenades will make a big bang. Are you sure we need them?"

"Yes, but it's not as quiet as you suggest; there is a large, upper-class pub opposite and quite a few cars and taxis coming and going. Anyway, let's think about it."

"Cars," said Cam. "Have you stolen one already?"

"Er, no," replied Freddie. "We have a problem with the car and the driver, but I'm hoping to sort it this afternoon. If I can't, I guess we must defer. But that's not ideal; these guys could move at any time."

CHAPTER 124

Cam was out for a run when Bea arrived. Freddie made her some coffee and got down to business. He had thought very carefully about how he might discuss the situation with her and how he could persuade her to help.

"No small talk, Freddie! Come on; spit it out. What's on your mind and how can I help? I imagine it's about those county lines people."

"Well, yes; it is. The police got the information they needed and raided a house in Chelsea. There were four men staying there, all with criminal records, none of them employed and no legitimate sources of income, but there were no drugs on the premises. They searched inside and out but found nothing at all. The NCA are one hundred percent sure they have the right guys, but there is nothing they can do, so the bastard criminals can just get on with the county lines and, possibly, arrange for me to be killed."

"Oh my God, Freddie; what are you going to do?"

"I've called up a very old friend and the two of us are going to Chelsea this evening to wipe them out."

"Just like that?"

"Yep."

Neither of them spoke for a while and then Bea asked Freddie a question.

"So, what is the favour you want from me?"

"The guy lined up to drive is stranded in New York. He's a pretty small bloke, not at all threatening. The plan was that he rings the bell and when someone inside has a look through the peephole they won't see any danger so that when the door opens we will throw in a stun grenade and charge inside. We should be back out in two or three minutes."

"So, you want me to drive and open the door?"

"Yes. We can go into the details when my pal, Cameron, comes back from his run, but I can't see any danger for you."

"Apart from being arrested, you mean?"

Freddie smiled.

"I don't think that is likely. Any problems, you just drive away and, by the way, if there was any interest from the police, I have a card up my sleeve."

"Which is?"

"The NCA provided me with the address and other information and they would be very embarrassed indeed if I revealed it. You would more likely be promoted than imprisoned."

Bea accepted this information and jumped to his previous mention of transport.

"What sort of car?" asked Bea.

"Er, well; that's a bit of a challenge. We have to steal one."

The doorbell buzzed. "Saved by the bell," said Freddie. "That will be Cameron."

And there he was, just a trace of perspiration on him, breathing steadily and putting out his hand to shake Bea's.

"Pleased to meet you, Bea; actually, *surprised* to meet you. If Freddie's been explaining what he calls his 'plan', I would have thought there was a fair chance you would be heading home by now."

Bea smiled.

"Are *you* thinking of heading home, Cameron?"

"No."

"Then neither am I."

"Any reservations, Bea?"

"Several, but it's the stun grenades that worry me the most. If people outside hear a loud bang they may become worried when they subsequently hear some smaller bangs and, to me, that spells trouble."

Cameron looked at Freddie.

"Looks like no stun grenades, then." He looked at his watch. "What about a car?"

"I'll deal with that," replied Bea. "Freddie, could you give me a fob for the car park? I'll bring the car in rather than leave it outside and I'd better get going. I'm off to Canary Wharf."

Freddie and Cameron looked at each other and shrugged.

CHAPTER 125

Bea walked to Hammersmith tube station, took the Piccadilly line to Green Park where she changed to the Jubilee line travelling to Canary Wharf. She had driven around that area more times than she could count, but had never walked. As a protection officer she was always looking around the environment and had seen Addison Lee cabs parked up without a fare, but positioned to move quickly if account customers booked through their app. Sometimes the driver was smoking a cigarette on the pavement, sometimes sitting in the car or sometimes leaning on the car. After walking around for just ten minutes she decided on her target.

The driver straightened up when he saw Bea approaching. Police officers were never good news. She showed him her warrant card; he didn't notice that she had her hand covering the area with her name and title.

"Excuse me, sir; are you responsible for this car?" she asked.

"Yeah," he replied. "What's the problem?"

"I'm not sure there is a problem, but please step out and back, sir!"

The driver did as he was told and stepped out and away from the car, looking puzzled. Bea opened the door and saw that the key was in the ignition. She got in, closed the door, clicked the central locking button, checked the mirror and drove away.

The drive from Canary Wharf to Fulham Reach took a lot longer than the journey on the tube, but it gave Bea time to figure out how to get rid of the car after Freddie and Cam had done what they had to do. She knew there would be CCTV all around Chelsea and the police could also use ANPR to see where they had driven, but she couldn't concern herself with that now. The first decision she made was that the three of them should separate when they dumped the car. The second decision was to dump it in a side street in Putney near the towpath. That provided several routes back to Hammersmith. The third decision was that they should take hoodies, baseball caps and other extra clothes to make it even more difficult for them to be identified and to make sure they didn't take anything back to Freddie's place that could incriminate them. And of course, she would swap her uniform jacket for a brightly-coloured sweatshirt after they had dumped the car.

Bea called Freddie from the Fulham Reach underground garage and she was in his living room at six-thirty. She explained how she got hold of the Addison Lee car and her suggestions as to how they could avoid being tracked after they left Cheyne Walk.

"Why an Addison Lee car, Bea?" asked Cam.

"Three reasons," she replied. "First, I knew where they would be parked and that they'd be unlocked. Second, I'm sure we will do what we can to eliminate anything that connects us to the car, but DNA is tricky; however, unlike a typical car, Addison Lee has a huge number of passengers, which means a huge number of samples. Even if one of us has DNA on the police database and even if one of us is a suspect, then who is to say when the DNA was left there? Better safe than sorry. And third, no one suspects an Addison Lee car idling in a street, it's ubiquitous."

Then it was time to get down to the details.

Freddie kicked off. "We leave here at eight. We will all be wearing vinyl gloves, the Kevlar vests and hoodies when we leave; I have them here. All of us will take a bag with replacement socks, shoes, trousers and sweatshirts, plus wet wipes. Cam and I will have an extra bag for our Ingrams. We will be in the back of the car and will keep our heads down for the first few minutes in case anyone notices us. We get to the area at about nine and park as close as possible to the house. When we are sure no one is near or observing us, we check we have the guns on single round mode with the safety on and we must ensure the suppressors are screwed on tightly. With masks on, Cam and I stand either side of the door and when you're ready, Bea, get out of the car and slam the door. You'll march up to the house and ring the bell, hold up your warrant card to the peephole and someone will open the door. If no one answers the bell, we abort."

"Wait! Wait a second, Freddie," said Cam. "Bea, when you were out finding the car, Freddie and I agreed that if you have any concerns, people looking at the car or, God forbid, cops, you just cruise away. Take the first turning on the left, and left again, which is a narrow road and stop where you think you will be opposite the back of the house and, one way or another, we'll meet you back there. And this is very important – drive away if we are not with you in four minutes. Drive away!"

Freddie continued.

"When the guy opens the door, Cam will shoot him in the chest. I will charge forward and Cam will shoot the chap in the head and follow. We will both check rooms until we find the other guys, then it's one in the chest followed by one in the head for all of them. I will deal with the ground floor; Cam will go upstairs and then we get the fuck out of there. Hopefully, you will be waiting for us, Bea."

CHAPTER 126

The trip to Chelsea was uneventful and the Addison Lee car pulled up outside the house. Bea looked around from the front while Cam and Freddie looked from the back. No spectators. Freddie and Cam took up position each side of the door. Bea slammed the door of the car, strode to the front door, took out her warrant card and pressed the bell. She assumed that someone had looked at it as the door opened straight away and she was confronted with a good-looking man wearing smart clothes and a grin that revealed very white teeth. Cam shot him and blood splashed on her face and jacket. As she closed the door and turned away, she heard another muffled shot within the house.

Freddie charged ahead. Bright lights on his right. Kitchen. No one there. Dimmer lights further on. Looked like a dining room. Three men playing cards. He hesitated for a moment; he'd never shot anyone in cold blood before. But an image stared him in the face. Jackie: Almost dead. Her clothes and face smeared with dog shit and covered with dog bites; just alive on the edge of death, trapped in that container. His Ingram hit each of them in the chest. Three rounds fired, blood all over the table and floor. Then three headshots, to be sure. Four rounds remaining. No time for screams. But, blood. God, so much blood. He'd been involved in several firefights in his career, but none so close and none so one-sided. He had to work hard not to vomit. He stood for a moment. No more violence, just the harsh smell of cordite and the sound of a clock ticking.

Cam had charged upstairs. Checking each room. Nothing! Nobody! Looking in wardrobes, looking under beds. Done! He joined Freddie in the room with the bodies. Blood everywhere. On the floor, on the table, soaking through clothes. Dead men. They touched knuckles and made for the door. Freddie opened it cautiously. The car was still outside, no one seemed at all interested in them. They got into the back and hunkered down. Cam looked at his watch. The operation had taken just less than four minutes.

Bea pulled away from the kerb and gasped. "What happened? What went wrong? Are they going to come after us? What went wrong?" she repeated.

Cam was as succinct, as usual.

"Nothing. It was smooth. Mission accomplished."

"But I only heard one gunshot!" said Bea.

"That's good to hear," Freddie replied. "Those suppressors are pretty effective and I think it all went very well. Is that blood on your face?"

Thirty minutes later they checked the car very carefully and then checked it again. They were at the end of a cul-de-sac running along the south side of the River Thames near Putney and they were ready to split up. All had changed into their new gear and used the wet wipes on the steering wheel and any other surfaces they might have touched, in spite of their gloves. Freddie threw the Kevlar vests into the river.

Bea had cleaned her face and had a bag ready for a rubbish bin. Cam had his ready as well. Freddie had two bags; one for his dirty gear for the rubbish bin, the other for the guns and spare rounds. They agreed that they would rendezvous at Fulham Reach, each taking a different route. Freddie and Cam had already opened some bottles when Bea arrived and the doors were opened to the terrace, but they weren't drinking and they weren't celebrating.

Freddie gave Bea a huge hug.

"Thank you, darling. Thank you! It all went brilliantly; not least because the guy opened the door with a smile, but also the Addison Lee transport!"

"So, why are you guys not celebrating?" she asked.

Cam frowned.

"Hard to say, Bea." Then he looked at Freddie and continued, "I guess, me and that man with his arm around you are used to defending ourselves rather than assassinating men sitting around a table. It's a bit like extermination. But, if killing them we have saved many other lives, then I'm OK with that." Then he smiled. "Actually, I'm *more* than OK. And you did well. You did *very* well, Bea, from start to finish. So, what would you like to drink?"

CHAPTER 127

Kurti had been in Wandsworth for more than six months and life in the privileged E wing 'Annex' was bearable although very boring. But at least they had a decent TV and he made a point of staying in touch with current affairs and never missed the early evening news followed by the London news. The timing for the programmes seemed to vary over the weekends and that irritated him. But when the London news opened on Saturday evening he went into shock. The picture showed the house in Cheyne Walk that he had rented for his top team and the voiceover was referring to a massacre, a shooting which had left four men dead.

"Oh fuck! Oh Christ!" he shouted. The other five men watching turned to him and then back to the screen.

"What's up?" asked one of them.

"My team, my four best men. Blown away! Killed. All of them. We've been friends since our village school days in Albania. I can't believe it." He put his head in his hands and closed his eyes.

The other men exchanged glances and left him to it. He didn't sleep at all that night.

The Christian Sunday Service was very popular in Wandsworth, not because many of the prisoners were religious, but because it provided an opportunity for them to get out of their cells. When Kurti returned to the Annex his grief had turned to anger and he had no problem in discussing the massacre of his team.

The undisputed boss of the Annex was Dave. He was doing 'life with no remission' and he asked the first question.

"Say, Tacic, you must have upset some serious people out there. Four people, for fuck's sake! Must have taken an army. Rivals?"

Kurti shook his head.

"We don't have rivals, we ask them to join us. If they don't, we kill them. Word gets around."

Dan, doing fifteen years for a massive fraud, joined in.

"If not rivals, who else?"

"I don't know, maybe someone in my operation. After all, who would even know where my friends were staying? I'm going to call my lawyer and tell him he'd better find out."

Later on, lying on his bunk, Kurti ran everyone through his mind. Then something clicked. *Elira!* He knew she had been picked up when the police raided the house in Acton Road, but he had heard nothing since. She knew the Chelsea location; perhaps she had done a deal. Maybe that Starling woman made her an offer she couldn't refuse. But, no! Impossible. The British police do not assassinate people, but no one would possibly believe they'd plant drugs in people's gardens, or at least they'd get someone to do it for them. But who? Of course… that fucking Bishop man! Got to be him.

Kurti had a quiet word with Dave.

"I think I know who it was that killed my men or at least organised it. I want him dead and I want him to die very slowly and very painfully. Do you have a contact that could deal with this for me?"

Dave was blunt.

"Yes, but you are probably looking at fifty thousand for the kill and ten thousand for my introduction. Are you good for that?"

"Of course," replied Kurti without hesitation.

"OK, let me have a chat with a pal and I'll get back to you."

"Thank you. The man's name is Miles Bishop, he lives in Fulham and I've had some people keeping an eye on him."

A few days later, Dave walked into Kurti's cell, closed the door and told him the news.

"It's all done. My pal has accepted the assignment. He's picked a bloke who gets off on hurting people. I won't give you his real name, but his nickname is Twenty-Four."

"Twenty-Four?"

"Yeah. That's the number of hours it took one of his victims to die. I've seen a clip from the video; it's the worst thing I have seen in my life. And the screaming. Terrible. I can still hear it."

"What does he do?"

"Do you really want to know? It's your choice."

"Yes."

"Well, it starts with the beating. He hangs them fully clothed on a hook and starts beating them with a cane until the clothes are all stripped off. Then he continues until quite a bit of skin has gone as well. He only stops when they pass out. Then it's the penis and testicles and a vice. We are only a couple of hours in at this stage."

"Enough!" said Kurti. "I've heard enough! I'll give you the details of my solicitor and he will give Mr Twenty-Four all the information we have on Bishop, including a photo. He will also hand over a deposit."

"No worries; I've already paid him, just to show good faith."

"Thanks, Dave. Thanks very much indeed."

CHAPTER 128

Twenty-Four met Kurti's solicitor who handed over the material on Bishop. He also introduced him to Roel who was now managing the existing surveillance on Freddie. Within a couple of weeks they were all prepared and it was just a question of waiting. The only challenge was grabbing him, but not killing him. That would come later, many hours after he had begged for death.

Freddie was well aware that he was being observed and followed but he wasn't too concerned. It was obvious that the people involved were young, inexperienced and lazy. He had no difficulty getting rid of them when he needed to, but he always stayed alert. Cycling back along the towpath with the letters he had collected from his pal near The Hurlingham Club, he was looking forward to dinner with Bea when a cyclist coming in the opposite direction crashed into him. He fell heavily and felt a rib crack, but he picked himself up swiftly to shout at the cyclist. It was then that he realised he was in deep shit. There was a moped roaring towards him, another cyclist coming from behind and an electric scooter in the distance. He started running. No point or time in shouting for help. The safest thing to do was to get into the nearest pub, which was The Crabtree, so he powered himself into the little path leading to the street entrance only to find it blocked by a large man pointing a gun at him.

"Hello Mr Bishop. Please don't do anything stupid. We have a car a few yards away. And just so you know, we mean business – feel this." He pulled a Taser from his pocket, aimed it at Freddie's groin and pulled the trigger. Freddie grunted. The pain was excruciating and his muscles contracted. He froze in place then collapsed on the ground.

"How's that?" asked the man. "Consider it a taste of things to come; many things to come – many *very* painful things to come." He opened a car's rear door and waited for Freddie to recover enough so he could haul him inside. The driver turned around to look at his new passenger and Freddie knew he had two choices: Get in the car and die painfully or fight. It took a nanosecond for him to decide. He spun, punched the man with the gun in the throat and started running – fast.

Of course, Freddie knew the area well and he took the first opportunity to get back on the towpath and, within seconds, he had a plan. Hammersmith Bridge was about five hundred yards away. It was getting dark. If he could get across the bridge he could lose anyone on the South Bank towpath, he knew it so well. And, of course, the bridge was closed to traffic so no cars could chase him down. Then a bike came out of Crisp Walk. The rider was almost a child. Freddie just swatted him away and heard the bike crashing onto the ground. Still running, no one in front of him, he reached the Hammersmith Bridge walkway and raised his pace even further. He looked back, no one following. His groin was aching, his chest was agony; it felt like at least two ribs had fractured, but his pace didn't slacken and he was confident he could escape.

A couple of minutes later he saw someone with an electric scooter on the walkway heading towards him at speed from the South Bank. As he got closer it looked as if he was holding a machete. Then Freddie turned around and he saw a bunch of guys coming from behind him. Just as the man with the machete arrived, Freddie kicked the scooter and he crashed into the metal pedestrian protection fence and dropped the machete. Freddie picked it up, ready to face the guys coming from behind, when a shot rang out and pinged off some metal nearby. The men were now about thirty yards away. Another shot, this time a clang and then a bullet hit him in the shoulder and he struggled to stay upright. He managed to use the body of the man who'd fallen from the scooter as a shield and he felt a bullet thud into it.

Freddie's brain was racing, his shoulder was burning; he could see that two of the men held handguns. All he had was the machete. Then the guy he was holding tried to grab him and, in spite of his wounded shoulder, Freddie managed to throw him over the guard rail. Then a second bullet hit him and he knew it was all over. He chose to jump down into the river. He didn't feel anything after that. No pain, just bright light, a clear blue sky and then nothing. His brain, his life, just closing down.

CHAPTER 129

William and Gill were in a black cab on their way to Charing Cross Hospital to confirm that the body was Freddie's and they were dreading the experience.

"Do you remember when we had to identify the body of that poor partner that the police thought was suicide, but it turned out that those money laundering people had killed him?" asked William. "God, what was his name?"

"I can't remember either," replied Gill. "What an epitaph! Anyway, at least we just had to look at photos then; I hope that's the same this time. Jesus, what a fucking mess! Anyway, Freddie will have loads of epitaphs at the event next week. There's been nothing like it before."

William sighed.

"Yeah, but so what? He doesn't get to hear it. I mean; does it really matter? How on earth did he get himself into this shit in the first place?"

Gill spoke gently.

"I think you know the answer to that question, William. First of all, he saved your life and that mad bitch wanted revenge; second, your friend, Diana, needed help and Freddie stepped up, and third, you guys rescued that Jackie woman, who seems to have been involved in all of this. Anyway, here we are. All we have to do is find the right entrance."

As William paid the fare, the cab driver spoke.

"Couldn't help overhearing you. Condolences. Go round to the right over there and you will see a sign marked 'Coroner's Office.'"

William pressed the bell by the door and they waited… and waited. Gill tried to open it, but no joy. After about ten minutes it finally opened and a harassed-looking woman with a grey coat and hair to match appeared round the door.

"Come this way," she said, turned her back and stalked off. Then she gestured to an open door. "Please wait there. I shall be back shortly."

"Christ!" said Gill. "We get condolences from the cab driver, but that woman has treated us like we have turned up for dinner at Benares without a reservation."

Finally, the lady with the grey coat and the grey hair returned.

"ID, please." Gill and William produced their passports, which they had been instructed to bring. "Follow me, please."

"Excuse me," began Gill, "it so happens we have had to identify someone before and we just looked at photos. Where are we going?"

The lady didn't stop walking and talked over her shoulder.

"The deceased has bullet wounds and has been classified as a murder victim, hence the need for your ID and hence the need to see the body."

"We need to see the body? Why?" Gill asked.

"No, just the face. And here we are. When I open this blind I need you each to answer one question: Do you recognise the deceased as Frederick Findlay?" She did so immediately without waiting to hear that they were okay with this.

William replied first: "Yes."

Then Gill: "Yes."

And after signing some forms, the ordeal was over.

They caught a cab outside the hospital and William spoke first.

"I've taken the liberty of asking Tina to make us some lunch. I thought we might need some sharpeners on the lawn followed by something to eat and I assumed you didn't have any meetings this afternoon."

"That would be lovely, William. Thank you!"

And it was. They both fell asleep in the sunshine on the river bank and didn't even hear Tina taking away the glasses, the plates, two empty wine bottles, an empty tonic bottle and an almost empty bottle of Sipsmith vodka.

Chapter 130

A couple of days later, Dave sauntered into Kurti's cell and sat down. He smiled.

"Your man, Miles Bishop, has been wasted!"

"Excellent! Thank you, Dave."

"No problem, but there were a couple of complications."

Kurti scowled.

"Complications? What sort of complications?"

"Well, the first thing is that the man was shot dead. He killed himself before the team could grab him."

"Not good, Dave. That man put me in here serving fifteen. I wanted him hurt."

"Well, he's dead, but there is another complication. This 'Miles Bishop' was, in fact, a guy called Findlay. Don't ask me why, don't ask me how, but Bishop was an alias. I hope to hell that he wasn't a spook or we will both be fucked!"

Kurti scowled again.

"Are you sure? Sure you had the right man?"

"I am one hundred per cent sure. And your chap, someone called Roel, was one of the guys that shot him, so if you have any doubts, speak to him!"

The next day Dave walked into Kurti's cell again.

"Have you checked with your man, Roel?"

"Yeah. It seems Bishop or Findlay or whoever, is dead, but I'm not happy that Twenty-Four didn't do his job."

Dave wasn't familiar with any form of criticism let alone coming from some third-rate drug dealer making a few quid from kids cooking and distributing crack cocaine. But he realised that Kurti was complaining.

"OK, squire, what do you want?"

"Nothing."

"Good."

"Nothing," repeated Kurti, "but don't expect I am going to pay for a promise that wasn't delivered."

"That's your choice, Tacic, but I put down a deposit and Twenty-Four will be looking to me for the balance. And I'm looking at you!"

"Look somewhere else."

Dave had a chat with the appropriate warden.

"Frank, do me a couple of favours, please. Worth five grand. Kurti has ripped me off. I'd like him out of the Annex as soon as possible, and if you could put the word out that anyone who wastes him will get ten grand, paid to whoever they want outside, I'd be very grateful."

When the warden visited the Annex the next day he passed a black bin liner to Kurti. "Put your stuff in this; you are being moved in with the general population."

"Why?"

"No idea, but you are off to a different landing. I'll take you there."

Kurti had been used to hearing some noise when he was in the Annex, but experiencing it first-hand was in a different league. Shouts, screams, alarms going off, whistles blowing and doors slamming. The warden looked at his piece of paper, opened the door, pushed Kurti inside, closed the door and walked off. There was a huge, naked man sitting on a lavatory looking at him curiously when he came in.

"Who the fuck are you?"

"I'm Tacic."

"Well, you must have seriously pissed someone off in this madhouse to be shut in with me."

"Why's that?"

The man stood up, wiped himself with some paper, walked towards Tacic and smiled.

"The crack. Sometimes it makes me feel good, but most of the time it gets me angry and then I start hitting things like the walls or the door or people. I don't know why. Do you?"

As the man came closer, Tacic could smell him – a combination of sweat, shit and something rancid. He stepped back but the man kept close to him.

"What's in that bag?" he asked.

"Just my stuff."

The man turned away and then turned back towards him.

"My name is Julian. It's my stuff now!"

Breakfast in the new wing was a nightmare for Tacic. Everyone seemed to be part of a group and the groups pushed him out of the way. Finally, he picked up his package of cereal and milk and walked back to his new cell, wondering if he could survive, but he was a strong man and felt that he could make it work. He was wrong.

Jonno Johnson had nothing to lose. He had killed three innocent women and was doing life without remission and Dave's ten grand would help his wife and kids for a few months. He followed Kurti into the cell, stabbed him in the belly, slashed his throat open, wiped the knife, handed it to Julian and walked out of the door. Kurti died within minutes.

CHAPTER 131

The event to commemorate Freddie's death, or 'passing' as some people preferred to describe it, was arranged by Alex Bracken and took place on the top floor of the DPK building. There were two large rooms, one for the drinks and the other for the eulogies. Many people had requested they attend but the space was sufficient for only forty. When they arrived, the mood was quite light-hearted. It was now over a month since they had heard about Freddie's murder and most of their shock had worn off, but there was still a great deal of speculation; after all, everyone knew about the incident when he shot someone and saved William's life and, of course, the fact that he had once been stabbed outside Fulham Football Club.

The invitation stated 'Drinks at six-thirty', but the room was filling up by six. This was the first event of this kind in the UK firm's history and no one wanted to miss it or miss the opportunity for unlimited drinks. The room was buzzing.

William approached 'Two Lunches' Lionel and spoke to him.

"This is more like a wedding than a wake."

"Think of it as a life well lived, William" he said, "because that's what it was. Let's drink to that and get a top-up before we go through and endure the well-meant but banal speeches. By the way, is it just DPK folk here or will we hear from his drug dealers, ex-wives, mistresses, cuckolded husbands and bookmakers?"

"No idea, old chap. We need to be quick to get that top-up!"

When everyone was assembled in the presentation room, Alex Bracken spoke; he was crisp and got the tone just right. He looked behind at the huge photo of Freddie for a moment. Then he thanked everyone for coming along and reminded those people who would be saying a few words to make sure they were just a *few* words. Then he introduced the first speaker and there was an audible gasp from some of the audience. It was Wendell Gunn.

Wendell was the recently retired global head of the firm, a man who had been responsible for two hundred and fifty thousand people in one hundred and sixty countries. A legend. A man of few words and respected by everyone. As usual, he was very brief.

"I had to come... Freddie was what we in the US would call 'A piece of work' and that's not always a compliment!" Many people nodded their heads in agreement.

"But he was a great asset to our firm in terms of the bottom line. And as some, but not many of you might know, he also alerted the SEC in the United States of some serious money laundering which we were able to close down and I was privileged to be invited to the White House and be thanked by the President! That has been very valuable to the firm over the past couple of years. So, please raise your glasses."

"To Freddie."

Next up, was Gill.

"When I joined DPK, Freddie was my mentor. I learned an incredible amount from him from day one; I could never have made it as a partner without his support. He was a huge man and a delight to know."

Then Freddie's executive assistant.

"Absolutely hopeless bloke. Expenses were a nightmare. Calendar a complete work of fiction, but clients loved him and he never let them down. But what can I say," she blinked back tears, "a wonderful man!"

Lionel lumbered up to the podium with drink in hand.

"As some of you may know, I do enjoy an occasional lunch and Freddie and I enjoyed several." A number of people laughed. "Alright – many. And like many of you in this room, I shall really miss him." He raised his glass. "Cheers, Freddie!"

It was William's turn next.

"Freddie was my best friend and he will be in my heart forever. You will all probably know that he saved my life, but it was his irrepressible approach to life that I loved. Now, some of you might still be wondering about the fact that Freddie got stabbed a couple of years ago and has now been killed. Perhaps I can shed some light on this and there's someone here who I'd like to introduce you to – Chief Superintendent Jackie Starling from the National Crime Agency."

The previously silent room was now interrupted by murmurings and mutterings of "What is this all about?" and "What's going on?" but the room was silent when Jackie Starling, in full uniform, walked from the back of the room to the podium to speak.

"Good evening ladies and gentlemen, and thank you, Alex, for allowing me to say a few words… and it *will* be a few words. Freddie had been very helpful to the NCA and to me personally. I would really like to tell you exactly how he helped us, but all I am able to say is that he risked his life twice and enabled us to secure convictions relating to major money launderers and drug dealers. And although I met William West for the first time today, we have something very important in common that I would like to share with you. Freddie saved his life. Freddie saved my life as well!" As she left the podium and strode to the exit, the mutterings had returned to the room.

Alex stood up.

"I think we have another thirty minutes to mix, mingle and maybe have another drink."

Somehow, Lionel reached the bar first. And he left the bar last.

CHAPTER 132

"Yes, please!" said Ina as she was offered another glass of Champagne. She smiled at William. "Do you think it's because I'm Scottish and the drinks are free?"

"No. I'm going to have another as well, and maybe another one after that!"

They were sitting in seats 2A and 2C on the eight-fifteen BA flight from Heathrow to Nice due to arrive at eleven-twenty.

"Is this the same flight we took when you transported me away to Saint-Paul-de-Vence almost three years ago?" asked Ina.

"Yes, it is and I will never forget the lovely lunch we had on the terrace and then walking up the hill to the Fondation Maeght."

"Of course! And, as I recall, we had some good fun in our room before dinner, but it was a sad ending, wasn't it. When we got back you found out that Felicity had been killed and then it went from bad to worse. Poor kid."

"Poor kid, indeed," William sighed.

Ina reached out and put her hand on his.

"What about you, William? A scar on your chest and a missing toe! Ah, good, here comes the Champagne. Let's look on the bright side!"

The flight arrived at Nice Côte d'Azur on time. As they only had hand baggage, they were in a taxi within ten minutes, arrived in Saint-Paul-de-Vence half an hour later, walked through the unmarked door to Colombe d'Or just before one o' clock and checked in. When they arrived in their room, Ina threw her arms around William.

"It's the same room, darling! Thank you, you old romantic! But don't look at me like that. I need to get changed into something a bit cooler. I remember how hot that terrace can be!"

Changed and unpacked, they went downstairs and passed the Alexander Calder mobile over the pool.

"Now I remember," recalled Ina, "there were a couple of children playing with that thing and you told me that Calder gave it to the hotel in the thirties and that many other artists donated their pictures over the years. What a magical place; I'm so glad you suggested we came here again!" And then they were taken to their table on the terrace with a view of the vineyards and trees below. Ina walked around to take a few photos.

When Ina returned there was a glass of rosé in front of her and a vodka in front of William.

"Sipsmith, William?" she enquired.

He smiled.

"Unlikely to find vodka from Chiswick in West London here in the South of France! This is Grey Goose."

"Why do they have it here?"

"It's made in France; Picardy, I th–"

"Look! No, don't look, William!" Ina interrupted him. "It's that actor, that film star – the one who was in those films. I said, 'don't look'! Oh God, I wish I could remember his name; he was in that Tarantino movie. He must be a regular; our waiter with the slow-motion walk has just rushed up to him."

The man looked about fifty. He was slim, tanned and wearing faded blue jeans, a T-shirt with a photo of Andy Warhol on it and Ray-Bans. He beamed at the waiter and shook his hand.

"Don't stare," said William. "There are often celebrities here. Don't you remember we saw Mick Jagger last time? And look, there's Bea!"

Bea looked incredibly beautiful. She had a white headband around her jet-black hair and was wearing a bright pink silk blouse with baggy white chinos and purple trainers. The chattering on the terrace stopped for a moment. People were asking themselves things like "Who is she? I must know her, I've seen her before," but she didn't seem to notice. William and Ina stood up as she approached.

William hugged her.

"Bea, you look fantastic! God, it's so good to see you."

Then Ina joined in with tears in her eyes.

"Bea, at one time we thought we might never see you again, but what happened to Freddie?"

Bea looked puzzled.

"He's there, just having a chat with the waiter."

Then it was Ina's turn to be puzzled.

"That man? Freddie? What on earth are you saying?"

CHAPTER 133

The film star was Freddie. But it wasn't him. William wasn't surprised.

"Fuck me, Freddie, you look like a film star, like that old git what's-his-name; I can't remember, but you look fucking amazing. Fuck*ing* ama*zing*! What have you done? Where have you been?"

Then Ina threw herself into Freddie's arms.

"Freddie, Freddie, oh Freddie. You look like a different man!" She looked him up and down. "Your broken nose has been fixed, your hair is grey and much shorter. Take off your sunglasses." He did. "I knew it! Your eyes are now bright blue, not grey. And your teeth are perfectly white. Good God, you've also lost some weight. I think you might have had some Botox. You are quite attractive!"

"I should be; I spent nearly two months in a clinic and it cost a fortune."

Finally, they all sat down. Their waiter brought the bottle of pink Champagne Freddie had ordered and, after they had toasted each other, William asked the question.

"Mate, it's wonderful to see you. It's almost three months since we spoke and then it was a two-minute call telling me that you were alive and – almost – kicking, and to tell no one apart from Gill and Ina! Do you want to tell all now or after lunch?"

"After lunch, please, Freddie. I haven't eaten since eight o'clock last night!" Ina suggested.

The Champagne bottles were empty by the time their food came and two bottles of very dry white Burgundy were polished off at the same time the food was finished. William ordered a bottle of Brouilly and asked for it to be cool. He wasn't surprised when the waiter sniffed at the request, but when it arrived it was perfect.

Then he said, "Freddie, or should I call you Lazarus? Gill and I committed perjury when we confirmed a complete stranger's body as yours. DPK organised an event to celebrate your life, which, as you can guess, was a major piss-up, but all the same, it was no joke. And your family, or should I say fami*lies*, were pretty upset, not least because there wasn't a penny for any of them in your 'will'. So, tell all!"

Freddie looked a little ashamed.

"First of all, I'll tell you about that evening. I was cycling back from a pal's flat and it was getting dark. I was attacked by a number of people on mopeds and bikes with knives and guns in Bishops Park. I thought I might lose some of them if I ran over the Hammersmith Bridge walkway, but somehow they had anticipated this might happen and had organised some people on the other side to intercept me and I was trapped in the middle of the bridge. The first bullet hit my shoulder. I managed to hit some guy and use his body for protection for a while, but the gunfire kept coming – banging and pinging against the metal structure of the bridge – near my feet, near my head; it was a nightmare. No, it was worse than that!"

"Where were the police?" asked Ina.

"Good question," Freddie replied. "I was praying that they would turn up, but I didn't even hear a siren. By then it was dark. Most of the shots were coming from the Hammersmith side and I thought I might be able to escape, but another guy on a moped with a fucking machete arrived from the south side and it was then that I realised I was in serious trouble. Then another round hit me in the leg and that was when I knew I was going to die."

"Knew?" asked William.

Freddie looked down at his lap, put down his coffee cup and replied to him.

"Yes, William. *Knew!*"

"But here you are, Freddie, thank God! What happened then?"

"I'm not really sure. I decided to go into the river; I'd already thrown one of the guys over the railings, I had to make a choice – stand there and die or take a chance with the water. I got hit by another round when I was in the air." At that, Freddie suddenly stood up and started walking. "Do you mind if I pop to the men's room?" William noticed he walked with a bit of a limp.

It was nearly four o'clock but the waiter was happy to serve them more drinks and he was patient as the three of them tried to agree what was required. After listening for at least five minutes, he suggested another bottle of the Brouilly and winked at William.

CHAPTER 134

Freddie came back. Ina looked around to make sure no one was in earshot and asked him to continue his story.

"OK, Freddie, you knew that you were going to die, but you didn't. And I have two questions. First, why *didn't* you die? Second, why did you pretend you were dead?"

The waiter arrived with the wine and that gave Freddie a few moments to compose his response. He spoke softly.

"I don't know why I didn't die. I was off the bridge, in the air and then everything was bright and then everything went dark, completely dark. I think my head must have hit the water first and I was concussed. The next thing I knew I was underwater and driving myself to the surface; just pure instinct. Fucking terrible though. Fucking cold. But I made it. I could see the bright lights of the bridge, nothing else, and even with my mind all fucked up I knew the guys up there would not be able to see me, otherwise they would have been blasting away. I couldn't move my left arm; it was hurting like hell, as was my right foot and the side of my neck was burning. But I knew where I was."

"Where were you?" asked Ina.

"I was close to the South Bank and the tide was coming in. I didn't fight it; I knew there was a slipway for St Paul's School further upstream quite near and, in spite of the pain, I tried to aim for where I thought it would be." Freddie smiled theatrically. "That's when I bumped into the body!"

'What?" whispered William. "What body?"

"The guy I had chucked over the bridge. His body was floating just under the surface and for some reason I towed it to the slipway. I've no idea why. I knew he was dead; I knew that I could hardly make it myself, but ten minutes later it and we were on the slipway. I was gasping and, I guess, bleeding quite a lot. The body was silent. There we were. I was getting weaker and that's when this idea, this stupid idea, came into my mind; 'Take any ID the man might have and chuck it in the river. Put my own ID in his pockets, leave him there and Freddie will be dead'. I knew I would have no more fear of being killed by drug dealers or being blackmailed by the NCA. No more being chased for money by kids that loathe me and no more signing off audits that could get me fined and fired."

William was visibly shocked.

"Are you nuts, Freddie?"

"Probably, yes," replied Freddie, "but then I've probably been nuts for most of my life!"

"What happened next, Freddie?" asked Ina.

"Well, I was completely fucked, so I phoned Bea."

"Christ!" exclaimed William. "How did you do that? If *you* were fucked, why wasn't your phone?"

"That's what *I* thought, mate. But I gave it a try anyway and it worked. Seems like my iPhone is good for thirty minutes at four metres' depth and I got through to Bea. Thank God!"

Bea put down her glass.

"I had just dropped off a US senator at their embassy in Vauxhall when I got the call. Freddie wasn't making much sense but, from what I heard, he was injured, bleeding and hiding behind some big logs from a felled tree and undergrowth on the South Bank towpath west of Hammersmith Bridge and I didn't hesitate."

"What do you mean?" asked Ina.

"I put on the blue lights and used the siren when I needed it – I'd only ever done that twice before – and pulled up by the bridge just fifteen minutes later. I ran down to the towpath and started shouting his name, found him and pretty much carried him to the car. Then I called Charing Cross Hospital, explained who I was and told them to get someone in A&E to be outside waiting for us. Thank God I was in uniform; they took me seriously when I arrived. Just before they wheeled him away, he whispered to me 'I'm Miles Bishop'. The next morning a runner came across the other body lying on the slipway and the police identified him as Frederick Findlay. And William, many thanks to you and your colleague for the identification. Can't have been much fun," she frowned. "Tell you what, cleaning the car wasn't much fun either – blood all over the place, the seat was soaked and, to cap it all, Freddie had been sick. I don't know how I could have explained that away!"

CHAPTER 135

It was five-thirty when the waiter brought the bill to William. He glanced at it and passed it to Freddie.

"Serious money, mate, and it's all down to you."

Freddie pulled a face.

"No problem about the money, but why not fifty-fifty? I mean, I'm happy to pay but I think there is something going on here."

"There is, indeed. Cast your mind back, Freddie. The two of us in the sunshine on the terrace at The Old Ship. You were explaining your hare-brained scheme to acquire some drugs and promised me that if I could come up with a better idea you would buy Ina and me lunch, in June on the terrace at Colombe d'Or. And, as you will recall, I did come up with a much better idea and here we are. So, thank you very much!"

Bea suggested they have a 'stroll' around the village. William and Freddie knew that really meant shopping, so decided they would be in the way, and found an outside table at Café de la Place opposite the hotel. It took a while to get the attention of a waiter, but when he returned with two glasses of red wine, Freddie and William relaxed and watched the locals playing pétanque, smoking Gitanes, scratching their backsides and arguing with each other.

Freddie gestured over in their direction.

"What a life those guys have. Just put on some dungarees and spend all afternoon with your mates and plenty of booze."

"Sounds familiar to me, mate, except we got paid for it and usually wore suits or something 'smart casual'," William responded. "Anyway, what are your plans, old chap? I guess you don't have to work now. Actually, that reminds me, we have a tenant for your flat, or should I say, Miles Bishop's flat. It's a corporate letting, two-year contract at eight thousand a month. Your pal, Rod Gladstone, really knows his stuff."

"Thank you, William. That's good to hear. Mr Bishop has also received his DPK death-in-service insurance money. Four times my last year's income, tax-free and last year was a very good year. So, money isn't an issue at the moment and won't be for a while."

"So, what is Miles Bishop going to do next, Freddie?"

Freddie scowled.

"I think he might have to be wiped out of existence. At the back of my mind is the faint possibility that he may cause me problems at some stage in the future so he's going to have to change his name."

"Isn't that terribly complicated?"

"Actually, no. My solicitor is already putting it all together. Of course, there are God alone knows how many people that need to be informed and some require something called a deed poll, but it's all pretty much straightforward. Takes about six weeks. Easier than opening a bank account or so he told me."

"What are you going to call yourself?"

"I think I have settled on Charles as a first name, but you can call me Charlie! We haven't chosen a surname yet. I quite like the name 'King.'"

"Why?"

"Couple of reasons; first, the king is the most important piece on the chess board. All the other players are there to protect him, including the bishop, and the other is how I might identify myself."

It was William's turn to make a face.

"What do you mean?"

"Well, you know 007, when he introduces himself he always says 'I'm Bond, James Bond'. I could introduce myself as 'King, King Charles.'"

William chuckled.

"Dream on, Charles, dream on! How about another drink?"

Freddie used his fluent French to organise two more glasses of red wine and leaned forward.

"Actually, I haven't a clue as to what the future holds. Bea has taken voluntary redundancy so we are both free as birds. In the meantime, we are going to stay where we are now. We are renting a lovely house with great views and a large pool. We have been making some good friends in Mougins, so life is good, but I guess we might get a bit bored, particularly when the weather turns chilly. Tell you something, though, William, I really hope we can keep in touch. You will always be my best friend. Always! Ah, here come the girls and what a surprise, they have carrier bags."

Two months later, Charlie King's mobile rang. He was doing his lengths in the pool – over water one way, under water the other way and a final underwater both ways. He was breathing heavily when he listened to the message.

"Freddie, sorry… Charlie! It's William. Could you call me back, please?"

Acknowledgements

Many thanks to my editor Caroline Ahearn and the team at Spiffing Covers.

Thanks also to the Roko coffee club and a number of my old EY colleagues. You know who you are!

As always, my thanks to my wonderful partner in crime Jenny Yamamoto. Without her this book would not have been written.

Reviews

Book Two. Terrible Brothers

"A dark page-turner. Truly gripping. Violence, sex, some very funny moments and details beautifully observed."

"I was looking forward to the second book and this certainly didn't disappoint. A great read full of excitement and intrigue. The new characters are well drawn and I thoroughly recommend this book to anyone who doesn't mind a bit of violence in the plot."

"Great storytelling in this strong follow up novel. I was on the edge of my seat till the final pages. Agog to read the final part of the trilogy."

"Simply Brilliant."

"Gripping read. The most terrible brothers you could have nightmares about."

Printed in Great Britain
by Amazon